BY THE SAME AUTHOR
ALL PUBLISHED BY HOUSE OF STRATUS

FICTION

ANN VERONICA
APROPOS OF DOLORES
THE AUTOCRACY OF MR PARHAM
BABES IN THE DARKLING WOOD
BEALBY
THE BROTHERS *AND*
   THE CROQUET PLAYER
THE BULPINGTON OF BLUP
THE DREAM
THE FIRST MEN IN THE MOON
THE FOOD OF THE GODS
THE HISTORY OF MR POLLY
THE HOLY TERROR
IN THE DAYS OF THE COMET
THE INVISIBLE MAN
THE ISLAND OF DR MOREAU
KIPPS: THE STORY OF A SIMPLE
   SOUL
LOVE AND MR LEWISHAM
MARRIAGE
MEANWHILE
MEN LIKE GODS
A MODERN UTOPIA
MR BRITLING SEES IT THROUGH
THE NEW MACHIAVELLI
THE PASSIONATE FRIENDS
THE SEA LADY
THE SHAPE OF THINGS TO COME
THE TIME MACHINE
TONO-BUNGAY

THE UNDYING FIRE
THE WAR IN THE AIR
THE WAR OF THE WORLDS
THE WHEELS OF CHANCE
WHEN THE SLEEPER WAKES
THE WIFE OF SIR ISAAC HARMAN
THE WONDERFUL VISIT
THE WORLD OF WILLIAM CLISSOLD
   VOLUMES 1, 2, 3

NON-FICTION

THE CONQUEST OF TIME *AND*
   THE HAPPY TURNING
EXPERIMENT IN AUTOBIOGRAPHY
   VOLUMES 1, 2
H G WELLS IN LOVE
THE OPEN CONSPIRACY AND OTHER
   WRITINGS

38

Brynhild

Brynhild

H G WELLS

HOUSE OF
STRATUS

First Published 1937

This edition published in 2002 by House of Stratus, an imprint of
House of Stratus Ltd, Thirsk Industrial Park, York Road, Thirsk,
North Yorkshire, YO7 3BX, UK.
Also at: House of Stratus Inc., 2 Neptune Road, Poughkeepsie, NY 12601, USA.

www.houseofstratus.com

Typeset, printed and bound by House of Stratus.

A catalogue record for this book is available from the British Library
and The Library of Congress.

ISBN 0-7551-0395-5

Contents

DISAVOWAL

All the characters in this book are fictitious characters. If by some accident they bear names already in use or happen to follow professions that living people follow, or live in houses like real existing houses, or play or work very much as actual persons do, that is so because fiction cannot but recall realities if it is to deal with life.

CHAPTER ONE

The Error of Judgment

Mr Rowland Palace woke up abruptly at seventeen minutes past three in the morning. A minute ago he had been in that uncharted region beyond dreamland where indeed the mind has its motions but their issue is stillborn and no trace survives, and now he was wide awake in a world of cheerless realities, persistent and inexorable. In that complete blackness he had blundered against an unpleasant memory, and the shock had hurled him back into the waking world.

Outside the house there was a gentle breeze. Across his ceiling the doubled shadows of two laburnum-trees thrown by two lamps in the roadway beyond his shrubbery, danced incessantly through intricate recurrent sequences. He was very weary of that dance, but in the daytime he could never remember to ask his wife to do something in the way of dark curtains. Now, though he stared hard at that all-too-familiar flickering, its irritation was subconscious. His mind was overwhelmed and possessed altogether by the thought of the desolating mistake he had made with those photographers.

'Why did I do it? Why did I ever consent to anything of the sort? Why did I let them get at me?'

1

The effect upon his special and appreciative public would, he felt, be incalculably bad. He had been made undignified – ridiculous.

How had it happened? How *could* it have happened?

It had been such a delightful afternoon up to that fatal moment. Nothing had warned him. He had been caught off his guard. He had not realized what was happening until it was too late.

'Oh, damn!' he said, and then much louder as if he feared the Recording Angel had not heard him, 'Oh, DAMN!'

The Recording Angel certainly could not have missed that. Mrs Palace in the next room heard it plainly. 'Trouble *again*,' she said. 'I wonder what it is *this* time?'

She speculated drowsily for a while, turned over and went to sleep. Either she would know in the morning or it wouldn't matter.

Like so many men who make their way to positions of importance in the world of thought and letters, Mr Rowland Palace was a man of acute sensibilities and incessant anxieties. He had been a delicate, prize-winning, magazine-starting sort of boy at school and already in his undergraduate days his literary bent had been conspicuous. His rise to prominence was, in the retrospect, rapid. His criticisms were listened to, he was already an influence before he came down from Cambridge. His very first book, *Bent Oars,* was a considerable success; it went beyond Britain, it excited the American colony in Paris and percolated thence to New York, Chicago, and the intellectual West. (That was in the pre-Joyce period, when Greenwich Village was in every sense young.) He became aware of himself as a figure of popular interest only very slowly. He distrusted the realization. If he could he would have concealed it from himself.

He hated to be self-conscious. He didn't like to feel that people looked at him. When he did he usually fell over things. His conception of himself was of a reserved, slenderish figure, delicate but opaque, observant, amused, kindly but enigmatical. His bearing, like his work, was pervaded by a gentle irony. (But Mrs Palace knew better.) He carried his faintly smiling face a little on one side. Few even of his intimates suspected his phases of irritation and neurasthenia.

His intellectual pose was to acquiesce in everything and believe in nothing. His dexterous depreciation could be turned left or right or where you would. He undermined and destroyed with a polished civility. His style was a witty style. This endeared him to youth, full of youth's natural suspicion that it is being dreadfully put upon and not quite clear how and why. He believed nothing; he clung to nothing. No trustful infantilism for him, he intimated. They envied that tremendously ripe grown-up attitude of his beyond measure. They imitated it in the *Granta* – not always, he felt, successfully. (A sedulous admirer can be a deadly parodist.) But plainly they regarded him as a liberator.

Being a liberator had not been in Mr Rowland Palace's original scheme of things. But it was borne in upon him steadily and continually that he *was* a liberator, and by imperceptible degrees he accepted the responsibility of the rôle. But there was nothing anarchistic or revolutionary about the liberation he purveyed; it was the liberation of a man of the world. It left you free to do anything – or nothing.

Yes.

3

But –

Those photographs.

2

Lady Burnish had taken her house-party across the corner of the park to see the vicar's May Day Festival. It was to be Great Fun. The vicar was much respected at Canham Towers, but with amusement. He was a round-faced, brown-eyed, loose-mouthed, button-nosed, excited-looking man, addicted to cassocks. He was a fluent tenor in the pulpit but on the level with you he spluttered. He had a natural tonsure with wiry intractable hair round it, and an aptitude for pageant, and he had greatly cleaned up and beautified his church. So that it didn't look a perfectly respectable church. It had just a suspicion of rouge in its appearance. And the new banners in the chancel were – though ever so little – *gay*.

He loved archaeology, but not for its laborious and often sordid facts. He hated excavations and stratigraphy, but he gloried in sudden finds and marvels. He had a rich confused sense of the romance of the past. He drew a loose-knit veil of folklore and ancient wisdom, unaccountable customs, semi-pagan mysticism and strange forgotten lovely things, across the harsh nakedness of the present. He was strong on the Druids; what he knew and inferred and invented about the Druids made a copious legend.

At times Lady Burnish, in her bright bantering way, said she thought he was almost more of a Druid than an Anglo-Catholic priest.

4

'We inherit,' he said, not denying the charge. 'Just as the Holy Father inherits the title of Pontifex Maximus.'

For he was the sort of vicar which calls the Pope the Holy Father and not the sort which calls him – disgusting phrase to apply to an old gentleman – the Whore of Babylon. He worked hard to restore Folk Dances, a belief in fairies, and a gilt and illuminated Merrie England of simple, dear, and plain but very rosy and lovable people. Which restoration was none the less difficult because manifestly nothing of the sort has ever existed.

He was holding a May Day Festival in the meadow between the churchyard and the almshouses. (He called the old ladies in the almshouses 'Goody Blake' and 'Goody Stonor' and so on, and they hated him like poison for it.) There was a garlanded maypole and a band and two tents for tenpenny and eighteen-penny teas respectively, there were omnibuses from Clutter-hamton and Bloor, there were no end of motor-cars and a crowd of people, village children in white and pink, and most of the vestry and choir robed as Druids, whether they liked it or not, with trousers and stout boots showing underneath, and there was our God-tonsured vicar, with flying arms and skirts and girdle tassels, leaving no one alone, the life and soul of it all.

At the outset Mr Rowland Palace had rather liked the man. There was a suggestion of infinite gallantry about this attempt to bring back the picturesque memories of a non-existent past and make them live again within sound and sight of an arterial way and an aerodrome.

'This is jolly,' he said to Lady Burnish, surveying the scene. 'Is that Robin Hood and Maid Marian I see before me? All the best people seem to be here. And is not that little troupe in top-hats and knee-breeches Ye Olde English Dancers, who have been capering round the country for years and years? They grow but they never grow up.'

'Their costumes are getting *very* tight,' said Lady Burnish.

Golstein, the professional refugee, made some comparison with similar beribboned festivities in Bavaria, but Sir Wilfred Blackstone, the literary atheist, bent as ever on anti-clerical controversy, was a little inclined to stress the originally phallic nature of the maypole dance.

'The Spring Queen and the Corn King and all that,' said Mr Penton-Grace, the novelist. 'And why not?'

That shut up Sir Wilfred.

The vicar made much of the presence of Mr Rowland Palace, flattered him and led him to his doom.

'A bard, a soothsayer,' cried the vicar. 'Merlin almost. You come, *cher maître*, apt to our occasion.'

He explained how he used these festivities insidiously for the intellectual stimulation of 'my yokel youth'. 'We have a prize to award for poetry and a prize essay. Yes, indeed. You shall see the three best poems and the three best essays and then, I am sure, you will give the prize.'

And Mr Palace read the unspeakable poems and glanced over the unreadable essays and, still without any premonition of evil, consented to award the prize.

There were two chairs almost like thrones on the dais, one for himself and one for dear Lady Burnish, and there were chairs behind for Druids and committee generally, and the vicar stood and officiated.

'You will wear a robe,' said the vicar.

'Do you think I need?'

'Oh, you mahst,' said Lady Cytherea Label.

'Crimson,' said the vicar.

'You'll look *splendid* in a crimson robe!' said Lady Cytherea.

She was a charming fresh young woman of one or two and twenty, unusually discriminating in things literary, modest and inquiring. She and Rowland had been great friends from the arrival tea-time of Friday onward, and it was now high Saturday. It was pleasant to find she had a critical, approving eye for his personal appearance.

And when it came to a fillet of gold braid, a bay wreath, and a daisy chain, she herself adjusted them and was lingering and fastidious about it.

'And the Bardic harp,' said the vicar, proffering an unreal wood, glue, and cardboard lyre.

The first shades of doubt fell upon Mr Palace as he walked in procession to the dais. He ascended the steps with that difficulty and uncertainty natural to a man unaccustomed to skirts (in this case far too long for him). He met the eye of his wife for a swift expressive instant.

She wasn't with him. She disapproved, distrusted. He never liked that dissentient expression of hers. Surely this robe was fine and dignified; he could throw it back in folds from his arms when he handled the rolled-up poems and prizes. Surely Lady Cytherea had fixed that fillet straight and well. He dismissed the doubt. His wife was just being sensitive about Lady Cytherea.

He did notice that there seemed to be an unusual number of Press photographers beside the dais. It had not occurred to him that this fantastic old-world vicar was a glutton for publicity. But the danger in the situation only bared its teeth after he had made his little gently ironical sympathetic speech and the prizes had been handed down. Then these pictorial news-hawks came

7

storming upon him. 'Just a moment, Mr Palace,' and, 'if we might get a shot of you, sir, beside Lady Burnish, handing the prize to the little girl. (Bill, where's that kid?)'

And, 'Just for a moment, sir – you speaking to Lady Cytherea Label. *Please*, sir.'

3

The photographs came out *awful*.

And they went round the world.

The scarlet robe wasn't a bit splendid. It was just a big dark robe obviously much too big for him and making him look stumpy – 'stumpy' was the only word for it. The fillet of gold was askew, if ever it had been straight; it came down over his forehead and rested over one eyebrow. The bay-leaves were crooked, too; they gave him dark, pointed ears. His genial expression was dreadfully overdone. (That perhaps was his own fault.) The harp got in edgeways – obviously pasteboard. He looked like one of the less respectable and less expensively dressed booncompanions of the Emperor Nero. Full of wine and wantonness. He looked much more like corrupting the village maiden than handing her a prize. Lady Burnish, at his side, had learnt early in life to hold her chin up and extend her backbone whenever cameras or observers were about. She seemed now to be looking down at him with infinite scorn. Well she might.

'Distinguished author relaxes,' was the legend of the first print of this he saw.

'Mr Rowland Palace Joins the Revels at Little Canham.'

They had done close-ups of him too. He had always been a little aloof and camera-shy in his publicity, and these Press photographers, knowing him by reputation as an inaccessible, had taken the fullest advantage of their opportunity. That enabled someone – apparently the writer of a syndicated letter and hostile to reaction – to stab him with, 'Modern Classicist dresses the Part'.

A considerable part of this syndicated critic's contribution to the mind of the race was printed in periodicals which made no use of photography. For their convenience, it seemed, a line drawing had been made of Mr Palace and reproduced upon metal for rough effective printing. 'Libellous' was all too mild a description of it. All over the United States, Canada, Australia, the statement that Mr Palace was a deboshed Druid would go.

'And one has no remedy!' said Mr Palace to the wavering shadows on his ceiling.

'Any combination of lines that they choose to present in zincography is a valid portrait according to the usage of the Press...

'Useless to sue.'

The shadows became still; they seemed to think it over for a moment or so, and then they gave way to hilarious approval.

For a week or so Mr Rowland Palace watched this dreadful perversion of his dignified and graceful presence, percolate through the British Press. Local papers in Oxford and Cambridge, where hitherto he had been a subtle voice speaking out of the shadows, now proclaimed him by picture and inference jovial and silly – but mostly silly. Then from New York onward these photographs passed across America. The letterpress, any explanation of the occasion, did not cross the Atlantic; it was just the pictures which travelled and the journalistic mind evoked what explanation it thought best.

'Mr Rowland Palace writes in Classical Attire. Garb of Suetonius best for his style.'

Some bright spirit in New York had discovered a wonderful connection between clothing and mood. He declared that Mr Rowland Palace found modern clothes mentally vulgarizing and resorted to loose robes to free his mind. And then in an exasperating patronizing way he told Mr Rowland Palace that more than robes might be necessary for that.

One bold editor made Lady Cytherea his daughter and another married him to Lady Burnish without further comment.

Texas guessed cheerfully, 'Rowland Palace as Old King Cole'.

The metal cliché, that absolutely libellous, hideous little face with its exaggerated woollen robe and its wreath making him at best a gnome askew – followed the photographs. It was evidently going into storage for the literary columns all over the world. Whenever he was reviewed or they had anything to say about him in the future, it would be dug up and used against him, sharpening the edge of hostility, poisoning praise.

'How can they get me *right?*' whispered Mr Rowland Palace to his ceiling. 'How can they ever get me right again?'

4

Mr Rowland Palace could lie there no longer. He stuck his feet out of bed and sat up. His fine hands clutched his shoulders.

'I have something to say,' he whispered. 'I deserve to be heard. I deserve to be read. Why should I be discredited and made preposterous? People will *dislike* me. They will refuse to read me. Who could *read* a man with a face like *that?*... Monstrous!'

In the stillness he had a faint intimation of the vastness and complexity of the answer. To keep some hold upon himself he repeated 'Why?'

He looked at his dim pillow. No good replacing his fretting head on that. He would put on his dressing-gown and slippers, make some tea, go downstairs to his study and write something – and so distract himself from this present overwhelming trouble. In an hour or so he might perhaps come back to that pillow with a reasonable prospect of sleep.

CHAPTER TWO

Nocturne

Mrs Palace was awakened by the sound of him bumping about in the little pantry on the landing in which tea-things were kept against just such occasions as this. He made a conclusive clatter by dropping the lid of the biscuit tin. She sighed but she knew what was expected of her.

She appeared, tall, slender, and shapely, holding her blue dressing-gown about her with a long, rather large hand. She was a fair-haired young woman, with a broad serene face and kind brown eyes that nowadays wore habitually an air of perplexity. She thought life more and more unreasonable but she did not care to condemn it. 'You are making tea again,' she remarked to his back.

'I haven't had a wink of sleep for three hours,' he said, turning a haggard face to her.

'Poor old Rowly! Let me get the tea for you and you go down to the study. I'll bring it down.'

'I just can't sleep. I lie there.'

'You've been worried by press-cuttings.'

'Now how do you know that?'

'Well you don't usually tear them up before you put them in the waste-paper basket. But this last week or so – '

'Do I tear them up! They deserve it.'

'Go to your study and let me manage. You'll only upset things. There's some bread and butter. I'll make you a bit of toast.'

When she brought down the tea-tray and toast to him he was sitting in his armchair staring miserably at the empty grate. He accepted his refreshment with a complete absence of thanks.

'Did you see those cuttings I tore up?' he asked abruptly.

'I guessed what they were about.'

'How?'

'I could see they were mostly pictures.'

'Gods! Why was I such a *fool?*'

Mrs Palace had no good answer for that.

'Why *was* I such a fool?'

She waited for a little while before she spoke. She stood weighing her words before she uttered them. 'Darling, don't you think perhaps you are making too much of all this? Maybe it wasn't very wise of you to let them dress you up like that. *I* didn't like it. But after all, does it matter so *very* much?'

'It matters vitally.'

'But how?'

'How little you understand the nuances of my position!' he said.

She received that unflinchingly. She knew there had to be that sort of accusation sooner or later. She made no answer.

'A writer,' he said, 'isn't what he is.'

She tried to weigh that. It was difficult to weigh.

'A writer, my dear Bryn, is what he *seems* to be. He is an effect – an impression. That's what we have to understand. We have to grasp that.'

'But really – after all – he's himself.'

'That is where you are wrong, Bryn. In fact,' he added generously, 'that's where we have *both* been wrong. Nobody's himself – nobody. There isn't such a thing. And we public characters, we politicians, writers, and so forth, are even less ourselves than most people.'

'*Need* you be, Rowly?'

He looked at her with the baleful eyes of one who encounters incredible stupidity. Then in the lonely hopeless tone of one who feels explanations are useless, he said, 'Yes'.

Deep in the heart of his wife there stirred a desire to spank him hard and good. It was one of those impulses from the subconscious that rush up into the light and instantly dive down again. She took a cup of tea instead and sat down with it opposite him in the smaller armchair.

He was always very sensitive to her feelings even when he disregarded them. Often he felt them before she was aware of them. He knew now that she was critical of the unjustifiable scorn in that 'Yes'. She had a way of perceiving things that were not meant for her. It was an impression to efface. He became elaborately explicit. 'You see, in this overcrowded world, every man who appeals to the public must put up – I won't say a false front – but a Large Simplified Façade. He must present a clear, plain version of himself. His appearance, the published anecdotes about him, his report, his prestige, must all tally with his work. I have felt that dimly, Bryn, long ago, but only tonight do I see it in its stark simplicity... Naturally to you it is a new idea.'

'Well... You don't mean, Rowly, you ought to be deliberately posing and pretending and play-acting.'

'No. No. Not posing and pretending and play-acting. Certainly not that. But one ought to keep one face to the public. We have to choose what we are and keep rigorously to that. The public has no time to conjugate us through a lot of moods and tenses. One firm, clear impression is all people have time for. I had – I believe – built up a sort of personality in their minds. Austere, rather aloof. They respected it. Martin called me a gentleman of letters. Ridiculous perhaps, but that was how I wanted to be taken – so as to pose myself and deliver what I had to say. That Elliot and Fry profile was all that was necessary then by way of a published portrait. It had dignity. *Now* – '

'Are they so very bad?'

'Hadn't you the curiosity even to smooth out one of those pictures?'

'I didn't want to pry.'

'No,' he said neutrally.

Mrs Palace became aware of that three in the morning chill that even early June cannot escape. She clicked on the radiant electric panel and replenished her husband's cup.

'Would you mind,' she asked, 'if I saw the next batch of cuttings before you tore them up?'

2

Soon, warmed by tea and stimulated by the tangible if unformulated resistances of his wife, Rowland Palace found his mental sources recovering strength and abundance. Soon he was in what is frequently called a mood of inspiration. That is to say, he did not know what was coming next. He talked more easily and listened with a deepening interest to the things he was saying.

'Why should I be disturbed by all this?' he asked. 'That's the revealing question. I am not vain.'

He paused on that. His wife accepted the proposition without a flicker of challenge. He did not look at her but he listened for the slightest sound from her.

'I may have a thousand faults and weaknesses,' he explained, 'but *certainly* I am not vain. No. This that I feel is something altogether different from wounded vanity.'

(Carried *nemine contradicente*.)

'But there *is* keeping up an appearance. That *is* a duty to oneself. Even in the past – Even before the newspaper and the camera abolished ordinary privacy... The world dressed up... Why did it dress up? Because dressing is a method of expression, a statement we make. It is a reassurance. It is a claim... What are crowns? What are robes? What is the wig of a judge? The robe of a priest? Or any sort of ceremony? With any but the lowest barbarians, a man who wishes to influence the crowd, win the attention of the crowd, must separate himself from the crowd – in some fashion. He owes it to the crowd itself. He must define himself. He must make his singularity clear. *Now* with our vast hurrying multitudes this is more than ever urgent. It has to be done. The pose. The difference.'

'But couldn't one write just for oneself?'

'Then why write it down?'

'Or for a select circle of readers?'

'Oddly enough – no. Writing is an appeal. Always. Its objective is attention. You want to be read by every possible congenial reader in the world. I don't argue whether it should or should not be like that, but that is in the nature of writing. At any rate that is the nature of *my* writing.'

'I suppose it is like that. I never thought.'

'No.'

But now the tide of thought was rising.

'I suppose, after all, the life of man with a public is only an exaggeration of the life of every one who lives among his fellows. Nobody simply *is*. Every one *presents* himself. Behaviour isn't what springs from oneself. It is what we allow ourselves to do. It may be the direct antagonist of impulse. We stand behind ourselves and pull the strings. Consider – the extremest cases – our public characters. Our statesmen. Every one of them is really a vast cartoon, a mask – almost like a carnival mask. With them the thing assumes gigantic proportions. But every one who lives in the public eye, every one indeed who passes even for a moment across the public scene, is really an effigy, a frontage, a deliberate misrepresentation. And if you cannot make an emphatic personage of yourself, hard, bright-coloured, and distinctive, you will not hold it, you will be swept away into the undistinguished crowd, disregarded, forgotten.'

'The whole world a masquerade,' said his wife. 'I have never realized – '

'A vast tumultuous masquerade, a clamour for attention. Even the common crowd have their cheap common masks and thrust them at one another. I see it all plainly now. Now that my public mask has been damaged, distorted, broken. I had my place on the car of critical thought – my essays, my poems. I cut the figure, as they say. Not so bad a figure. And now I've just tumbled off the car and these jokers have clapped an ugly visor of fun upon me...'

'Darling it isn't so bad as that! Really it isn't!'

'Let me go on with my image. It does me good to expand the facts. There's real truth in it, and if I blow out my trouble like a bladder I shall presently be able to burst it, it will shrivel to nothing. Come to think of it, Bryn, no one has ever really *seen* a human being. No human beings have ever really seen themselves. They tell themselves stories about themselves. They pose and act. They tell stories about themselves to other people. Life is a battle of make-believe, a universal bluff. Only in the shock of some violent self-contradiction do we get a glimpse of the truth. So – There we are.'

He stopped abruptly.

'Darling,' she ventured, 'I'm sure it's done you good to say all that.'

'It wasn't bad of you to listen.'

She decided to sit on the arm of his chair. 'Poor busy little head,' she said, and kissed his forehead. 'It doesn't taste a bit like cardboard.'

He pretended to be still deep with thought.

'I will do something about it in the morning,' he promised himself.

'Bryn,' he said, 'you're pretty good for me. It would be awful to get up for this sort of thing and have to face it alone.'

She rested her cheek against his forehead for a moment. He put his arm about her and looked up at her almost shyly.

'I'll come up with you and smooth your pillow and uncrumple your sheets and put you to sleep,' she said, as if in answer to a question.

3

He went to sleep as soon as she left him.

But Mrs Palace slept no more that night. This nocturnal soothing always left her restless and active-minded. She found something between a memory of his talk and a dream procession going through her head. It was a parade of the world, she saw, the world of mankind wearing artificial faces, artificial bodies, on stilts and crutches and floats, mounted on horses, which themselves were caparisoned. All sorts of familiar people went by – and their faces were masks and never before had she seen that they were masks. The servants, the tradesmen's boys, her mother and father, her school teachers, every one she had taken for granted and believed in. Obviously masks. And pervading this spectacle was a strange, vast apprehension. Something was going to happen. Suddenly there was to be a miracle and the whole world would be stripped bare in a second. Every one would cease to pose, cease to behave. They would be instantaneously aware of the futility of conducting themselves.

Suppose all the trappings and behavings set aside, what sort of things would run out? What sort of queer creatures would come snarling out or scuttle for shelter?

Then from the general she came to the particular. What was there hiding behind that fine arras of kindly gentility, that clean, semi-athletic, cultured critic of life, Mr Rowland Palace? What was he really?

20

And what if presently she began to turn round and look for her own unmasked self? Not that, according to this new view of life, it seemed wise or necessary to turn one's attention that way. But if she wasn't really the honest, fairly sane and presentable young woman who for the last few years had been doing her duty (and on the whole liking it fairly well) by a fitful, sensitive, distinguished author – though she was beginning to think she would have preferred to have started a family three or four years ago – what on earth might she not be?

And so the rediscovery by Mr Rowland Palace of Schopenhauer's realization of the importance of Show (*Vorstellung*) sent him and his wife off in diametrically opposite directions, for while it started him upon the idea of the extreme importance of enlarging and strengthening the façade he presented to the world, a façade obviously perilously vulnerable at present, it sent her inquiring into all the neglected possibilities that might be pining and fretting behind the façade she had hitherto unquestioningly supposed to be herself.

CHAPTER THREE

The World Begins Every Morning

After Mr Rowland Palace had relieved his mind by talking, he was apt to forget much of what he had said. He rose late next day and it was only as he shaved that, with an effect of extreme novelty and detachment, the idea that all conscious life is masquerade, returned to him. Then for some seconds he paused, a lathered man on the left-hand side of his face and a smooth new-born Rowland on the right, uncertain whether he had been visited by a profound discovery or a fantastic dream. He looked himself in the eyes, questioning how much of his overnight activities was now eluding him. Not the faintest shade of the nocturnal despair that had coloured his memory of those Druidical snapshots remained. He saw them now as the repercussion of a slight tactical blunder, that ruffled but could not reverse the general strategy of his life, a mere incident, controllable and reparable.

As every military man knows, the brightest of opportunities may be revealed by a reparable blunder.

When he came down his wife had breakfasted and was sitting at the little desk between the fireplace and window, from which she directed her household. The shade of sympathetic anxiety in her eyes vanished at the sight of his general pinkness. She kissed him, considered him for a moment and rang for fresh toast.

He did not immediately open the plump bundle of press-cuttings among his letters and when he did, he did so with no apparent distaste.

His words when he spoke astonished her. 'Not so bad,' he said.

'I've seen none of them,' she said, and came round behind him.

'This one in profile.'

He was always at his best in profile because then one did not get a certain inequality of his eyes, which made one of them seem always just a little astonished at and inclined to protest against its fellow. It was quite a large picture form the *World Made Visible* that he held out to her. It formed part of the double page called 'In the Public Eye'. She saw him robed and garlanded and looking silly – but amiably silly. He was bending forward to give the prize to the village maiden, who regarded him with unquestionable awe. The letterpress said 'The Critic turns Bard'.

Mrs Palace ran her eye over the rest of the cuttings. There were no other pictures. 'The thing's dying out,' she said.

'Yes,' he said slowly, finished his tea and took up the picture again. 'Yes.'

He got up, still holding the illustrated cutting and straddled the hearthrug. 'Now if *that* had gone to the Oxford and Cambridge papers, it wouldn't have mattered so much. They could have stood that.'

'Rowly,' she asked, 'why do you think so much of under-graduates?'

'Every writer in his sense writes for undergraduates. Using the word for practically all the adolescents who read books. The clerk, the shopman, the young miner, and so on are just donless undergraduates nowadays. They read the same stuff, they talk the same stuff. Real social differences disappear. A few dons more or less and a little disregarded Gothic, don't matter. What's the Backs? What's Magdalen tower? Just scenery. Inside they are all the same now, Cambridge or Camberwell. And these undergraduates, donned and donless, are the *living core* of the public. Nothing else matters.'

'But – real undergraduates are so *silly!* They're sillier than young girls.'

'Possibly. Softer anyhow. They take impressions very readily and then they grow up very fast. They get beefy. Voices deepen. Self-confidence. Whiskers. And it's all over. Plasticity has ended. The print is there for life. What undergraduates think today, the world thinks tomorrow. You can mould undergraduates. You can put things over on them and push their minds about. They resent it very quickly if they see you at it, but it has to happen to them. Somebody gets them. They can't think alone. You can't push adult minds about. Adults have *set*. They resist. Print yourself on minds between seventeen and three-and-twenty, Bryn – and the rest you need not bother about. Either you've won them or lost them. The fear of the undergraduates is the beginning of fame. For a writer. For a politician.'

He put the picture-cutting on the table before him where he could see it, took the tobacco-jar from the mantelshelf and began to fill his pipe. Mrs Palace rang for the girl to clear away and returned to her accounts. Her husband smoked and reflected.

Presently he tried over a few propositions.

'The undergraduate is soft-witted and yet dangerous. He is as suspicious as a nervous dog. He is resolved that nobody shall make a fool of him. He longs to do brave things. You must keep your façade towards him *always*. Once he gets a glimpse of something soft and sensitive behind it – his mouth waters – he bites! That was what I feared about this Druid business. Why I took it so seriously. I seemed to be showing my unprotected pants. The contempt of the undergraduate when he thinks he sees round you is implacable. And the more idiotic it is the more implacable it is... But with that last picture now – I could get past them.'

Mrs Palace had one ear for him, and thrice she added up the butcher's bill and got a different result. Then she left the question of the butcher altogether and stared at this remarkable husband of hers. She was trying to match him with the sensitive, suffering, indistinctly grateful thing she had parted from in the night.

She looked at the cutting on the table and then back at his face.

2

'Why *not* a touch of geniality, Bryn? Why *not* a touch of geniality? I've long had an idea that the impression I made on people was a little cold and stiff. One shouldn't be too aloof. You see – the way this little affair at Canham was taken up... It looks as if they didn't quite like me – as if they had been waiting for some slip on my part... Growing inpatient... It hasn't been like that before.'

He was now quite evidently talking to himself. 'Suppose one had a personality – a public personality – that *included* slips of this sort. If one were known to be a little careless...

'In the end they might like one better.'

He seemed to become faintly aware of his wife again.

'There's a sort of turning-point in the literary life, Bryn – in our world. A change of phase. To begin with, one, *oneself*, is an undergraduate. One is just part of the general undergraduate pack, a thing that responds easily, shouts loudly. Condemns, adheres. One is irresponsible. One says, does, or believes – anything. Nobody observes you. Nobody minds. Whatever you do is a rag and you are forgiven. "Bright boy," they remark. Then, as people say, you arrive. Almost with a jolt. It is like the sudden expansion of water when it freezes. You are *de-liquidated*. You become larger. You are looked at, judged, *placed*. That is what has happened to me. I am the least self-conscious of men, but I perceive that I have become an audible visible figure.'

'You've had press-cuttings for years,' said his wife.

'But for those cuttings I should hardly realize it now.'

She reflected and returned to the household accounts.

Presently, having got a new and unprecedented total for the butcher's bill, she became aware that he was speaking again. 'Oh!' she said. 'What *is* it, dear?'

'Well – this is the point, Bryn. I have *really* arrived. I mean in a popular sense. I suppose *The Supple Willow Wand* has done it. Or a general accumulation of reputation. The world-wide distribution of these photographs shows that. We are seen. We have to be seen. We have ceased to be supers in the World Carnival. And we have to meet the occasion.'

He seemed to hesitate. She helped him with 'How?'

'Yes – how?'

She waited. She was no good at answering counter-questions.

'We have to make up our minds about the figure we mean to cut in the world. And we have to stick to that. From now on.

Otherwise these young gentlemen with the cameras and the paragraph writers and the gossip correspondents will invent something about us for themselves. And they will get us wrong. All wrong. And people will open my books in the wrong key. Almost as though each volume came out wrapped up in a more vulgarizing blurb than the last, adorned with an uglier portrait and a hostile preface. "That fellow," they will say.'

'But even if we do invent – Dearest, can't we *be* what we *are*?'

'Yes. Yes. We don't have to change. I don't mean that. But – we have to *seem* what we are. We have to be what we are night and day. And let them into it. And see that they get it.'

'And avoid inferior intimations,' she said. 'I don't see how it can be done, darling.'

She stood up with the butcher's book in her hand. She felt it would add up quite differently in her own room. Possibly it would begin to settle down to something like a uniform total. 'I really don't see what we can do about it,' she said.

But her husband wanted to talk to her.

3

'Wait a moment, Bryn, I don't think you quite get me. No. I see what you think, of course. But simplification of behaviour isn't insincerity. I don't think it deceit to put one's cards on the table. Either we walk up to the newspaper camera and face it, or we are surprised and assassinated. That's the modern alternative. You give yourself out or you are dragged out. People want to imagine a writer while they read him. And hear about him. He owes them a good personality just as he owes them a good style. From publication to publicity is a necessary step.'

He pulled himself up in front of her. 'Well. Isn't it?' he asked.

'I'm thinking,' she said.

'Dear, I don't quite see what you are getting at. Can't one write books and still be private?'

'Not now. Not in this world of mass effects. Not if one means to influence opinion.'

'But Kipling, for instance. People heard very little about him intimately. And there's no portrait of Virginia Woolf that I know of. Elizabeth of the *German Garden* again. You never see a portrait of her or hear anything about her home or her habits.'

'Invisibility once in a way may be a sort of personality. As a matter of fact the Elizabeth books are full of personality. She is delightfully there, even if she isn't at home to photographers and callers. Once in a way you can do that. I grant you, too, that the Waverley novels were published incognito. Scott cut a bigger figure as the Great Unknown than he did at Abbotsford. But the day for that sort of thing is past. Reputations were made then by social gossip. Not now. In these rushing times the public has no patience for masks and mysteries. If you don't give them something, they'll snatch at something. Or just rush by.'

'But Rowly, what does *giving them something* mean?'

'Choose our own battleground. Be prepared for them. Tell them to come and look when we are ready for them.'

'Interviews?'

'Possibly.'

'Anecdotes about you?'

'Look at that.' He indicated the cutting.

'Rowly,' she said. 'Does that mean you think we ought to have photographers in the house and me telling interviewers what it is like to be married to you – and things like that?'

'Not exactly *that*.'

'But something very like it,' she said. She reflected, and he saw what to his private self he called her obstinate expression, stealing over her face. She gave her decision with a gentle mulishness: 'Rowly, dear; I don't think I could stand it.'

He raised his eyebrows and shoulders and said no more and she went thoughtfully out of the room, the household books in her hand almost forgotten.

CHAPTER FOUR

Mr Rowland Palace in Search of Himself

For some days Mr Rowland Palace talked no more to his wife about this uneasy urge of his towards a planned, controlled, and effective publicity. But he was thinking with extraordinary animation, discursiveness, and abundance about it. He was indeed launched upon a very wide and congenial flow of thought. It was almost as if the dam penning up some great reservoir of imaginations had given way.

In a sense no doubt, like every rational creature that has to conduct itself, he was always thinking about himself. But like most rational self-conducting creatures the self he thought about was taken for granted in most of its details. It was apprehended superficially and habitually, but now, under this new and stimulating suggestion of putting over a personality on the world, he could yield freely to a long-restrained impulse, and think about himself amply and continually. He could wallow in his own characteristics. Instead of asking 'What shall I do?' he could vary his questions between: 'What am I? What can I be? What had I best be? What had they best think I am?' And 'How do I look to them?' and find unlimited interest in the ensuing exercises.

There had been phases in his life before when with greater or less intensity Mr Rowland Palace had been the main subject of his own attention. His great friendship with Montague Mansbridge in the last year at Shonts, had been a long orgy of mutual self-explanation, terminated only when Mansbridge, who was not only a bad letter writer but, it proved, a bad letter reader, went to the East. Palace had been head of the school and Mansbridge had been captain of games and when they talked it seemed to them that the world was like a red carpet put down before their feet. At the price of rather overrating Mansbridge he did for a while get a satisfactorily objective impression of himself. And there had been the time of his engagement to Brynhild and their honeymoon.

That had happened when Rowland was thirty-two and Bryn was twenty. At the university he had had literary associates but no close friends, and still less had there been scope for the exploration of his ego when he returned from Cambridge to teach history and English in Shonts and develop the literary career that had been opened so auspiciously with *Bent Oars*. The feeling of his colleagues there had been against any accentuation of personality and the games master said openly that it was *infra dig.* for a teacher of literature to 'publish things'. The atmosphere of Shonts was full of that menacing modesty that so well becomes an Englishman. He had been forced back upon himself and upon the ironical style. He realized now for the first time that perhaps irony was not really his quality.

Then had come growing success, the unexpected death in an automobile accident, of a tough rich aunt godmother, twenty years before her time, the consequent release from the assistant-mastership at Shonts and his meeting with his distant cousin Brynhild with the dark eyes. Both were stimulatingly unrich but well provided for and they were both reasonably addicted to tennis, boating, and mountain climbing. She was the daughter of a country rector who had been a great classic and had not so much educated her as made up his old classical clothing for her mind to wear. It fitted very loosely but it kept her out of contact with vulgar ideas. Six terms at the celebrated High-farthing school after his death had affected his influence very little. He had done his utmost to impress upon her that there was something contemptibly unscholarly and inaccurate about most contemporary things and that though sin was highly reprehensible, meanness and mental disingenuousness were far more hateful to both God and man. One was in the world, of course, but that was no reason why one should mix oneself up with it in an indiscriminating way. She grew up reserved, but not shy, a good listener and anxious to learn. She had an air of being taken by surprise by the human spectacle and wanting to know what it was about as it thrust itself upon her. She was the sort of young woman who does not like dogs.

Palace's literary prestige impressed her greatly, and on their honeymoon, loitering and rambling in the Bernese Alps and over the Theodule, he opened his heart to her about himself – and life generally – and his ambitions and how he was almost in spite of himself an intellectual liberator. He was a good enough lover to tell her continually how lovely she was, and he said she was as simple as dawning and direct as the flight of an arrow. His own much more complicated make-up was consequently the main substance of his discourse.

He was not always easy to follow and sometimes the old habit of irony asserted itself. She loved to hear him talk in those days, she had never met any one so clever or any one who stretched her mind so much since her father died, she followed his words intently and remembered them all, but at times she found it difficult to say quite the right thing in reply.

One day they were sitting on a low wall near one of those sanctuaries at Orta. He sat with his back to the figures and talked about his influence in the world. He said he wanted to release people. That was his aim.

'Release from what?'

'From all the clotted nonsense, new and old, in which they are – embedded.'

'And, dearest, what *then?*'

It seemed natural enough to ask that. She looked at him expectantly but all he did was to frown slightly and wave an arm.

'What *would* you?' he asked.

'But what would you?' she countered.

'Art, freedom, a sufficient life.'

Was he embarrassed at expounding the obvious or was he evading the inexplicable? Art, freedom, a sufficient life? She felt, but she did not know how to say, that these words meant nothing until they were defined. But her mind suddenly bristled with questions like a hedgehog's quills. And as immediately it came to her that not a single quill could be shot at him profitably. What was this 'art', what was this 'freedom', what was this 'sufficient life' that justified his widespread scorn for the rest of humanity and in particular the rest of humanity which wrote and practised the arts? She had better not ask it. Somehow it wasn't the time. And yet there she was thinking it. This realization gave her her first twinge of disloyalty.

Her dream had been of two lovers living a life of perfect candour. Was she now holding back her questions because she was not clever enough to put them, or was she holding them back because he might think the answers would be too subtle for her capacity? And she hardly dared think that these two alternatives did not by any means exhaust the possibility of the situation. She hardly dared think that perhaps he would just throw his arms and his phrases about with an increasing irritation in his voice.

She awoke one night and he was sleeping with his cheek touching her shoulder. How dear he was and how manly! Maybe imperfection is a part of manliness. What a wonderful abundant realization of life this love in marriage was, this intensive exploration of personality into which one flowed and which flowed into one. It was like going through a vast gift mansion of treasures and discovering unsuspected rooms and corridors of quaint and amusing things. He had some quite endearing absurdities and appealing defects she had never anticipated. And then came the thought that all of that content was not at the same level of dearness. Down some of the passages the exhibits were not quite – not *quite* – of the same quality. There were traits that it was not pure joy to discover. She lay very still and tried to think exclusively of a thousand lovely things that had come to her in the past few weeks, lovely things she had been able to get out of it all, in order to banish the disagreeable realization that was taking hold of her that in certain respects she was becoming distinctly critical of him. She was holding back insidious realizations. As, for instance, that his voice had just a shade of needlessly aggressive defiance in it, that he pitched it too high and his face a little too high when he delivered it, and indulged too frequently in weak, fastidious gestures of the hands. And that he was apt to interrupt and override her remarks when they attempted to deflect him into elucidation. And that nearly all his discourse was deprecatory. For him even the Alps never rose to their highest, and generally he thought the sun might have set with a better grace.

No. It wasn't like that. It couldn't be like that.

Should young lovers be critical of each other? It was human to be imperfect. It was lovable to be as absurdly exacting with life as he was.

Something brought Milton's 'safest and seemliest by her husband stays' across her drowsy mind; there was a certain disloyalty in wandering away from him even in her thoughts. She must stop this thinking. She stirred about and withdrew her shoulder and woke Rowly up and kissed him.

And one day they were out among the reeds upon the lake in a canopied boat. They had swum and lunched and been everything to each other that lovers should be. Then, wrapped only in a towel and smoking an indolent cigarette, she did her best to broach the gist of her private trouble and abolish the rising barrier of reserve on her part that threatened their perfect intimacy.

'Darling,' she said, 'one can be too critical, don't you think? Too soon, too often, and too much.'

She was thinking simply of this queer new uncontrollable disposition of her awakening mind to criticize him and note points against him, but the one face that leapt up in him to meet her observation was that his published essays were saturated with the critical spirit.

'My dear Bryn,' he protested, 'criticism is the touchstone of life. I could not love thee half as much, loved I not criticism more. I couldn't appreciate your loveliness if I didn't know acutely what Bad is.'

'But between friends and lovers?'

'I've said it.'

He didn't see, she realized, which way the point was turned. 'But suppose suddenly I began finding fault with *you?*'

He let that slip by him.

'How can one find perfection if one can't find fault?'

She looked at his remark for some moments. It seemed to have got loose from some other discussion. She just stared at him. When he found she had nothing more to say he stared back between interrogation and surprise.

'Things are so difficult to say,' she apologized at last. She felt she was being very stupid.

'Maybe I've been rhetorical at times,' he tried. 'But do you find, dear, that on the whole my intelligence seems over-critical? Is that what you mean?'

It wasn't at all what she had meant. But she felt she could never get back to that original intention and so she went on with the new thread.

'Darling, I know so little. There's all sorts of things that you don't say because probably you think I know all about them. You don't know how many backward people like me there are in the world. So you seem to be condemning. Very often you seem to be condemning. Just condemning. When really, if I knew your standards, I should understand why you look down on so many people.'

'You mean I look down on too many people?'

'You have a right to look down on them.'

He surveyed her lovely pose of stark inquiry. It was almost as though she had caught his weapon of irony and turned it against him. But there was nothing but receptive simplicity in her eyes.

37

'Well, *haven't* you?' she said very simply and earnestly.

'Haven't *we?*'

She detached herself. 'I'm nothing.'

Something like a metal bar seemed to him to fall between them. He looked away from her across the lake to where the little town basked on its island. 'I suppose I am preposterous,' he said, and something seemed to go out of the sunlight.

A faint resentment came into his voice. 'I suppose it is preposterous to regret the common things of life; their limitations, compromises, desolating self-sufficiency... There is striving behind every scorn... Rejection of the second best... Am I nothing more than bitter-tongued? Maybe. I thought you understood me better, Bryn. Perhaps I don't even understand myself... The haunting impalpable presence of an infinite desire.'

He stopped. She was soundless. She might not have been there. He turned from the lake and looked at her. Her expression was earnest and her lips were silently repeating those last words. She was committing them to memory, she was taking them down for later examination, she was going off with them to gnaw them in quiet.

And immediately he knew that they were – innutritious.

Then it was for the first time that it dawned upon Rowland Palace that there was something obtuse about his lovely Brynhild, that the peculiar quality needed to understand him was lacking in her. She didn't quite know how to take things like that. She was joining up one thing he said with another and keeping an account for reference.

He did not want her to remember; he wanted her to sympathize and accept. And pass on. He had been too careless with her, too lavishly open. Against her too, against her literal seriousness, her meticulous interrogativeness, he must protect his soul. And in this fashion it was that his second great flow of self-expression turned to ebb. Again he began to fall back into the solitude of his inner self. And upon the distractions of work and events.

Which did not prevent their being quite happy lovers and tourists throughout that honeymoon. He was the best of company now that self-revelation was ebbing. He attempted less and less talk about the inner significance of love, and there was a truce to mutual criticism. His ironies and comments on contemporary things diminished. The thoughts of Brynhild remained as deep and unfathomable as the depths of her dark eyes. They were as shapeless even to her as things peered at in an overshadowed pool. Only slowly did she realize that for her also Rowland was becoming self-protective and ironical and that her beautiful dream of a limitless mutual explicitness was fading away.

2

So in this third expedition of Mr Rowland Palace in search of his hidden self which we are now recording, Brynhild had no place. Indeed, her mere presence was sufficient to arrest the pursuit altogether.

He had tried to break down his immense reserves and produce a real self for his friend Mansbridge. And Mansbridge had never really answered his letters. He had tried again to produce a hidden self for Brynhild and she had betrayed – to his sensitive observation at least, she had betrayed – a critical searching curiosity about the solidity of that hidden self of his. He had recoiled before the mute questions in her eyes. She had made him doubt even himself. Now like a great light breaking in upon him had come this realization that the time for the long-deferred disrobing of his ironies and disbeliefs had arrived. The egg-shell of negation had been tapped by those photographers and he had to come forth of his own accord or be for ever made ridiculous.

He was proposing to release a new and more intimate self, not now to any single person but to an indefinite public; he was going to ask for understanding from the unknown. The mistake hitherto had been to look to single individuals as the mirrors in which the self was to be discovered and seen. It was to a public he must address himself.

Much of Mr Rowland Palace's meditations upon his definitive self was conducted that May in the gardens of the Royal Botanical Society in Regent's Park. In those days the Inner Circle was still cut off from public intrusion, a pleasant rather untidy arrangement of glass-houses, lawns, shrubs, flower-beds, and ornamental water which might have been a hundred miles from London for any sign of town or population at hand. One felt like the house guest at some country seat. It was very peaceful and delightful for every one who subscribed to the society.

Some of his thinking he did in his study or in bed at nights. He was a fellow of the Zoological Society, but he went there more rarely because of the greater distance from his house in Gloucester Place, and for any one gathering ideas about a true self he found the Zoo almost too suggestive. Many of the higher animals, he perceived, were acutely self-conscious. The lions posed, the wolves would not meet his eye, the howler showed off, the mandrill was as frankly self-revelatory as any modern author. Such beasts are in a society of their own imagining. But the ducks and gulls and the reptiles seemed still in the age of innocence, unaware that there could be anything to conceal or exhibit or explain.

Now as soon as Rowland Palace was fairly launched upon the flood of self-investigation and self-construction, he found himself in trouble with something that had always been lying in wait for him since those impalpable honeymoon discordances. It was not an accusation Brynhild had levelled at him. It was not that she had ever done more than seemed to imply. And yet he was as convinced that she thought it, as if since those first weeks together she had not only maintained the completest disbelief in him but reminded him of it continually. He had nothing to go upon for this but the merest shadow of a suggestion in a careless phrase, and something that looked out at him ever and again from her candid and yet mysterious eyes.

He had indeed thought this thing *for* her, made it hers in his mind, and worn it like a tender place that must not be touched too closely, through nine years of marriage. Now, if he was to go out into the open before his public, he would have to come to some decision about their unformulated discordance.

This deterrent idea which had barred him from the pleasures of unrestrained Narcissism for nearly a decade and kept him on the rails of objective irony, was this, that it is unjustifiable to despise or belittle anything in the world unless one has a definite conception of something better. And that, save for a few phrases and mere emotional gestures, he had nothing whatever to set against the poor commonly accepted things he battered. He was recognized as a 'liberating' writer. 'Liberation,' asked the disturbing inner questioner who bore the face of Brynhild, 'for what?'

'For what?' he said aloud in the brightness of the after-glow, watching a dabchick lead a trail of diminutive offspring across the shining water towards a headland of reeds.

'*I* know. As a Christian devotee knows his God. But how to make *them* know? How to convince them that I am not merely hollow – a hollow resonance making rebellious noises?'

He found a good phrase.

'You can't invite inspectors into the Holy of Holies...'

That beautiful pellucid evening glowered with acceptance, everything was magically real, and that seemed a very satisfactory and restful conclusion to the matter.

But that evening he went round with Brynhild to the Oscar Gecks' to dine, and as he sat over the coffee with two other men he asked suddenly: 'I wonder if Ever there was Anything in the Holy of Holies?'

3

One of the men was historical and archaeological, but Oscar Geck was nearer Palace's point. 'You think that maybe there is nothing at the heart of things?'

'The general idea,' said the historian, 'has been that God is at the heart of things.'

'For endless people nowadays,' said Geck, 'God is merely a title conferred on nothing. The modern God cannot move because he is omnipresent, cannot think because he is omniscient, cannot act because he is outside time and eternal and omnipotent, while action can only go on in time against resistance. Logic has blown him out like a soap-bubble until he has no substance left at all.'

'And when you have abolished God by intellectual wind,' said Palace, 'still he is there. At the heart of things. Still there is Beauty. Still there is a living judge who makes some values immeasurably greater than others.'

'Are you so sure that's not in yourself?' asked Geck.

'Does it matter where it is?' said Palace.

The historian made an irrevelant remark. 'I am like a palaeontologist who cannot deal with life until it is reduced to dead bones. I deal with the remains of dead gods. Cathedrals, mosques, a coral reef of temples, religious wars. I cannot deal with living gods or gods alleged to be living. They are not history. Sometimes I feel that this modern God of yours is so impalpable that he will leave nothing whatever behind to fossilize. Which will make the religious history of the period very difficult when it comes to be written...'

He went his way for some five minutes of talk and then died out. Oscar Geck suggested they should go upstairs, and Mr Palace's Holy of Holies remained obscure.

4

He found himself discussing his Holy of Holies with the tree shadows on his ceiling in the middle of the night.

'It is plain I am a Mystic,' he said.

'The spirit of the Innermost, the spirit of *my* innermost, can only be known by its outer manifestations. Demigods are the facets of God. I believe in Beethoven, Mozart, Leonardo da

Vinci... Shakespeare. There is an inner light that recognizes the divine.

'The divine is hieratic. Behind the great Demigods are the lesser Gods. And Angels. Angels... I am becoming Swedenborgian.'

He dozed pleasantly through a dream of tiers above tiers of exalted beings. Very Swedenborgian indeed, circle above circle. He also had his place in one of these tiers serving the ineffable, the transcendent, the ultimate beauty. He found himself murmuring 'Metaphorical. All thought is metaphor.'

Sleep obliterated him for an unmarked period of minutes and when he was awake again a slanting bar of moonlight leant against the north-west wall of his room. It had not been there before.

'Mystics cannot explain. Mystics cannot be called upon to explain. But nevertheless they can have the clearest sense of values. They are not merely justified in condemning and deprecating certain things; it is their duty. To some of us is given the spear of Ithuriel.'

The run of phrases in his mind became abruptly audible. 'And that is where *I* come in,' he said aloud.

He was now wide awake. He sat up in bed with a sense of complete *éclaircissement*.

He was one of the great company that served the supreme mystery. Some had to make and create; there were infinite varieties of service, but his rôle was clearly to wield the spear of Ithuriel. And somehow it had to be made evident to the great public that that was what he amounted to.

Of this fundamental rightness of his life he was not perhaps explicitly sure but he was mystically sure. Which is on the whole a far securer defensive certainty.

And now having found his essential self and his essential function and defeated and dismissed that long rankling doubt, that nine-year-old doubt, about his fundamental self, having assured himself that at heart he was not practically empty and envious but mystically full, he could deal with the problem of putting himself over to the public with a steadfast and confident mind.

It was admitted that he had been doing that part of his Ithuriel business negligently. At the proper time Ithuriel should come out commandingly, not lurk for ever among the shrubs. He had kept up his reserve too long. He had incurred the suspicion of being a Superior Person, supercilious, precious, loftily genteel, a Prig. He had to give that figure warmth and colour before it was too late. He had to become a character. That maypole day at Canham had been not a disaster but a saving shock. One of the photographs he had realized had not been so bad. It had set the key for what he had to do.

He had to make it plain that he was not high and disdainful but sympathetic and jolly – as he felt sure he really was. He had to smile spontaneously; laugh aloud, bring his ironies into the thick of things. 'Rowland Palace; the Second Phase.'

He had as a matter of fact been changing very profoundly during the last decade. It was not a thing he admitted freely even to himself, but his youth had been a *timid* youth. It was just because he was generally timid that he had developed a certain aggressive vigour in his writing. None so poor that cannot swagger at a writing-desk. A sheet of paper is your faithful partisan and the ink in a fountain-pen, however much it may clog or blot, never blanches.

But success had given him courage, his marriage, too, had given him a certain courage with people. Though Bryn baffled him, it was very plain she loved him. His looks and bearing had improved with her approval. He had become something of a talker at lunches and dinners, and more particularly when Bryn was out of earshot. He had found out that all women did not regard him with eyes in which affectionate scepticism was becoming more and more apparent. There was an offhand easiness of understanding about women like Lady Burnish and Lady Cytherea. They did not consider his good things suspiciously; they swallowed them whole.

He was developing a discursive liking for women. He was the sort of man who would rather talk to any woman not absolutely obese or ugly or decrepit than to any man. They were responsive.

A few little things had happened. Going downstairs on Sunday night at Empton Lodge a tall and extremely good-looking housemaid had passed him on the stairs and looked at him with, he fancied, exceptional intentness. On the landing he had glanced back to verify this odd impression and she had paused above and was standing looking down at him. There was an instant of still frankness and she turned away and he went on down. She never appeared again. It meant nothing. It meant everything.

Then when he loitered behind the house-party that was being taken round the great gardens of Hangar Hoe, to show Miss Sheila Dalrymple how quaint the infloresence of a moss could look through a pocket lens, and just for a moment her eyelash brushed his cheek – lingeringly. His heart stopped for a moment. 'Never anything so lovely,' he said, and except for a roguish smile from her at the station on Monday morning that was all.

But the moment when he went out on the balcony with the tall dark Miss Gambard, the elder one, after the second act of *Tristan*, was more wonderful still. For she looked at him in a mutuality of appreciative exaltation and kissed him there and then. Just that. Not a word. A stillness and they went in again.

Such little things confirm a man.

But an increasing appreciation of variety in women did not withdraw him from association with men; it invigorated his association with men. He found it was no longer necessary to fend them off with an enigmatical shy haughtiness. He could take and give. He had joined the Thespian Club and in the smoking-room he would twit and be twitted.

So this new Rowland Palace he felt he was now capable of releasing for the Market Place of life, was shaping as an altogether more human, smiling, kinky, playful fellow, broader, larger, more various and unexpected, stabbing his victims as though he loved them, then the quiet, aloof, but just a trifle adolescent figure with the curling lip that had hitherto stood in the shop window.

Mr Palace was filling out.

'A touch of the Anatolian,' he said, with France rather than Nearer Asia in his mind.

'That's what I am,' he said. 'That's what I am *as I ripen.*'

And then turning to the actual business of putting it over: 'It has to be done properly.'

CHAPTER FIVE

Elements of the Science and Art of Publicity

It had to be done properly. It had to be done without Brynhild knowing anything about it. Because if once he knew that she knew that he had the deliberate intention of making a public figure of himself, more explicit to the public than he was to her, then without a word, without a gesture, his intention would collapse. She was a difficult wife, though she did not mean to be. She was often totally unaware of the wordless things she said to him, of the initiatives she killed. And over and above her obstruction, he had as yet only the faintest idea how to set about this business of self-exposure.

He felt he had to go warily, taking soundings, charting these intricate and dangerous channels that led at last to the public recognition of an established personality. He must get people who knew about this sort of thing to talk to him and show him the ropes.

He began with Desmond Blatch, his agent.

Desmond Blatch suggested a streaky blend of family solicitor with a commercial traveller in fancy foods, and sometimes the family solicitor stuff was on the surface and sometimes the drummer swirled up. When he was talking strict business he kept his glasses on; when he talked art they immediately fell off and he used them as a baton to conduct his conversation. He had an imposing office to justify a uniform ten per cent and its walls were hung with signed enlargements of all that was prominent and successful in contemporary literature.

'I was in the Strand and it occurred to me – as I had a quarter of an hour or so free – to drop in and hear how things are going with me,' said Mr Palace.

There was a pause. 'How *are* they going?' asked Mr Palace.

'Steadily,' said Mr Blatch, 'steadily. How is the – the new work – going on?'

'*Which* new work?'

'The – èr – the novel.'

'They were both novels I had in mind.'

'Of course,' said Mr Blatch, making his glasses flash intelligently. 'I understand that. And I may say that I have one or two developments... Preparatory work... But I hope to be able to put something like a firm proposal before you very soon. From an unexpected quarter. That I think you will find attractive – to say the least of it.'

'It wasn't *offers* I had in mind,' said Mr Palace.

Mr Blatch became silently interrogative.

'At least not today. No. It's the question of my position, my attitude generally, *vis-à-vis* with the public. It seemed to me – as I was passing... Well, an agent isn't merely a haggler for prices.'

'Oh, no.'

'Shouldn't be.'

Mr Blatch tried to keep touch. 'One has to think of all sorts of – collateral – considerations.'

50

'Exactly. For instance, the general growth and one's reputation. The rôle of criticism, rumour, anecdote...'

'I watch it,' Mr Blatch asserted in a voice that wasn't quite assured as it might be. 'I watch it.'

'You have press-cutting, I presume?'

'Generally – about *all* my authors,' said Mr Blatch, having difficulties with his glasses. They fell off suddenly. He ended with a flourish of them to show the comprehensiveness of his 'generally'.

'Yes – but nowadays...' Mr Palace hung fire for a moment and then came to it abruptly. 'Is that enough?'

He expanded. 'Times have changed. In the past, in the time of Dickens and Thackeray and Longfellow and Tennyson and so forth – it was a simple, steadfast, unencumbered world. There was a definite reading public, a compact world of criticism. It was a room, a large room but not an overwhelming room, full of similarly cultivated people into which the author came. He made his bow. He was introduced. That was all. After all, I suppose the original literary agent – by the by, who *was* the original literary agent?'

'A P Watt – a friend of Walter Besant and Wilkie Collins and James Payn.'

'Yes. Well, I suppose all he had to do was to sell novels and serial rights?'

'Practically that was all.'

'And that only in Great Britain?'

'There was no American copyright.'

'America did not matter.'

Mr Blatch threw something of the wonder of life's changes into his voice. 'America,' he echoed, 'did not matter.'

'*Now,*' said Mr Palace, and his gesture made the contrast.

'Nowadays,' he expanded, 'I observe that the simple straightforward relationship of author, buyers of books and library subscribers, has swollen and blossomed out and branched and divided. There is no longer a reading public; there are innumerable little transitory reading publics. They come and go. They are attracted with more difficulty, they forget more readily, and they misunderstand – swiftly.'

Mr Blatch wondering more and more what Mr Palace was driving at, tightened his lips, nodded his head, and replaced his glasses.

'A reputation in the old days was made – for good,' said Mr Palace. 'You were labelled. And there you were.'

'Perfectly true,' said Mr Blatch. 'Perfectly true. There you were.'

'But now,' said Mr Palace, 'a personal reputation is infinitely more exposed and precarious; it has to be sown, watched, fostered, protected from wilting, protected from parasites and enemies of all sorts, developed, guarded, magnified. What are you doing for my reputation, Blatch? What idea have you of me? What, so to speak, is the Rowland Palace idea? What is the idea you are – what is the expression? – putting over on them on my behalf?'

'A very good reputation,' said Mr Blatch. 'A steadily growing reputation.'

'As what?'

Mr Blatch felt he was undergoing a cross-examination that might become hostile. He had to develop his line of defence quickly. He had been leaning back in his chair. Now he sat up, handled papers on his desk and looked steadfastly at Mr Palace.

'The best of all reputations, the reputation of being *a better seller every time*.'

'You miss my point,' said Mr Palace.

'No,' said Mr Blatch, 'I don't miss your point. But I know where my business begins and ends. I am not agent between author and public. I am agent between author and editor, author and publisher, author and producer.'

'But *they* have to have a conception of me!'

'As a producer of saleable goods.'

'But that is dependent on what the public thinks of me. So *you* have to have an idea of what idea the publisher has of the idea of me that the public has.' Mr Blatch frowned with mental effort.

'And all these ideas, mind you,' pressed Mr Palace, 'based in the last resort on one's reputation with the public or with some section of the public, are, I suggest, notions that can be made, sustained, damaged, improved...'

Mr Palace threw up a hand of lively fingers, to express the variegated activities of reputation-making.

Mr Blatch felt that the time had come to escape from this issue by a little confusing talk. Mr Palace had to be distracted from himself.

'I don't know whether *every* literary reputation isn't ultimately an Act of God,' said Mr Blatch. 'I think you are inclined to stress its artificiality.' His eyes searched for something on his spacious desk and he lifted up a little volume in an unwholesome-looking mauve and blue wrapper. 'Here, for instance, is Phyllis Pelmet. God alone knows how this book of hers came to sell – but it sells like hot cakes. It goes on selling. She knew no one. She had no introductions. Batley thought he wouldn't sell two thousand of her. It just happens. Old

Schroederer has her. A thousand in advance. It's a good spring for Phyllis Pelmet just as it may be a good spring for bluebells. Are you a gardener, Mr Palace? One year the bluebells make a delightful patch under your beech-trees; the next they are noxious weeds swarming all over your flower-beds. And nobody knows why.'

'People in your position ought to know,' said Mr Palace harshly. 'Some day some one will.'

'I doubt it,' said Mr Blatch.

'And what I am talking about is not these – these spasmodic sales. Your Phyllis Pelmets are here today and gone tomorrow. They are daily-paper reputations. People of that sort are like the last murderess or the new boy golfer. *I* am talking about the establishment of a permanent reputation, of the way in which some men and women seem to loom larger and root deeper with the years.'

'Ah, *that!*' said Mr Blatch, and dropped and waved his glasses. 'Quality, abundance, a continual freshness. That sort of thing makes me a bit of a mystic. It transcends business. You have to be always the same and always novel, give 'em exactly what they expect – with a little touch of surprise each time. But that, you know, is something innate. No man, as the Bible puts it, by taking thought can add an inch to his reputation. No. And is that kind of thing going on now, as it used to go on? Maybe there are not going to be many more Great Names at all. Do you ever, in your leisure nowadays, do any literary criticism? Apart from the Phyllis Pelmets and that sort of – well – *epidemic*, do you ever see any one really coming along? Some one with staying power?'

Mr Palace appeared to reflect, and shook his head. He was not in the least interested in any one who might be coming along except himself.

'This new man Alfred Bunter, for instance. Is *he* going to last?'

'I've never read a line of him. They say he has a sort of rude vigour. It's not for me to judge.'

'I see his name in the advertisements. *H*e certainly gets advertised.'

'And sold. He sells well.'

'Every time?'

'So far.'

'I don't know anything at all about this Alfred Bunter, but you must allow me to believe that nowadays, just as formerly, Great Names – names as relatively great as those of Scott and Dickens and Tolstoy in the past – will still emerge. Only you see, my dear Blatch, and that brings me to what I have in mind, the scale of operations is different and the operations have to be more designed, more complicated, more broadly planned. There's the straddle of Britain and America, for example...'

'You might lecture over there.'

'The travelling salesman of one's own goods.'

'Bunter is going to lecture. It needn't be just ordinary lecturing.'

'I don't see that Bunter supplies any precedent for me.'

'He shows himself about. You know, Mr Palace, the real maker of an author's personality is the author himself. An agent cannot create that for him.'

'Ah, now we come to grips. The agent cannot fabricate a personality – I agree. But the agent can seize upon it and –

disseminate it. He can magnify, he can repeat and recall. He may even enhance.'

'If you give him a chance,' said Mr Blatch. 'Now Shaw, for example – '

'Pure exhibitionism. And so far as I know he has no agent.'

Mr Palace perceived that there was no more to be said just then. 'We've had a good talk,' he said, 'I wanted to get your point of view.'

He rose.

Blatch came round his desk to show him out. He seemed to have already dismissed all that they had been talking about from his mind. 'You *should* read something of Alfred Bunter's,' he said, 'apart from anything we've been saying, the man has a quality. I'd like your reactions.'

As Mr Palace made his way towards the Thespian Club he considered the difficulties and advantages that might arise if he got a new agent altogether. 'Fellows like Blatch can reap a harvest,' he reflected, 'at ten per cent. But can they sow and cherish a harvest? They needn't. That's the trouble; they needn't! There are too many authors. Blatch is able to live by snatch crops. And anyhow – *damn* this *Alfred Bunter!* Who's agent *is* Blatch? – Bunter's or mine?'

2

Brooding still on the untilled field of his personal fame Mr Palace entered the club. As he passed the big circle about the hall fire on his way to the hat-pegs he heard old Cummington saying: 'This fellow Bunter can knock spots off any one else writing

56

novels today. He had a vitality. Oh! A tremendous vitality. He just pours out.'

'Give *me* restraint,' said Mr Palace softly to himself, hanging up his hat in the long passage.

He decided not to join the big circle for cocktails. Cummington's enthusiasms always annoyed him and this last enthusiasm just now he felt might annoy him very much. He would be asked to participate. No! He went into the dining-room a little in advance of the general crowd and sat down by a habit at one of the small tables. It had been his pose at his club as elsewhere not to mingle too indiscriminately with his fellows. Now as they filtered into the room he watched them. They were barristers accustomed to act, actors accustomed to under-act; journalists, writers, and so forth, all evidently conscious in an embarrassed way of themselves, and going through the daily ritual of being interested in each other and pleased to meet. Greetings were exchanged, hands were raised in brisk and agreeable gestures of fellowship to distant friends. Very few noticed Mr Palace. In his highly sensitized state this was exaggerated.

'Aloof or effaced?' he questioned. 'It's gone on too long. They've lost interest.'

Scraps of conversation floated to him. Nobody was saying anything about him although one set at the general table was firing disconnected comments at one another across the board about new poetry and new poets. Three or four years ago, surely they would at any rate have mentioned him... One should disregard such things? But *can* one disregard such things?...

He overheard Bradbrook, just back from Hollywood and entertaining a guest at the next small table, describing the intense unconfessed struggle for recognition that went on in the film world. He became acutely interested. 'It's reduced to a system,' said Bradbrook. 'It's fundamental. It pushes sex and gain into a secondary position. When I was there, a fellow who had something to do with building the sets, committed suicide, simply and solely because he was mortified by not being given a credit – credits they call 'em – on the screen…'

After lunch Mr Palace went into the smoking-room and sat down deliberately by the side of Bradbrook.

'Have a good time in Hollywood?' said Mr Palace, and Bradbrook with a certain weary facility began to unload and spread out his impressions for the fifty-ninth time or so.

'The psychology of film production is wonderful, I'm told,' said Mr Palace.

'The psychology is wonderful. Never was the assurance of a group of men so built up as that of the Hollywood magnates.'

Bradbrook seemed to be exploring some reservoir of resentment. 'They believe in themselves,' he said. And then infusing awe into his voice: 'They believe that the films as we see them are *good*.'

'Really? Good?'

'Yes, good. Good in themselves. As good as can be done. They congratulate each other on triumphs and masterpieces. And they *believe* it, Palace!'

'Their organization of Yes-Men is marvellous,' continued Bradbrook. 'It is like reinforcing a radio message. They have to find out what the weary Boss is weakly trying to think or believe, sustain it by inflated endorsement, reinforce it, remove objections. So the great bosses remain stout-hearted and sure of themselves and resolute against intruders and they continue to repeat the dear old silent film with small variations time after time, with a feeling of great novelty and refreshment. Every invention that comes along, sound, colour, music, what-not, they subdue to the measure of their old organization and remain in a state of immovable enterprise, as they were...'

'What I think even more interesting than all that extraordinary unprogressiveness of the film world,' said Mr Palace, 'is the *way* in which reputations are fostered and pressed home. There's those names on the screen. What did I hear you call them just now? – Credits?'

'Credits. Yes, your name on the screen in letters so high and not an inch smaller. Everybody has credits. Everybody lives by credits. The film world is an immense pile, an invincible pile, of credits – for the most part richly undeserved.'

Mr Bradbrook being now well launched on his sixtieth or so recital of his Hollywood grievances, needed little stimulation to continue. He had gone out to show them. They had tacitly refused to be shown. Charming they had been in every other way – exasperatingly charming. He was sore with a sense of neglected merit and at every repetition he felt more convinced of the soothing rightness of his judgment.

'This piling up of reputations in the film world is one of the most curious exhibitions of modern social psychology. You would imagine that an art as popular as the film would depend for its reputations almost entirely on the public choice. But it is only a few of the very prominent actors or actresses who represent public selection. Even they have to hold on to it by incessant advertisement. The rest are trying to impress each other. Convince themselves and each other they are the brightest and best producers, directors, scenarists, cameramen, special effects men, editors, cutters, music-men, that ever. Presently there will be colour experts and stereoscopists setting up their special hoots. It's a hooting competition. They run periodicals that the outside public scarcely ever sees, special periodicals with immense photogravure illustrations telling each other. All those credits on the screen – do you ever remember a name of them?'

'Never.'

'Nor I. Nor any one. Any one normal. They are just shouting across the audience at their producers and financiers – and the film critics. Keeping it up that the public is attending. And the public *isn't* attending. The public is incapable of that sort of attention. And their periodicals! Pretending that the public is there, greedy to read all about their blessed personalities.'

'Something of the same sort does happen with literature,' mused Mr Palace.

'The public doesn't heed.'

'Who *is* the public, anyhow?'

'It goes to the cinemas, it drifts in, it drifts out. It never reads those Credits on the screen. It never reads the film critics. It takes what is given it – like a pig in a sty. It refuses little. It would take almost anything else just as meekly as it takes the stuff it gets. Nobody really knows what moves it to come and come again or stay away. Bad homes, I suppose. Now and then something or somebody really tickles it and it follows that name about. Very rarely. It happened to Charles Chaplin. It happened to husky Greta. Most of the so-called popular stars are names shouted to deaf ears. The cinema public really doesn't care about them. Whatever the cinema public was in the past, *now* it is advertisement deaf.'

'But in the end solid worth, outstanding quality, intrinsic merit, must tell.'

'If it can get to the public,' said Bradbrook with a sudden access of bitterness. 'If ever it can get through to the public. And hold its attention. Past the meretricious clamour. Solid worth! Outstanding quality! It has to be as solid as a rock and as outstanding as the Eiffel Tower. Given that – !'

'I wonder,' said Mr Palace, 'has Fame always been a put-up job? It's only that nowadays it is plainer. Caesar, I suppose, ran publicity stunts.'

'Fame has never been so barefaced and naked before. Once she blew a trumpet. Now she makes indecent noises. It would be interesting to write a history of Fame. It has certainly never been run as a business before and made into a big-scale industry.'

'One thing puzzles me; how do these publicity fellows get their job? I mean these reputation agents. How do they get paid?'

This was a line of thought that did not interest Bradbrook.

'Commissions on contracts, I imagine. Or a percentage of the gross income. I don't know.'

'I suppose,' said Mr Palace with an effort, 'that even some authors – writers shall we call them? – do something of the sort.'

'Well, isn't a publisher supposed to do that kind of thing for his author?' asked Bradbrook. 'They always *pretend* they do.'

'Do they?' said Mr Palace, wary not to betray too keen an interest in the question. 'I don't know.'

'Nor I. Give me a crust and liberty. I observe all these things, I deplore them, and that's far as I seem able to go...'

The attention of Mr Palace wandered. Publicity *was*, after all, the publisher's business – however much he neglected it. Of course it was. He determined suddenly to look up Schroederer and speak his mind to him. Generally he left the handling of Schroederer to Blatch. It was Blatch who had 'placed' him with Schroederer years ago. But perhaps it had been a mistake to maintain a certain aloofness from Schroederer. Just because of a certain unattractiveness in Schroederer's appearance and bearing. An author is as unwise to cut his publisher as he would be to cut the mother of his children if he wants them to turn out well.

3

Schroederer listened with a lacklustre eye to Mr Palace's exposition of his views about the duties of a publisher as a fame maker. The idea that his business was to make and foster fame – except his own fame – had manifestly never entered Schroederer's head and was not entering his head now. It was flowing by and passing away.

Schroederer was a realist and his concern was with his firm. Authors were merely the material you arrange upon your list so as to make the pattern of Schroederer clear and bright. They rose somehow to fame and you paid for them; they declined and you dropped them. The thing to do was to put them all in uniform mauve-green wrappers with red and buff covers underneath, so that ultimately the public would recognize these chromatic signs for good reading and bother no more who the authors were. 'I read Schroederer's books,' the public would say, and then there would be an end to authors and their airs and graces, and he would get intelligent female labour at reasonable rates to write the stuff inside under his direction. When the mauve-green wrappers were securely established, it might be possible to indicate whether the flavouring were sexual, intellectual, left, right, or detective, by some variation in the general design, an obelisk, for example, the hammer and sickle, the swastika or what-not.

Meanwhile, so long as authors were selling as authors, you had to listen to stuff like this that Palace was talking.

Schroederer was a large, massive man, with abundant curly hair and by Western standards, an extensive face. His normal expression was one of patient self-confidence, varied by lapses into great mobility when he was exercised by a business suggestion or anxious to be effective. Then he gesticulated, brought his face nearer to his interlocutor and spat slightly as he became emphatic. Finally, he would wipe himself up so to speak and become suddenly immobile again, with his face interrogative and a little askew.

After their first greetings he allowed Mr Palace to proceed with his discourse and occupied himself with a small silver-mounted pocket toothpick. Occasionally he nodded to indicate that his attention was not entirely concentrated within his mouth.

Mr Palace found something disconcerting in this detachment of Mr Schroederer. He did not open his demand for artificial publicity with anything like the vigour with which he had tackled Mr Blatch. But he managed to unfold his case.

'Well,' he said at last, petering out rather than concluding; 'that's how I see it.'

'It's all wrong,' said Schroederer, putting the toothpick away carefully and regarding Mr Palace with instructive eyes. 'From my point of view, you've got everything wrong. All this Fame business. This Great Man system. It's over. It's finished.'

He leant an elbow on his desk and emphasized his words with plump red fingers.

'It's when a thing begins that there's Fame. Adam! After Adam, my dear chap, any amount of men as good as him. But do we hear of them? Adam got it first – Adam *the* man. After that any one could be a man – wasn't thought anything of. Then again, Abraham, Isaac, Jacob, celebrated Jews and after them any amount of Jews, but nothing like the same fuss about them. Abraham, Isaac, and Jacob – *the* Jews. Same thing with literature, just the same. Scott, Dickens, Tolstoy – I've got writers on my list could write any of them into a cocked hat, but all the same they don't stand out. Scott! Good heavens! if he brought that Waverley stuff along to me here, I'd tell him to go and cut it. Cut it to hell! And then burn the rest. But what was I saying? Getting there first. Look at the generals in the Great War. Do you think they were *all* so second-rate? Not a bit of it. It's just that there was such a lot of them, and just because what they did had been done first long ago by some one else who did it no better but did it earlier. What would Frederick the Great have done in the Great War, father? Nothing great. What would Alexander? You're not up to date. There never was more than a certain amount of literary Fame possible in the world and that cake's been all cut up and given away.'

'Then why do you advertise your writers at all?' said Mr Palace.

'I advertise their books. And I don't go on advertising those after the crest of the sales. 'I'd like to do it sometimes but, my dear fellow, it's no good. *You simply just can't do it.*'

'I don't agree with you,' said Mr Palace after a slight pause.

'If you had been in publishing as long as I have you would...'

Schroederer withdrew his face for a brief interval and with his head slightly on one side considered Mr Palace.

'Publishing,' he resumed suddenly, advancing his face again, this time with a sort of confidential intimacy and protruding his lower lip, 'is the most extraordinary business. You don't publish this book or that book nowadays, you publish a *list*. A list, my dear fellow.' He made what he evidently considered to be a list-like gesture. 'You don't sell books by ones or twos, you sell them in parcels and thirteens. What the bookseller wants is a selection. That's where *I* come in. My list is my battlefront. I look over my list. I study my list. My list is the best-balanced list in London. My authors are a team. I don't care what authors come along nowadays: Milton, Shakespeare – God himself and his Holy Bible; if he wasn't properly placed on a list you couldn't market him. Only the big shops would look at a parcel of him and even they wouldn't repeat. You've got to face the facts, Mr Palace,' hissed Mr Schroederer, inadvertently moistening the inquiring face before him and hammering his desk with the back of one hand. 'You've got to face facts. People *read* all right – they still read, but it's books they read – not authors...

'Now just look at these lists of mine, Mr Palace. They're balanced like a menu.'

He held out his printed matter in one large hand and slapped it with the other bunch of fingers. 'Here they are! Everything in season. Early peas and hothouse grapes for you. They take some getting. But I look out. *My* readers look out. I choose critics and book reviewers in London as my manuscript readers; no bright young ladies of culture for me; my readers know the ropes and they know what's coming a year ahead. They choose it as readers and they welcome it as critics. Phyllis Pelmet. We spotted her. No one else did. *I've* got her now. I got her before she *began* to sell. This new fellow, Alfred Bunter – I've got him.'

'Who on earth is Alfred Bunter?' asked Palace, stung sharply. 'I've never heard of him until a few weeks ago.'

'He's just come up with a rush. Don't ask me what he writes about, because I don't know. "Raw expressiveness" is on the blurb. He's my ham.'

'Your *what?*' said Mr Palace.

'My ham – Westphalia ham. Raw – you know. All I know about him is that he opens his mouth pretty wide. But he has to be on the autumn list this year – and here he is.'

The outburst was over and Mr Schroederer began to withdraw his face in good order. Mr Palace decided that everything necessary had been said – and even a little more – in this conversation. The world has changed indeed. It is a new world. Mr Murray never talked about his 'list' to Lord Byron as though that nobleman was hors-d'oeuvres or entrée, nor Mr Chapman to Dickens in the rôle of boiled mutton with trimmings.

Somebody, of course, must decide somewhere that Mr Alfred Bunter had to be on the autumn list this year…

But, oh! What was the good of talking about things like that to this – this *grocer?*

4

It was in the quality of the brain of Mr Rowland Palace to be easily worked-up. At times ideas were like germs in his intelligence and increased mightily in it and made it feverishly active and impatient. This idea of a watched and cherished publicity which had started so casually after the festivities at Little Canham, was now in a myriad repetitions keeping his brain heated and busy; it gathered force with opposition; it accumulated against obstacles. He felt more and more acutely that the mighty traditions of English literature were being undermined or stifled or betrayed or starved (Mr Palace was undecided about the best metaphor) by the short-sighted commercialism of such guardians as Blatch and Schroederer. Great names need to be built up and great names are not being built up. Less and less were they being built up on either side of the Atlantic. What would the teacher of English literature do when he came to instruct the young about our present age? Not a name. Not a date. What sort of Period would that be?

Seen from this angle Fame became almost a duty.

If it was his duty to write, and he had never questioned that, then it was equally his duty to foster that Fame without which he would go unread.

Essentially, he reflected, an author is a performer, he performs upon his readers. There is no authorship *in vacuo*. His business merely starts when he has set down his thoughts upon paper. Then only begins the chase – in so many cases a hopeless chase – to find some one to read his thoughts. That some one must in the next stage be wooed by legible printing, by an ingeniously attractive title, by a charming cover. Make-up. And before that some one is wooed he has to be located and approached. Readers do not follow an author about. They do not sit on his doorstep waiting. They elude. While writing is a sedentary affair, the chase is mobile. You cannot sit and hunt. A division of labour has long been recognized here. Poets, as Petronius tells us, once pursued their readers, their hearers rather than readers, into the market-place in person, but for centuries this chase of the reader fell to the bookseller, let Schroederer say what he chose. The bookseller-publisher saw to the printing that it was clear, and the binding that it was alluring; he got his shop window and began telling people how good the author's writing was, how very good it was.

As the world grew larger the division of labour came into play again and bookseller-publisher split into bookseller and publisher. The bookseller became a mere retailer. It fell to the publisher to sustain the author's praise. He did it so well for a time that profits accumulated, considerable profits – which it was presently discovered did not reach the author. And so the era of the author's agent dawned.

But authors multiplied. (How much wiser it would be to teach people to read and not to write!) 'We are living in an era of over-production – of everything,' said Mr Palace. 'One has to face the facts – as Schroederer said. Even literary distinction is becoming commonplace. We need to accentuate distinction among distinctions. I have been fortunate so far, but my position is precarious...'

Precarious. It was a new distressful idea to him. Rivalry was arising. Newer writers were already galling his kibe. He was being hustled. He had never realized it until today; he was being hustled off the lists – off Schroederer's lists.

He had thought these publishers' lists were like state barges on a tranquil river. Now he saw them as the insufficient crowded boats that toss round a sinking liner.

A week or so ago Bunter had been nothing to him. Had not existed for him. Now – he was a challenge, a warning, a menace. While he had been wrapped in a pleasant self-complacency

Bunter had been stealing a march on him. Bunter the Coming Man! But for all Blatch's mysticism these things did not happen spontaneously. Somehow the thing was done. Distasteful as the job was, he must find out about this Bunter. How did he do it? How was he doing it?

One idea jostled another in his mind.

'I want an impresario,' said Mr Palace aloud, in Long Acre.

And then inaudibly: 'God send me that impresario.'

His brain-pressure rose to a level that demanded action.

He returned to the Thespians, which at that hour was almost deserted. He went up to the celebrated library and sat at one of the writing-desks for a time, nibbling a knuckle in tense meditation. Then carefully selecting one of those sheets of paper that are without the club heading, he wrote:

'An author needs an impresario, a young man of energy, understanding, imagination, and a knowledge of the literary world in Europe and America, who will direct not merely the advertisement of his publications but his public appearances and his general publicity so as to consolidate his effect. Write in the first instance, giving your ideas of how your task should be done, as well as your requirements. Apply – '

'Aye, there's the rub,' said Mr Palace and mused.

Then suddenly there drifted into his mind that years ago he had acquired a monomark. He pulled out his keys and examined the tab: 'BM/HUTO.' All he had to do was to write to Monomark House, alter his registered address from his home to the Thespian Club and wind up his advertisements with: 'Apply BM/HUTO. London, W.'

He sat weighing all the possibilities of his action. In no way could anything of this reach Brynhild's ears? Not directly – no. But was there anything in the phrasing or spirit of that advertisement which might betray him to any acute contemporary? Would Bradbrook, for example, after their talk in the smoking-room, spot anything?

He had a cup of tea before his mind was made up, then he dismissed his fears. Stamps and a postal order in a plain envelope – nothing would show.

And now where was this advertisement to appear? The *Times* agony column? The *New Statesman?* The *Spectator?* The *Author?*

Each channel had its advantages and its limitations. T? N? S? A? He would turn over a page in a book and whichever letter came first should decide.

CHAPTER SIX

Expert in Publicity

A few afternoons later Mr Rowland Palace was seated in a remote defensive corner of the Thespian Club library examining the enclosures in three considerable envelopes directed to him by the Monomark Company.

A faint irrational sense of guilt tinged the background of his mind. Yet, he assured himself, what he was doing was perfectly reasonable and proper. He had thought it out and re-thought it from this angle and that. Fame was necessarily artificial – but why go over that again?

No less than nineteen persons he learnt were willing to act as his impresario and there might be others to follow. Two were ladies, three, so they intimated, were men of age and experience, the other fourteen were young men. Mr Palace savoured their stationery, their handwriting, their phrasing with keen appreciation. One man wrote from a Rowton lodging-house on ruled paper torn from an exercise book. A certain bashfulness about the business was apparent on the applicant side. Queer that they too should have this same irrational feeling of a slight indelicacy. One lady and one young man wanted to be answered Poste Restante.

The lady who wanted an answer Poste Restante was employed by a typewriting firm and had 'personally copied several difficult authors' MSS in quadruplicate'. She did not want either her employers or her half-sister to know she was restless, hence the address at a post office. She had worked previously in a responsible capacity in the office of a firm of publishers connected with the hop and kindred trades and had had a thorough insight into their business methods and particularly into the advertising side. She had 'good elementary' French and German and 'some Italian' and had travelled extensively during her vacations on the Baltic, the Mediterranean, and North Africa. She was thirty-three, Church of England and had been engaged eight years.

The other lady was younger and she wanted to 'get out of my stuffy home to the world I really belong to'. She did not disguise that she regarded Mr Palace chiefly as a means to that end. A glowing enthusiasm for writing possessed her. 'As soon as I begin to see how you do it I believe I shall write novels myself. Many of the people I have been connected with have been most peculiar and amusing.' At school she had been the sort of girl who is the life and soul of everything. She had been hostess of a municipal whist drive several times, had run a very successful bazaar stall ('profit of £17 11s. 4d. on £25 cost'), and so felt thoroughly capable of assisting you at your public appearances 'without gaucherie'. Feminist tendencies were evident in her in spite of her tender years. 'I admit you advertise for an impresario, but I do not see why you should not find an *impresaria* quite as efficient and far more *sympathetic*.' Finally she added: 'Of course, if you are a woman it will not make the slightest difference to me.'

'M'yes,' said Mr Palace, and tore up the letter carefully as though he was destroying the writer in the process.

The Rowton House correspondent betrayed himself a begging letter writer before he got to the end, and two of the applicants were facetious – Mr Palace thought very stupidly facetious – in intention. Five were green young public school men in various stages of after-school disillusionment about their prospects in the world, and there was also an army captain and a bank clerk in the same class with them, all comprehensively ignorant of most things, all extraordinarily clever, they said, and eager and willing to learn and serve. Just tell them exactly what to do and, by Gosh! wouldn't they do it! The army captain said he was prepared to be 'unscrupulously loyal'. He had had some experience as a blackshirt in a 'trusted position'. But Mr Palace was looking for fame rather than thuggery.

After the elimination of these undesirables he had nine letters left which promised at least a faint realization of his needs. Two applicants who were too concise, promising fuller particulars at a later stage, also went into the discard. The remaining seven followed his instructions and expatiated.

He read these essays upon publicity, shot with alluring autobiographical detail, with intelligent interest. He held a pencil in his hand and occasionally underlined outstanding phrases or corrected flaws in the prose. They had ideas, these seven; they had an inkling of the realities of the problem. They dispelled any lingering doubt he may have had in his mind that show is the only reality.

They ranged in age from twenty-three to thirty-four. One with previous experience, chiefly in the field of selling 'novelties and small patented proprietary articles', approached the problem of selling Mr Palace to himself and the world, through a highly scientific-looking terminology. He talked of the *advertiser*, the *advertisand*, being the thing advertised or put over, and the *advertisee*, being the person induced to buy, respect, or otherwise respond to the advertisement. And first, said he, Mr Palace must have a clear persuasion about his own merits. 'To create belief in an advertisand, the advertiser must believe in it himself. Intrinsic value is always indeterminate and may in some cases be non-existent, but a sustaining sense of honest worth in the travellers, distributors, and purchasers concerned, whether it be faith in a monetary medium, proprietary medicine, political organization, religious movement, literary reputation, automobile accessory, food substance, tobacco mixture, domestic gadget or what-not, is a *sine qua non* to a maintained effective functioning of that advertisement. Doubt is the ultimate enemy of the advertiser; nothing is safe from it; the whole social order would collapse and does tend to collapse (*vide* Christianity in the last hundred years) when and in so far as its confidence is not sustained.'

'This young man,' said Mr Palace, turning over a score or more of sheets still unread, 'his the makings of a successful popular philosophical writer. But – '

He glanced on to page 46 and found the deployment of general principles was still going on; he turned to the end and there was still nothing really concrete.

'Such copiousness ought to win him respect in academic circles... I doubt if we should ever get down to brass tacks together. No. I want some one nearer the surface than this. Me as the Great Advertisand. It won't do.'

A second of the seven experts had been in succession in the reception-room of a fashionable photographer, partner to a small

Bloomsbury publisher, publicity and social manager of a Kensington Hotel, and a motor-car salesman. He seemed to be greatly obsessed and enslaved by the fact that he had once designed a very successful book wrapper; he reverted to it repeatedly, illustrated his discourse by it, and made Mr Palace feel that his own exploitation in these hands would certainly follow as closely on the lines of that memorable piece of attractiveness as the difference in circumstance and material permitted.

A third of the seven had been working with Blatch for a while in some rather indefinite capacity. 'He'd know too much about me,' said Mr Palace. Two other of the applicants had 'done publicity' for movie stars and one had run a casting agency. One of the former enclosed a great number of large photographs of alleged stars, several of whom, said he, he had 'practically made'. Mr Palace, after studying these photographs for a time, decided that even God was a better maker.

Finally, as the most satisfying and promising of the nineteen, emerged a certain Mr Immanuel Cloote. He had written his letter very clearly and precisely on a typewriter. He told little of his qualifications. He set himself to the task in hand. He underlined all his cardinal statements. He used capitals for emphasis and paragraphed with skill. 'I will put my views as briefly as possible,' he began, and proceeded: 'The essence of success is personality, that is to say, *individual distinction*.'

'*Now* we get at things,' said Mr Palace.

'Personality is a reality. Perhaps it is the only reality. It is certainly the most fascinating in the world. But in a world that *becomes continually more emphatic*, it must be accentuated. Every effective woman knows that. In her make-up, what does she do?

75

First, she accepts herself. Then she enhances herself. Keys herself up to modern lighting. And so fascinates. The modern writer is in exactly the same position.'

'Precisely what I am saying,' said Mr Palace, and read on with increasing approval.

'Let me consider some of the ways in which a real personality may be presented to public attention.'

'Exactly,' said Mr Palace.

Mr Cloote divided his matter into sections, spaced out from each other and headed in underlined capitals. First of all he dealt with *The Impression Sought*. Then with the great truth *The Impression must have Facets or it is not Solid*. You must not harp too much on one aspect of a writer's quality. Gissing, for instance, was handicapped by his irony; they called him depressing; Chesterton was pigeon-holed as paradoxical even when he was doing his simple utmost to speak plainly; Wells was pinned down by his being always linked with 'The Future of – this or that.' (But Wells at the best was a discursive intractable writer with no real sense of dignity. A man is not called 'HG' by all his friends for nothing.)

Having got your contemplated Impression solid and assured, came *The Display*. Under this head Mr Cloote put 'the General Claim and Assertion of the author or other personality being publicized'. Under this head the impresario would have to watch advertisements, insist upon 'relative prominence' so as not to have one's name subordinated through smaller type or secondary position to another, keep an eye on shop windows, bookstalls, check the publishers' salesmen about what they told the booksellers, etc., etc. (Mr Cloote was very good at the use of 'etc., etc.')

Thence he swept on to collateral methods of 'intensifying the Impression sought'. There was The Anecdote. It was very important that 'interesting things should happen or *be made to have happened* to the personality concerned'. Some people seemed to be sought out by accidents of an illuminating quality. They are accosted by remarkable characters, they provoke children to comments good enough for *Punch*. They emerge from it very creditably.

'*Such things*,' Mr Cloote italicized, '*are not necessarily accidents.*'

Then the *dispute*, best in a weekly paper, about some grave, distinguished subject, is a good reputation sustainer. Under-graduates read disputes, delight in them, take sides and 'imitate them'.

'He understands my point about undergraduates,' Mr Palace approved. 'He really is intelligent.'

The whole art of discussions and collateral displays of interest is in its infancy. 'I should delight,' Mr Cloote confessed, 'to explore its fascinating possibilities to the utmost.' 'Spontaneous recognition is still uncultivated. The long letters written by people in hydropathic establishments, law agents' offices, hotels on wet days, rest cures, etc., etc., should be *followed up*. The letter-writer should become a personal friend, an instructed unpaid canvasser.' '*Quote his own letter back to him.*'

'Following up' is an 'art carried to a high level by the bucket-shop and by the sellers of many proprietary articles, etc., etc.,' but it is none the less to be practised on that account. Ordinary literary men disregarded it and allowed it to die away. 'Their paths are littered, literally littered, with the dead letters of discouraged correspondents. They do not sustain correspondence and none that I know of adopt the useful expedient of signing correspondence prepared for them by competent hands.'

'The *Protection of a Reputation from Distracting Suggestions* which may set a writer askew with public opinion and his own real performances, is also fascinating field for new work...'

'The man knows his business,' said Mr Palace.

He laughed shortly. 'It's utterly absurd.'

He nodded gravely to Mr Cloote's letter. 'It's profoundly true.'

He sat with frowning brows. 'So it is the world must know me... So it is I must come to know myself... To begin with I admit it is – artificial...

'As that other fellow said, the advertisand must believe in himself, as being exact to specification...'

He had read Kant in his time. 'What, after all, *is* Conduct?' he asked. 'It is to make oneself a consistent phenomenon. What else can it be? The noumenon is for ever unknown. *Gnothi seauton.* Provocative but impossible. *Can* a man know himself? Can he ever know as much about himself as other people do?'

Like a sigh upon the wind came the name of 'Pirandello'.

Then coming to reality again Mr Palace asked himself: 'I wonder if a psychoanalyst would make anything of that fellow's continual use of the word "fascination"?'

2

'And now,' said Mr Palace, putting the selected application into his pocket and dropping its torn envelope into a Thespian Club waste-paper basket already choked with the letters of the rejected; 'how to reveal ourselves to Mr Immanuel Cloote?

'First – his references for trustworthiness. Yes.

'But then I must meet him face to face. Not here. Club walls have ears. And damned curious eyes. Some hotel? Where I am known in the Restaurant. I can make that all right...

'Curious how I hesitate about this...'

But his hesitations were overcome and he found himself in the character of one who has a suite upstairs, walking across the Grand Embassy lounge to his indicated guest. The young man had a broad head of the Alpine type and a lot of dark, close, curly hair; his features seemed to have been flattened vertically into a permanent frown and when he spoke he spoke deliberately in a tone of strangulating restraint. Speech did not flow out of him; he produced with a faint flavour of preliminary internal struggle. It was as though he had to hold energy back to avoid either an excess of emphasis or volubility. Nevertheless he produced a lot. There was a marked vertical cast in his eyes. One regarded Mr Palace intently; the other carried over his right shoulder, as it were, to higher and better things.

He was biting the nails of a large competent-looking reddish hand with considerable animus, when he became aware of the approach of Mr Palace. Then he desisted from his auto-cannibalism and leapt to his feet to greet his prospective client. He leapt up so swiftly that Mr Palace expected him to leave the floor for an inch or so. Happily he stopped in time.

'It's Mr Rowland Palace,' he exclaimed. 'Yes. It's Mr Rowland Palace. Delightful! Forgive my recognizing you, sir. I remember the frontispiece to *Sago Lane*.'

'Let us sit down and talk,' said Mr Palace, feeling that Mr Cloote had rather too emphatic a voice for lounge conversation and looking round for the most secluded corner. 'You wrote me a very interesting letter.'

'The one thing I have always desired, sir, is to make a literary career,' Mr Cloote opened as they sat down. 'The atmosphere, the importance of literature had always fascinated me – fascinated me. Yet, oddly enough, I have never wanted actually to write myself. Never. Oddly enough. I realized – what so few people realize – that I have no invention as a writer, no creative drive whatever. None. Even when I have tried to be just descriptive of things seen, I have found I invented no phrases, I used no new constructions. I was trite. Abundant but trite. A marine store of phrases; not a workshop. And still the fascination of literature remained. Here is something, I said – I say – that alters people's ideas, alters people's lives, alters everything. Literature still fascinates me, sir. Writers fascinate me more. They could do what I could not do. You forgive me entering into these particulars about myself?'

'They are necessary,' said Mr Palace.

'How shall I serve literature, I asked myself. I thought of going into publishing and treating authors with a fostering care. But as I had no capital, and as most authors I found have a premature receptivity – often a real need – for cash payment, that was impossible. I expected it to be pleasant. It was unpleasant. No. I did a certain amount of small publicity – too trivial to talk about. And other things. I have sold organs to Indian rajahs.'

'Organs?'

'Musical instruments, sir. Large wind instruments with the most remarkable stops. A fascinating adventure. But let that pass. My peculiar gift is appreciation. For a time I wrote the screen announcements for Walworth Films. Crescendos of superlatives

– cascades of superlatives – an easy task. At times my appreciation was strained to the utmost, but I got my results. Now I find myself to the utmost, but I got my results. Now I find myself with my hands on opportunity – the great opportunity of my life. Did you read my letter? It said almost everything I had to say. It is for you to do the talking now, Mr Palace. I know exactly what you want. You want building up. To me, Mr Palace – you mustn't mind my saying it – to me you have to be the Clay that I can make into a Living Speaking Image. Perhaps not exactly Clay. No – that has associations!' He cut up the space before him with gestures of his hands. It was as if he cut out bits of it and threw them away. The piece he kept was: 'Glorious living material, fine and subtle. But there it is – you see what I mean. It is an adventure which – I can only say' – he hesitated for a moment seeking the right word, and produced it at last with an air of triumph – 'fascinates me.'

'I find,' said Mr Palace, getting into the pause, 'you put things with a certain intensity but – '

'I am too excitable,' injected Mr Cloote.

'But I think you do really *get* the sort of enterprise I have in mind.'

Mr Cloote brought his large strong hand flat before Mr Palace's face. 'I have to study you.'

'Study essentials.'

'Magnify you.'

'For the sake of visibility.'

'Proclaim you. Be your Aaron. Your John the Baptist. Your – Stooge!'

'Of course, there has to be a restraint in enterprise.'

81

'Leave that to me. Of course I must warn you. One part we must make clear. To a man of your fascinating refinement and delicacy – '

'Irony is a quality I – '

'Yes, irony. Some of the first strokes of the portrait I shall draw may seem *Crude*.'

'One must be careful of that.'

'The intensest care. Meticulous. It may not happen at all. But I am anxious to anticipate any little – what shall I say? – birth pangs? Not exactly "birth pangs". Saddle soreness? Chafing? Difference of phase? Breaking the arrangement in. You understand me?'

Mr Palace nodded not too reassuringly.

'Perfect!' cried Mr Cloote, triumphantly.

He seemed to appeal to some unseen presence to witness the swift intelligence between himself and Mr Palace.

'I speak four languages well,' he added, out of the void. 'And six or seven indifferently. I have travelled widely – in various capacities. Before the mast – and behind. My mother was a Pole. I associate my literary ineptitude – no milder word will do – with my poly-glottery. The gift for languages is a gift for learning phrases quickly – that is to say *cliché*. It is an uncritical gift. A child learns languages more readily than an adult because criticism is not yet born in it. You, Mr Palace, speak French badly.'

'I'm afraid that is so.'

'I *knew* it, Mr Palace – from the fascinating subtlety of your style. Every word weighed in the balance and none found wanting. You can only do that with one language in a lifetime. If I may, I shall make capital out of your bad French.'

'But speaking of Poles, Joseph Conrad spoke several languages.'

'Badly, sir – all badly. And he wrote Conradese. That's by the way. Let us come to our work. The Task before us. I am inclined to think we could best map it out in a series of campaigns or operations – operations. Operations on the Nobel Prize Campaign, for example. Operations in respect to America...'

'But don't you think the Nobel Prize – ?'

'Mr Palace, the planning of a literary career nowadays which excluded consideration of that great distinction would be imperfect. And similarly I have to assume that your name *must* become a byword for literary excellence in America. There is no success without it. A byword – you have to be. Far beyond the mere reading public. In the gutter. You can't possibly scale the heavens if the feet of the ladder aren't firmly in the gutter. The east-side gutter. No other American gutter had ever heard of a book. There you must be, with the Bible and Shakespeare. *And* Carlyle and Mrs Humphry Ward *and* Bergson *and* Conrad *and* Aldous Huxley *and* Charles Morgan *and* all the other discoveries America has made. They're wonderful over there on the appreciation trail. Once they discover. Kind of high and fastidious to begin with – waiting for the other chap to speak first – almost one might say "snifty", and then a sort of Appreciation Stampede. There ought to be a history, a natural history of American criticism. Take Conrad, of whom you spoke just now. Beautiful but abstruse writer. Colorado. Pink caviare. Special taste, I mean. Such richness. Turns the simplest ideas into mysteries. Adds a complication of life on every page. Says nothing in a kind of literary agony. Most effective. Novelettes ennobled. Platitudes – with a passionate patina. The gnome, the fairy changeling who ran away to sea and was scared to death by a ship. You'd think he was above their heads. Buy that's what *got* them. They don't respect you if they understand you. Naturally. In a sort of way. They don't like being told what they think they know. Such a lot of them have been taught literature at college and they naturally despise the elementary stage. If you ask a child in New York to name the greatest of English writers, it will certainly give you the immortal Joseph in the first half-dozen. Any American woman. Any American. With – perhaps – Lindenburg. Not that they know anything about it, they just *know* it. How *that* was established – '

He paused.

'Fascinates you,' laughed Mr Palace with a gleam of his mocking charm.

3

That night Mr Palace woke up and had the most fearful doubts, remorse, and perplexity about his engagement of Mr Cloote. He had engaged him, though much remained to be settled, because at the time there did not seem to be any other way out of the Grand Embassy Hotel. He was to have three hundred a year – it seemed cheap for so energetic and comprehensive a being – for an experimental year. Then they would see. There had been vague intimations of an office for him; still vaguer of material needed, running expenses. Expenses?

'What have I brought upon myself?' Mr Palace asked his ceiling reflections. 'What monstrous system of new worries – new preoccupations – have I not incurred?'

The tree shadows did not stir. Never had they been so still before. They seemed to be mourning the irretrievable.

Imposed upon that familiar thought-background was a shadowy face, which became intensified and distorted whenever he turned over and shut his eyes. It had a deep earnestness in its eyes, both in the one that fascinated you directly – *what* a word, '*fascinated*'! – and the other which looked over your shoulder; it had a slow, deep, explanatory, compelling voice that pushed against you and a flat, red, expository hand that cut the space about you into compartments...

Cloote would be a difficult man to get away from...

There were moments when Mr Palace felt like a man who has gone out into the jungle to find a piece of rope and picked up an Anaconda.

An overwhelming problem of that night-watch was the exact way in which to introduce this Cloote and all his activities into the hitherto simple and orderly Palace life. He was attracted by the idea of not telling Brynhild or any one at all about Cloote – making him a secret agent. Rowland saw himself leading a double life, scorning the tricks and vulgarities of publicity at home and then slipping away on all sorts of excuses to foster a gigantic publicity at some office in the city.

From this his dreaming mind carried him into visions of masks and disguises. If he and Cloote had presently to go about on some jointly enterprise. Would Cloote consent to travel as a valet? He might not like being asked to be a valet. 'Private Secretary' was certainly the proper title so far as a title was needed. Agent? 'Agent' of unspecified standing...

He awoke from a dream in which he and Cloote in masks had been sacking Schroederer's office, to waking clearness again. What exactly was he thinking about? What had to be done?

He had to intimate...he perceived there were some difficult intimations ahead of him. He had to intimate to Brynhild, that he felt a need for some sort of secretary-agent at his elbow. She was bound to ask questions – no, not exactly ask questions but seem to be thinking questions. He knew her. He saw, what he had not seen before, that Miss Pardlow, his present typist, might have to be – dislocated – during the reconstruction.

Out of a mass of dreamlike suggestions one idea became clearer and clearer. The need for an office away from his home. Anthony Hope Hawkins in his time, he knew, had found it very conducive to his work to go down to an office on the Embankment and work there with the punctuality of a business man. He could plead this precedent. He might say a lot about the office and very little about Cloote. Then Brynhild and Cloote need never come into anything but the most incidental contact...

She might, of course, insist on furnishing the office. But then he might have it furnished and tell her before she saw it that it was a furnished office.

The office idea had everything in its favour. Then Palace need not be seen about with Cloote – or hardly ever. He could be represented as simply a secretarial helper. He could be minimized.

Not only had he to intimate all these things to Brynhild and put them over with her in the face of whatever objection she made, but, far more difficult in the way of intimations, was that without for one moment casting the faintest aspersions upon his wife and his relations with his wife, without descending to any detail or analysis whatever, he had to make it perfectly clear to Cloote that for unspecified and inexplicable reasons it was desirable, it was imperative – if and when she met him – that he should breathe no word about his essential task of consolidating and expanding Mr Palace's fame.

CHAPTER SEVEN

Weekend at Valliant Chevrell

For some days Mrs Palace had been aware that something unusual was going on in her husband's mind. She sat now at the breakfast-table unobtrusively observant and turned over her letters. He was preoccupied. He was bothered. He was not interested in the morning papers. And it was one of those things – they were becoming innumerable nowadays – about which he would tell her nothing. Was he having sentimental troubles or was he digesting some particularly hostile or belittling criticism or was there trouble about the next book?

Why was it he could not talk of such things to her?

She opened a large pale-blue envelope with a coronet. It was from Spencer Dispenser, Lord Valliant Chevrell's marvellous factotum, giving full and engaging particulars of the forth-coming weekend. 'You will meet Lady Cytherea Label, who is one of your husband's most ardent fans, and Lady Burnish and Mrs Penton Grace who is in her way a novelist – literature has many mansions, remember – and there's Mr Alfred Bunter – the new sensation, and the Swope-Petershams.'

She looked up. 'We're going to meet Alfred Bunter at Valliant Chevrell,' she told him.

'That's the man who makes the running,' he said. 'I'll be curious to see him.'

'Makes the running?' she asked softly.

'Oh! He's heading fast to be a Best Seller. Everybody is taking him up. I don't understand these things.'

So that was it. He was still worrying about his publicity. The thorn had festered. Pity he should be bothered by things like that. Why couldn't a man just think and write? She reflected for a moment and then opened another letter.

Her husband was saying something. 'I'm beginning to think Valliant Chevrell is getting a trifle too promiscuous in his invitations, Bryn. A little too – *topical*. It's just a bit of a shock to find the latest boomster from nowhere is going to be present.'

'It may be just his curiosity,' said Brynhild. 'You know he *is* curious. The rest of the party – . Quite nice people. The Swope-Petershams he says and Lady Cytherea Label.'

The trouble vanished from Rowland's brow. 'I like the Swope-Petershams,' he said.

Brynhild's smile was imperceptible. 'And Lady Burnish,' she added softly. 'You like *her*.'

2

Lord Valliant Chevrel's appetite for big parties, Brynhild thought, was growing with indulgence. This was the very biggest party she had ever seen even in that insatiably hospitable house. But later she found that a number of callers from the neighbourhood were swelling the assembly beneath the great cedar on the lawn. It was like a garden-party. Cissy Parkington, the host's cousin, who could never catch a name and lost it at once if she caught it, was acting distractedly as hostess. She welcomed the guests by saying, 'I don't know where any one is. The new chimpanzee has melancholia and Roddy has gone off to hold its hand.'

After which she left the newcomers to their own devices and prepared to greet the next.

Brynhild was hailed by a woman she had met, it seemed, in London who wanted to talk about some alleged mutual acquaintance with the quite unfamiliar name of Fanny. Fanny, it seemed, had gone off very suddenly to Biskra. Brynhild accepted a cup of tea from Spencer Dispenser, while she ran about in her mind trying to match up Fanny to anything whatever. Rowland drifted off towards a little group which opened out to receive him. She heard the voice of Lady Cytherea. 'You mahst settle, Mr Palace. You're just in taim. You know everything. Can a chimpanzee be crossed in love?'

'It's the only way you *could* cross a chimpanzee,' said Mr Palace, right on the spur of the moment and wondering what on earth he meant.

It was accepted as suggestively brilliant.

Brynhild, looking round over her tea-cup and trying to remember any one of the name of Fanny – Fanny Anything? Frances Anything? who might go off to Biskra, was struck by the appearance of a man standing alone with a most unintroduced air about him, who she instantly divined was Mr Alfred Bunter. 'I *can't* imagine in the least why she has gone so suddenly,' she said, playing for time.

'You're too charitable,' said the lady.

Brynhild raised her eyebrows and did that perfectly.

91

'I expect you know all about it,' said the lady. 'Well, I won't cross-examine you if you don't care to talk.'

'I'm not so well-informed as you think,' said Brynhild. 'Have you ever seen larger hydrangeas?'

Brynhild gradually detached her attention from her interlocutor behind a series of conversational parries, and watched the unintroduced man. He was ruddy and rather tall, a brown-haired man, in a brown hat and a brown suit to match that was somehow – she couldn't quite tell – out of key with the party. He was surveying his prospective company with a detached interest; he was lonely but not embarrassed. She knew his type, the newly arrived, the last social mouthful. In most of these large weekend parties there is some one who doesn't belong and never quite begins to belong – The Stranger. He does not assimilate from the outset and gradually he becomes inassimilable. This man she perceived, was probably cast for the rôle of The Stranger for this weekend.

Unless something was speedily done for him.

He was cast for the rôle of The Stranger just as she was cast for the rôle of a Quiet Lovely. That seemed to be her invariable lot at weekend parties, and nothing was ever done for her to save her from it. Because only herself could do that. Men you can save, but not women. It was always the same story. She stood about, she sat about, she played tennis or golf or rowed or swam or went with the walking party. Men and even women were attracted to her; they came to her; they visibly remarked to one another that she was lovely; they started duologues with her, pleasant duologues that floated over the surface of things. Over the surface and away. Then they drifted off. As Sunday wore on many of them paired off with other women. They showed a dispositon to go off into secluded places with them. They seemed in some way to have penetrated the surface of things with them, to have become confidential and in some queer way more *real*. How did they do it? Others of the women became dramatic, conspicuous, addressed circles, made amazing confessions to the company at tea. How did they break through themselves to do that? Anyhow she could not. She had never broken through herself yet. She remained a Quiet Lovely, an onlooker, disregarded.

'Do you think that is the new writer, Mr Bunter?' she asked, realizing that she had to account for her wandering attention.

'Oh, *yes!*' said the lady, turning to look. 'That's certainly Alfred Bunter. I met him last Thursday at Chlorinda's. Or Friday was it? He's – he's quite shy, but rather nice.'

As she spoke Mr Bunter's tranquil regard came round to them. 'Mr Bunter!' she cried. 'Mr Bun – ter.'

He looked at them for a moment and particularly at Brynhild, and his expression brightened. He came to them.

'You'll remember me,' said the lady. 'You were at Chlorinda's – at Lady Shatc's last week. You do remember? When they talked about Fascism. And the Fifth Dimension and neon lights and all that.'

'I seem to remember,' he said, trying to recall her.

'I *love* good talk,' said the lady, and to Brynhild: 'Don't you?'

'Who were the talkers?' asked Brynhild...

It was clear the lady who knew Fanny was now beginning to suspect that she had mistaken Brynhild for some one else and had no idea of her real name and no intention of experimenting in introductions. Mr Bunter took Brynhild's tea-cup and returned to them and presently Brynhild found herself agreeably incognito – agreeably because she was spared the usual compliments about *Bent Oars* and *The Supple Willow Wand* – walking alone with Mr Bunter towards the rose garden.

'I am rather a novice in this sort of thing,' said Mr Bunter. 'Who was the lady who – introduced us? Who had met me at Lady Shate's?'

'I hoped you'd tell me that,' said Brynhild.

He smiled and she found something very vivid and appealing in his smile.

'Things get clearer at dinner,' he said.

'We all get labelled at dinner.'

'Labelled,' he said softly, as though he criticized the phrase and found some riddle in it. Then he went on: 'I'm really a very inexperienced person indeed here. I'm an outsider. Why not be frank? I was thinking – Tell me, doesn't a place like this and a party like this mean a great deal of money?'

'I suppose it does.'

'And how is it done?'

'Mines and shipping, I believe, in this case,' said Brynhild.

'There's largeness… I wish I understood better how it was done and why it is done.'

He explained that he had recently, 'in the last year or so', written a couple of books that had sold a lot – 'anyhow, it seemed a lot to me' – and suddenly, 'Oh, in the last two months or so,' first one hostess and then another had asked him to a weekend party. And to houses and places like this. Outside his world. 'I had no idea,' he said, 'what these places were like and how many there seem to be. I've lived in England all my life and I've never suspected what lay behind the gates and the palings and the notices about Trespassing. It's amazing.'

3

Now this promised to be interesting talk.

'There are not so very many places as large and fine as Valliant Chevrell now,' she said, 'and few people as able to keep them up as Lord Valliant Chevrell can. Some great houses have decayed a lot, many have been sold – and Americanized. Maybe it isn't going to last very much longer.'

'One hears that. But is there much in that?'

'A few years back the advertisements of houses and parks in *The Times* used to be headed, "England changing Hands".'

'But has it changed its butlers?' he asked, with a glance back at the disciplined service on the lawn. 'It's a stout old system with a lot of inertia. These trees – there's something for-ever-ish about them.'

She began a short history of the house from its Jacobean days. She felt pleasantly at an advantage with him. All this belonged to her as it did not belong to him. She had been here before five times. She had to be something of a hostess to him.

She showed him the rose garden with care and appreciation. She hunted for a corner of cream and white roses she remembered from last year. She liked and admired the place herself and she took him through to where a sundial, a sunken garden, and a lily-pond grouped graciously towards a glimpse of the lake and an emphatic sustained line of old yew-trees – trees full of personality. Here again a vast generous red wall ran out protectively between the yew-trees and the sunk garden, and ended in a flourish of stone. There was a long white seat that she had appreciated in a former visit, and to that she conducted him and sat down beside him.

'There!' she said with an intonation of proprietary triumph.

'By Jove!' said he. 'Serenity!'

He looked at her as though she and the mellow assured garden were all of a piece.

'Now this was worth coming for! Do you know I hesitated about coming down here today. I'm glad I did.'

'These lovely walls. This place would be nothing without these walls. How lavish they were with their walls,' she said.

'Lavish,' said he, and reflected. 'I suppose – They could be just as lavish today. They have the clay, the labour unemployed – but they don't do it. Nobody builds walls for the sake of walls today. Walls just for the grace of it. Why has this sort of thing stopped? With resources a hundred times as great as those old seventeenth-century garden-makers'? This place is a wonder because it is rare. And yet we could make all our island a garden, an estate like this and as mellow as this, from Land's End to John o' Groats. We don't. That makes me Angry. It brings my Anger back. I am an Angry Man. Did you know I was an Angry Man? Almost professionally. You don't know my books? No? But that is what they say of me – the Angry Man. The world angers me. I am ashamed to be an Angry Man. What is the good of being Angry? I get angry and shout. I don't write books, I shout them. And what is the good of that?'

Brynhild felt that any one but a Quiet Lovely would have something apt to say here, but she had nothing.

Her silence did not seem to discourage Mr Bunter. He dug his heels into the turf in a way that somehow reminded Brynhild of a happy cat clawing a rug. The he went on with his thoughts.

'You know. I am silly. I am silly to be Angry and silly in myself. I am really the answer to my own question, why don't we make all the world a garden? Why don't we turn everything in nature to loveliness? Because I am as silly as I am angry. That is the answer. What I want,' said Mr Bunter, with a sudden chuckle, 'is a head *so* big.' He put his hands about his temples to indicate a linear extension of six inches or so. 'And heart and lungs – oxygen to ginger it up. Then I'd have a nice large brain-room to think in, I'd be able to pigeon-hole things properly and set about them seriously and I wouldn't be ineffective and angry any more.'

She nodded appreciatively. She had at times wished something of the sort herself.

'Bigger and better heads. You can't get them. I suppose I'm greedy. I want to do too much. Then I fall over my silliness and I get Angry. I am too intelligent for my silliness. I know and I am incapable. If only I could turn off thinking. If one could turn a tap and reduce one's thoughts and ideas to a manageable trickle. I can't tell you how I envy at times the coolness, the empty, self-satisfied self-possession of that damned façade, Palace.'

Brynhild sat up slightly. She controlled an impulse to laugh aloud. Instead she laid a cool restraining hand on Mr Bunter's freckled fist and pressed it softly.

He glanced at her in mild surprise.

'Mr Bunter,' she said, regretting the phantom of a chuckle in her voice and pointing with her other hand, 'look over there. Isn't it lovely?'

'What's lovely?'

'Oh! All of it. You know. Those cluster roses and all that. I ought to tell you, Mr Bunter – I'm Mrs Rowland Palace.'

'*What?*'

'Just that.'

'I got you all wrong. I wanted to know who you were as soon as I saw you. I liked you – somehow. And – preposterously – I jumped at the idea that you were Lady Cytherea. Lady Cytherea Lamb or Label or something. I had seen her name on a bag at the station and wondered what she would be like... Cytherea! A lovely name, anyhow. And instead it's Mrs Rowland Palace... I just don't know what to say about that remark of mine. Don't take what I said too seriously. It's envy, Mrs Palace. Envy. There's a *polish* in his work. A poise, a fineness in his irony...'

He paused. He fixed his eye on the clustering roses, as though he was trying very hard to remember more of Rowland's good points.

Brynhild's desire to laugh returned.

'Tell me some more about making red garden walls all over England, Mr Bunter. Is the world a miser – if it is rich enough to do that and yet won't?'

'Not even a good hard vice like miserliness. It's just silliness, clumsiness, not being quick and clear-minded, blundering – all thumbs. Stupid fool I was – saying that.'

She looked at his troubled face and resentful eyes. He was absurdly rueful and reproachful. Yes – reproachful. And some quality that came close to her, she did not know what. Her self-restraint deserted her and she laughed gaily at his plight. His puzzled expression changed slowly to a grin of the completest understanding. Then both became serious again as though they drew down a blind that had for a moment been raised, improperly. His eyes went away from her.

'I wonder where that little gate down there goes,' he said.

'It leads to the swimming-place and boat-house. There is quite a pretty stretch of lake beyond and the path runs round it.'

They both stood up.

'Let's,' he said. 'We have half an hour before the dressing bell...'

But a tarnish of embarrassment had fallen upon them both. The afternoon that had seemed for a while to be crystalline was now at most indistinctly translucent. 'I'm slipping back to a Quiet Lovely,' she told herself. 'I can't help myself. It was just the shock got me out of it for a minute.'

They talked not very easily now, and chiefly about spiraea and loosestrife and water-rats and water-beetles and about the jade and brown of still water and about trout and carp and how to cook carp and a miscellany of things like that; and they said nothing more about themselves or the world in general until it was time to part in the hall for dressing. It was as if something almost completely impalpable had frightened them away from any reality of conversation. And yet what was there to it? He had just made a quite natural mistake and she had behaved as a semi-hostess should. What had checked them? And what was it had been checked?

4

When Brynhild had dressed she went through the connecting bathroom to her husband's room to tell him she was ready to go down.

She found him sitting in a deep chintz-covered armchair, before a cheerful little unnecessary fire he had lit. He was so lost in thought he did not hear the slight rustle of her entrance. He was sitting without jacket or vest, looking neat and healthy in his shirt and black tie.

If his thoughts were deep they were manifestly not disagreeable. He was – what was the word? – ruminating – pleasantly.

'Has there been a gong yet?' she asked, and roused him.

A certain softness of self-satisfaction flattened out as he became aware of her presence.

'Did you play tennis?' he asked politely.

'No foursome,' she said truthfully but disingenuously.

He stood up before the fire. 'The Coming Man disappeared,' he remarked. 'Shy, I suppose.'

'Alfred Bunter?'

'Who else? It's an interesting party this time. He'll find his level. These young, very aristocratic, fairly rich girls – They have a curious freshness and boldness. A sort of modern vicious freshness. Tremendously outspoken. Startling. They know so much by hearsay and so little by experience.'

'I suppose, though, they do what they can to remedy that.'

Mr Palace smiled and nodded. 'They certainly get on with life.'

('Smirk' was the word that came into her mind and was instantly ejected again.)

'Interesting types,' he repeated. 'One has to know about them. If only as a novelist.'

A gong began to boom like China, Further India, and the Coromandel Coast. Mr Palace moved towards his dinner-jacket.

Brynhild perceived that among two or three other new books on the table was *The Cramped Village*, by Alfred Bunter. She picked it up. 'I'll take something to read for the night,' she said with the air of an accidental choice, as though it was just any old book, and carried it off to her own room.

5

When the Palaces came down the great staircase, a good half of the company were already standing about with cocktails in their hands. Mr Alfred Bunter had got himself isolated again and regarded Brynhild with a faint appeal which evoked an insufficient spasm of the sub-hostess in her. He was no longer dressed a little out of key. What an excellent leveller is your dinner-jacket! But the impulse to go over to him was checked by a score of sufficient considerations. Raymond was invited by a common movement of Lady Cytherea and her two companions. He made no difficulty about what was evidently a resumption. 'Well,' he said, 'and what did the third pig say?'

'We still don't know,' said Lady Cytherea, and they all giggled, a trio of quite nice well-regulated giggles.

Brynhild took in their quality as she moved across the room, seeing them without looking as a woman can. They were all dressed simply – with a simple insufficiency that made the most of their slight young bodies. For the first time in her life Brynhild realized that she must soon be just handsome, dignified, and early middle-aged. She resigned herself to the attentions of old Swope-Petersham.

The idea that she was inescapably a Quiet Lovely floated through her mind again at dinner. She liked Valliant Chevrell's long table, all glass, silver, and well-chosen flowers, extremely. People could talk earnestly, intimately, formally, according to their natures, by twos and threes and fours, and if one sat out, so to speak, one had no embarrassing sense of being exposed. What a lot most of them had to say and how quick they were in getting to it! She didn't want in the least to talk to either of her neighbours. Each in his due turn was sociable for a time and she was intelligent but unhelpful. The gentleman on her right told her things about Valliant Chevrell's old silver. Afterwards the gentleman on her left made conversation about the silver and she was able to use several of the facts and appreciations she had got from the gentleman on her right.

Meanwhile her observation wandered up and down the table. She saw many little things that were happening and even some that were not. Was her host in love with that very delicate blonde woman on his right – she was the Countess something or other from Rome? Would he ever marry? He was the nimblest, most evasive of eligibles. Rowland was between the Countess and Lady Burnish, out of harm's way for a time. Halfway down the table were Lady Dynover and young Mr Bates, and in some occult way Brynhild realized that knee was pressed against knee and neither of them knew quite what to do about it next. Beyond Lady Dynover sat Bunter, quietly alone, with conversation to the left of him and tongue-tied passion to the right. He was making no attempt to talk; he might have been dining alone. Then presently he began to look up and down the table seeking somebody. He was doing this very unobtrusively. She knew he was seeking somebody because whenever his view was obstructed by flowers or a glass candelabra, he moved his head to see round it. He was looking for some one. He was looking for her.

She met his eyes for a moment and smiled ever so faintly. Which evoked an answering friendly smile.

After which she looked at him no more, though she perceived that ever and again he sought to repeat that flash of mutual recognition.

And after all, what was it they were smiling about?

After dinner and the recess Valliant Chevrell and Spencer Dispenser appeared among the ladies with a trail of men behind them, and set themselves to sort out the bridge addicts and such dull guests as are better put to bridge lest worse befall, and then to instruct the residue for Valliant Chevrell's particular delight, charades.

'Charades,' Valliant Chevrell would say, 'mix people nicely,' and there is no doubt that charades as they played them under his direction mixed them a good deal. There was a considerable amount of going off together and going off apart, necessary whispering and conspiring close to the pink receptive ear, a running about passages for needed properties, much dressing-up and undressing and helping to dress and undress.

Sometimes the charade was done by syllables, but more often the 'Whole' was spelt out a letter at a time. There was much confused secrecy about it all. Everybody knew the one or two letters in which they acted, but only their host alone or with some chosen confederate was supposed to know the 'Whole'.

Valliant Chevrell was generally the director of his scenes, but the direction of the first light was taken out of his hands by Lady Cytherea. He drew her apart to tell her that the first letter was P. He had Pluto in mind as the whole, and for P he wanted her to produce '*Paris*'. She leapt at the idea. 'We three'll do it,' she cried. 'Oh, let us. We mahst. We know it so well. You think of the next one, Roddy.' The trio were ready. It was only after she and her two friends had bundled out and consulted outside with cries and giggles, that they changed their minds from the town to the Trojan and called out Mr Palace to assist them. And afterwards they called out old Mrs Checkshalton.

Meanwhile Valliant Chevrell arranged to resume his usurped leadership, and made extensive confidential preparations for L, Laocoon. The butler was summoned and told in a loud whisper to 'bring in about three long lengths of hose. Black or grey? It doesn't matter.'

'We'll do the group. You and I and Hickson,' he said to Bunter – because here he perceived was a way of getting his new guest tousled and deprived of tie and collar and generally mixing him in.

He came across to Brynhild. 'Would you do U? Undine – you know – sorrowing under the water?'

'*I* can manage it,' he reassured her.

Spencer Dispenser who was acting as general property man and scene-shifter, came in to arrange the slopes of Mount Ida by means of a green window-curtain, thrown over a sofa. Then entered Rowland as Paris.

The three young ladies had undressed Mr Palace very thoroughly. In place of a Phrygian cap they had put a red ribbon round his hair. He was wearing his bathing-shorts under an arrangement of sheepskin rugs held together by brown luggage-straps, and he carried a long alpenstock to which a crook-handled walking-stick had been tied. A pair of plimsolls had been deprived of their uppers and converted into sandals with the aid of a tape-measure which ran up his two shins and round his calves saying 23, 24, 25, 26, and 58, 59, 60 respectively. He had been slightly rouged and his hair arranged for him and he carried himself as though he had recently been told – as indeed he had been told – that he was 'aw'fly handsome'. He came forward, surveyed an imaginary landscape from under his flattened hands, slowly and calmly, moved pensively across the scene, entered his cave behind the sofa, picked up the greensward on the sofa, selected a cushion from beneath it (laughter) and, extending himself upon the floor, feigned sleep.

Thereupon old Mrs Checkshalton partly entered and was partly pushed on the scene, dishevelled, looking indeed very like a real Goddess of Discord. She was carrying a large orange. She complained in loud whispers she was still uncertain what to do. 'You throw down the apple when we come,' said a voice at the door. 'Yes, just throw the apple down.'

'But fwhat's the good of calling an orange an apple, when it isun't? And I tell ye it's ripe to bursting and not to be thrown about,' she protested, and then remembering her audience, she mopped and mowed towards the company, held up the orange before her face in a cruel and sinister manner and made the most terrible faces at it with an anxious eye on the entrance.

Whereupon the goddesses appeared. The thoroughness with which Mr Palace had been undressed was nothing to the liberality of their disclosures. Lady Cytherea as Venus wore practically nothing but the thinnest muslin and a girdle of broad metal links (cestus) and she had powdered her person and enhanced her charms with rouge very attractively. She was as rosy-fingered as the dawn and in fact generally rosy. It had never dawned on Brynhild before that rouge might be used on any part of the person except the face. Florrie Caterham, crowned as Juno, had lengths of serene white calico before her and behind

105

her, and practically nothing at the sides. She was brown and svelte and the glimpse was startling but delightful. Mess Brew Samson as Pallas had a certain translucent charm in a lawn night-gown and a laurel crown, but she lacked the frank assurance of her companions.

'And fwhat am I supposed to do *now?*' said Mrs Checkshalton, disregarding the rules that limited her to pantomime. 'Here's the orange for ye,' and having put it down on a convenient card-table she seated herself in the audience.

The three goddesses then executed a brief but effective dance of jealousy and pride. Each in turn reached towards the golden apple and was restrained by the other two. Then Venus discovered Paris who was awakened and brought forward to decide them. There was a further dance about him as a pivot.

Brynhild found she was disliking the way Rowland was being handled by these young women, and she reproached herself bitterly for her illiberal turn of mind. And still more did she reproach herself for disliking Rowland. She had no right – She became aware of Valliant Chevrell seated on a hassock nursing his knees and regarding Palace with an expression of sour but restrained impatience, and then she met frank interrogation in Bunter's eyes.

She had no reply for him. She turned back to the scene.

The three goddesses were now posed for the Judgment of Paris, and Rowland in his attitude was recalling all the worst excesses of all the pseudo-Russian ballets she had ever seen. Then with an elaborate assumption of grace he was down and kneeling at Lady Cytherea's feet, offering her the orange. Juno and Pallas featured resentment; Venus looked almost over-kind, dropping forward, hands extended to receive the prize.

They held this for a moment, the company burst into applause, and then all four actors became human again.

'Can you *guess* it?' said Lady Cytherea.

'Can we *not?*' cried the Countess something or other from Rome.

'That's a great tableau. Where did you get the sheepskins?' asked young Mr Bates.

'The crook was *my* discovery,' said Miss Samson. 'I remembered seeing it.'

'Paris,' said a quiet gentleman in the corner. 'Letter P,' and involved himself in some regrettable but incomplete joke about 'P's and Q's'. He evidently meant to say something neat and found he was saying something quite untidy.

'And now off you go and make yourselves decent again,' said Valliant Chevrell, pushing his cousin Cytherea towards the door with a certain cousinly violence. 'And Bunter and Hickson and I will purge their corrupted minds with terror and pity.'

The Laocoon group was done, after a careful study of the picture in the *Dictionnaire Larousse*, with dignity and decorum. The hose made almost excessive snakes. In fact some one guessed 'M – Michelin tyres'. Both Valliant Chevrell and Hickson were revealed in patches and fragments as very white men, but it was made manifest that Bunter had been cast, and cast rather well, in light bronze. All the Laocoon family, it seemed, wore wrist-watches.

Applause.

The actors of 'Paris' reappeared at another door, restored a little untidily to normal costumes, while the tableau was in progress.

'Well,' said Palace, 'Paris may have been easy, but your Laocoon I call obvious.'

'Why *not?*' asked Valliant Chevrell almost disagreeably from among coils of hose that were getting unmanageable.

Meanwhile Brynhild had been doing her best to think out a difficult mixture of immediate problems. They were problems of the most diverse values: little problems and big problems, problems of emotion and problems of dramatic direction. They had jumped upon her simultaneously. One was the inopportune question whether she wasn't altogether too meek a wife and whether she ought to allow her Rowland to be raped from her under her eyes in this fashion and whether it wasn't possible to do something quietly firm about it there and then. And the next was just how Rowland was feeling about her and whether he was forgetting even his customary reluctant awareness of her observant presence, and whether it might not be possible – though she had never done anything of the sort before – to rouse his facile competitiveness with some display of wandering interest. And as for the show – ?

She must think about Undine.

It seemed to her that something better could be done with Undine than just moping under water for her lost soul and her lost knight. She felt far too much like the part to want to display herself in that fashion. She didn't know La Motte Fouqué's story – and indeed who does? – and she imagined she might improvise a scene in which a water sprite who has married a Christian gentleman is exorcised by a crucifix. There had to be the knight in the scene – she had a great idea about that; there was a suit of armour in the broad passage. Why should she not take Rowland for the knight? After all he was her man. She had a right to take him. She would just take Rowland away from these brisk sirens and have a scene in which she was torn away from his arms. He would like wearing that armour...

'Time to go out I think, Mrs Palace,' said Valliant Chevrell. 'Who will you take?'

She had no time to realize the immense bare self-exposure of her next step before she had taken it.

'Rowland,' she said. 'Will you come?'

He was saying something in an undertone to Florrie Caterham who had to direct his attention to Brynhild. He looked up startled and grasped the situation. His expression became defensive.

'You mustn't make me do all the acting, Bryn,' he said, as if he addressed an unreasonable child. 'No.'

For a moment Brynhild felt that she and Rowland held the stage and that every one was observing them.

'This, my dear,' said her guardian angel within her, 'is going to be a Scene – unless you hold tight. So hold tight.'

She held tight.

'Of course,' she said, without a flicker, with a perfect indifference of manner, and paused for a moment to seek a substitute. The impulse to call upon Bunter was so strong and his restrained alertness so plain to her that she suppressed it at once. 'Keep your chin up and your voice soft and hold tight,' said her guardian angel in complete control of the situation.

'Will *you* come?' she said, and young Mr Bates rose in ready compliance.

'And some one else.' Again her eyes floated over Mr Bunter and she picked the man who had sat on her right at dinner.

'I'll tell you,' she said to Valliant Chevrell. 'Can we have some of that suit of armour?'

'Oh! *great* idea!' said Valliant Chevrell.

6

Brynhild did not think her Undine scene very good, but it was passable and there was much friendly applause. Young Bates wore the armour and relinquished his changeling wife reluctantly over the battlements of the sofa, to a fierce Water Sprite clad mostly in a strange fireplace ornament of weed-like green streamers that some one had unearthed in the housekeeper's room, and bearing a toasting-fork trident from the same locality, and Brynhild, in a retreating conical head-dress of paper and gauze and a slight medievalization of her dinner-frock, was just torn away and sat down to grieve in a not very well suggested cavern in the corner. Afterwards there was some little delay in helping young Bates out of his armour, there were moments when his extraction seemed doubtful; and when Brynhild rejoined the audience, T – it turned out to be Timon – was well under way.

She went to sit on a cushioned window-sill at the back, thinking now abundantly of all the bright things she might have done, which she hadn't done, to make that Undine more effective, and feeling how uninventive and unenterprising she was, so that she did not realize immediately that something had happened to Rowland. Then she forgot about her own deficiencies completely in her observation of him. Something *had* happened to him. He was no longer in the mood of conquering assurance that had distinguished his rendering of Paris. He was suddenly being tremendously left out. The trio had discovered a new and more difficult quarry in Mr Bunter. Some probably tacit and intuitive conspiracy had set them upon drawing out Mr Bunter. They had thought he was shy and afraid of them and so quite negligible, and then they had suddenly suspected that for some inscrutable reason he was not in the least interested in them and rather bored by them. That had changed everything. Mr Bunter had to be seen to. They had dropped Mr Palace simply and frankly.

They had grouped themselves round Mr Bunter and clamoured for him to act with them. They got at Valliant Chevrell, almost visibly pleased to have Palace put back in his place at last, and Brynhild heard Lady Cytherea insisting, 'Oh, but he mahst. He can't refuse.' Finally they led away the new victim.

Mr Bunter's Pluto was felt by many to be the best piece of acting that evening. He sat crowned in regal state on a chair on a table and contrived to look as though he really detested the damned (the Honourable Florence Caterham, the Honourable Alfred Bates, and Lady Dynover) who writhed sinfully but ignored and despised beneath his feet. Persephone enthroned beside him was unable to soften his infernal, his inspissated, gloom. When Mercury (Theodore Hickson, Esq.), in a zephyr silk shirt and shorts, wearing a rather small copper basin, bearing a tolerable caduceus and provided also with a red-covered Baedeker and a Cook's ticket wallet (applause), appeared and poised himself gracefully on one foot to summon her for her annual trip to the upper world, a grim smile of acquiescence lit the monarch's face. He waved off her farewell embraces, indicated irritably that she must not keep the car waiting, featured all the natural relief of a husband who is seeing off a too-attentive spouse, and then with an expression of impish sadism, a god left free at last to do as he pleased, bent forward, glanced over his shoulder to be sure she had really gone and prodded his sceptre into young Bates with the gusto of a long-deferred pleasure. 'Ouch!' said young Bates. Then Pluto, clawing his face with a glare of incredible malignity, considered what he should do to the two lady damned. Florrie looked up, met his expression of perfectly genuine dislike and uttered a perfectly genuine little scream. Mr Bunter sat up, smiled triumphantly at the audience and relaxed to show that the scene was over. (Prolonged applause.)

Rowland was applauding, Brynhild noted. He clapped hard, harder than anybody else almost, but the mask of cold irony had returned to his expressive face. He seemed disposed to become lofty and aloof.

This was interesting. What was he going to do about it?

Scarcely ever was he out of her thoughts and observation for the rest of the evening. She was the freer to concentrate upon him, because in his perplexed efforts to recall the errant trio, he seemed to be exceptionally oblivious of her. His first impulse, she perceived, was to be sulkily aloof in a scornfully dignified manner, 'if they chose to fool about with that bounder', etc., etc., but his intelligence would, she knew, be fully alive to the fact that they would probably not give a second thought to a mere Byronic disdain. He had to go on being 'amused' by them whether he liked it or not. He intended to be in the foreground of their scene when the first freshness of Bunter's unresponsiveness wore off. From one or two slight intimations, Brynhild was disposed to think he was trying to bring either Lady Dynover or the Italian countess into comparison and competition, but in that matter it seemed to his wife, he was reckoning without young Bates or their host. After that he was quietly charming to Cissie Parkington. Later it became plain from small movements and intimations, that he would if he could, detach Lady Cytherea from her two more trivial allies...

Somehow he did it. Something happened in undertones or in a movement. He must have made a direct appeal, because when about midnight the next charade (Nero) was over and the charade people made their way back to the little tables of flustered, pertinacious bridge players and the barley water and drinks in the central hall, he and Lady Cytherea disappeared through a door in the corridor in the most concerted manner possible and reappeared ten minutes afterwards from the direction of the front entrance, with a cleared-up expression on their candid faces.

The pair of them took the centre of the stage.

'It's the mahst wonderful moon!' cried Lady Cytherea.

'It's magic out there,' said Rowland.

Evidently it had been magic out there and he wanted every one to realize it. There was something proprietorial in his bearing, there was an assertion. Whatever had happened in the garden out there was as nothing to him in comparison with the dramatic assertion of close association, conveyed by this entry.

Brynhild stood with a glass of barley water in her hand marvelling quietly at life.

It had become necessary to both these remarkable people to intimate that in moonlight anyhow, they were of importance to each other, and that for all the finer purposes of life, people like Mr Alfred Bunter did not exist. *Why?* They were playing this at

Alfred Bunter, at the company generally, at Brynhild and at themselves, and why they were moved to play this small drama and make this show, Omniscience only knew.

'Am I different?' thought Brynhild; 'or is it just that I can watch other people and not myself? *Do* I do things in that way?

'I'm passive. After all' – moment of deep thought – 'for action one must act.'

She finished her barley water and put down the glass before she realized that there might be something a little defective about that profound philosophical discovery. 'For action one must act?' Yet it had seemed to mean something. Act? She smiled at herself with so amused a smile that Valliant Chevrell, watching her across the room and thinking how pleasant it would be to paint her portrait not merely as a lovely subject but a good still sitter, was suddenly struck with the idea that Palace was probably the damnedest ass he had ever known.

7

Late at night Brynhild, in a mood of scientific comparison, surveyed herself as God had made her in her bedroom mirror and weighed her own clear skin and her long and gracious lines against Lady Cytherea's lively assemblage of blobs, brisk curvatures, and flashes of enhanced and assisted pink.

'A secret beauty is nothing to him,' she said to the living Venus before her. '*The show's the thing…*

'You chose him. You're married to him.'

She looked into the drooping face before her and suddenly turned and went softly and locked her door very carefully and noiselessly against his still possible intrusion.

That was something she had never done before. And it was something she felt she was going to do now quite frequently.

She returned to scrutinize herself again. 'I'm beautiful,' she decided. 'And what good has it been to me? And what good is it now?

'I thought life was going to be lovely – and it turns out to be *this*. This sort of thing. And again this sort of thing. And then more of this sort of thing.'

She put on her white silk pyjamas slowly and absent-mindedly. She hadn't the slightest desire to go to bed. She opened her curtains and pulled up her blind and surveyed the moonlit garden. It was like a stage scene, an empty stage scene now, set for love.

Love? The universal desire; the universal frustration.

She had begun loving very well. And then somehow it had not gone on. Somehow it had faded into habits and associations. Why had it gone like that? Was that her fault? She couldn't think so. It might have been so different. For a long time it had kept on seeming that it was presently going to be different. And suddenly for no plain reason now it had become manifest that it could never be different until the end of everything...

That was the gist of it.

She turned away from the moonlight. She did not like her thoughts. This was self-pity! This wasn't the sort of thing one ought to be thinking. Think about something else? But somehow she could not think of anything else. What is reading for? Wasn't there a book?... Of course! There on the table. Alfred Bunter!

Maybe it would be just a novel. Anyhow it would be better to read the silliest story than to go on just at present thinking about herself.

8

She read Mr Bunter for two hours. It was an extremely turgid story about hampered and defeated people. 'Turgid' was the word for it. They lived in London as well as in the country; *The Cramped Village*, it seemed, was not a place, but life. They paralysed each other. Dreams tormented them from above and lusts and savage passions from below. They flattened themselves out to the decent exigencies of the Cramped Village. They distressed their poor heads whenever they raised them and they stumbled and fell down whenever they touched earth. Bunter was distressed for them and puzzled by them, and every now and then he broke out into that 'Anger' that people found characteristic and rather amusing in him. The style was rough and yet stimulating and – ? – the word was: *patchy*. In places it gobbled, in places it boomed, and then – it soared.

She knew quite well enough how prose becomes patchy if you worry it too much. How it works into raw places and holes. In her rôle of sympathetic helper and occasional typist she had had to watch that happen and say nothing, many times. He was plainly trying to get more into his narrative than his narrative prose could stand. He used disconnected unfused words so that at times his picture had less the effect of a painting than mosaic. He was plainly dissatisfied with the account he was giving of the motives of his characters. He was not quite sure of them himself and also he was not quite sure of the uptake of his readers.

'It's a splutter,' she thought... 'Like a cat with its head in a bag... A man trying most desperately to say something more than *can* be said... But he never fakes. He never walks out from it with an air of having settled it when he hasn't.

'He wants to get into things and under things. He wants to over-feel. He doesn't *believe* in the surface. He doesn't care how things look; he wants to know what things they are...

'Of course, there's a sort of indecency about that...'

She mused along these lines for a while and then she uttered one word out loud – because she wanted to hear it.

'Façade!

'Yes, Mr Bunter,' she reflected, 'you can hit upon the just word at times. The precise word... Among others. Among quite a lot of others.'

She put the book on the table beside her and paused for a moment, sitting up in her bed before she put out the light.

She looked towards the locked door – listening.

Rowland had a way of opening doors very softly and maybe he had been at the door and found it locked. He was quite capable of coming to her like that for consolation, in spite of all the appearances of the evening. Such revulsions had happened before. And if he *had* turned the handle – !

But perhaps he wasn't in need of consolation.

Perhaps that entry from moonlight had put everything square again and he was just sleeping on it happily.

How often had she listened like this to the mystery of Rowland and what he might be doing or feeling in another room!

He couldn't be no better than he seemed to be!

In through those two doors there was perhaps a real Rowland now.

Perhaps the Façade like a discarded garment was hanging over the back of a chair.

At times when he was asleep there was something about him helpless, quite unpretending, faintly silly and very, very, *very* dear and inviting indeed.

'Don't be a fool, Bryn,' she said, and sat up very still for the better part of a minute.

'Good night, Façade,' she whispered, clicked down the switch resolutely and thrust her shoulder into her pillow.

CHAPTER EIGHT

Exploring the Laurel Grove

No insurmountable difficulties arose about the installation of Mr Immanuel Cloote. Indeed, so far as installation was concerned, it all went much more smoothly than Mr Palace had ever dared to hope. Brynhild was unexpectedly indifferent to his explanation that he needed an office and an amanuensis, a new amanuensis – Mr Cloote as yet not named – away from home. 'Then I get a walk every morning – every morning that I want to, that is. A change of atmosphere. You understand?'

'It's so reasonable,' she said, 'I wonder you haven't done it long ago,' and he dismissed the thought that there was something enigmatical in her acquiescence.

A suitable office was found on the upper floor of Multiple Building, High Holborn, Mr Cloote displayed great energy and swiftness, and thither presently Mr Palace, feeling unnaturally and excessively modern, repaired to take over the intelligent control of his hitherto neglected and casual growth of laurels. 'It's like the difference between plantation rubber and forest rubber,' said Mr Cloote, displaying his preparations for the great campaign. 'Exactly like – for all practical purposes, that is. It's *grown* now. It used to be *collected*. There you are.'

Mr Palace surveyed the office equipment with interest and a certain doubt whether Mr Cloote could have kept within the estimate agreed upon. To a man who, for the sake of graciousness, had often written on parchment surface paper with a goose quill pen, there was something disconcerting in all this apparatus for the achievement of celebrity. He felt as a medieval swordsman may have felt in the presence of a cannon. He felt like one of King Arthur's Knights who had somehow been given a machine gun, least gentlemanly of weapons. And had been told the other side would certainly use it – unless he shot first.

Mr Cloote had set about his business with manifest gusto. Along one side of the room were fixtures with files and indexes and shelves containing books of reference, *Who's Who, Who's Who in America*, a Peerage, Literary Year Books, *Europa*, Gazetteers, Press guides, an encyclopaedic dictionary. Upon the opposite wall were maps of the world, of Europe, of England, with flags, and a number of large sheets of squared paper on which the daily number of 'Press mentions' and other indications of the health and well-being of Mr Palace's fame were to be traced. The actual furniture consisted of a sofa, an austere chair, an armchair, a bureau with an office chair, two telephones, an electric clock, and much writing and blotting material. Two large framed portraits of Mr Palace, a table portrait of Mr Palace in childhood, and a bust of a laureated Julius Caesar on a bookcase, completed the adornment of the room.

'Here,' said Mr Cloote, 'in this shelf of folders, assembled under letters of the alphabet, are projects for what I may call our Campaigns – each with it definite, thought-out, duly subordinated and duly co-ordinated, objective. All at present absolutely tentative, subject to your approval. I have been at work upon them – in the night – in trains – on Sunday afternoons – making notes – afterwards transferred. Re-sorted. On this system. On that. Re-shuffled. Masticated. Insalivated. Digested. You must glance over all this. I don't want to give you unnecessary trouble, but here is the plan of campaign. There' – he extended himself and his arms and his large hands towards the shelf of folders with the widening gesture of a swimmer – 'there is the reputation of my greatest writer – folded at present like the wings of a new-hatched moth. Slowly we shall see those wings quiver, extend, grow strong. A moth coming out into the limelight! Out of your cocoon, Mr Palace! And away!'

He turned and stared at and above Mr Palace and then brought his hot face nearer. 'Forgive me if I am excited,' he said. 'But I am very much excited.'

'These folders,' inquired Mr Palace, remaining cool and dignified by an effort. 'What have you in them?'

'Let us take one haphazard,' said Mr Cloote, and chose a folder with great deliberation. '*This*, I think – H'm.

'Now here' – he opened the folder and poised it on one large hand while he indicated much order, division, and sweeping intentions by the other. 'Here we have "Academic Prestige – cultivation of". First, a preliminary discussion whether it is really worth having – and a carefully reasoned estimate – I will discuss that later – and next a list – I add to it constantly – of what I call Founts, Founts of Honour, distinctions, prizes. In the universal struggle for recognition there are not only universities and fully equipped academies organized to place the palms on such brows, or rather laurels, I should say, where they are most likely to be a credit to the conferrer, but also a number of organizations, societies, prize-giving committees, of very unequal prestige – many of them – which assemble with dignity, with social Eclat, and read important papers to themselves – importantly. Usually on what you might call *distinguished* subjects. The *highest* tone – the very highest. They honour themselves in honouring each other.

'But they have to be chosen. It is a most delicate task. Those Prizes. American women of the socially enterprising sort with titles; *their* prizes are apt to be Bad – thoroughly Bad. I am trying here, by a system of mark-giving, to estimate just what relative value attaches to the better advertised of these Prizes. I give so much for names, on a scale I have worked out.

'If the social element enters ambiguously into the Prize-givings, Mr Palace, what you might call the meretricious element – commercial factors, to be plain – is apt to enter into Book of the Month selections. Through their professional readers, through the *esprit de corps* of their authors. It's natural, it was to be expected that Schroederer, for example, would get his fingers into that. It one Book Club won't do what he wants, he can always start another.'

'That,' said Mr Palace, 'is where the universities come in. They at least – '

'*Would* come in,' said Mr Cloote, 'if you could eliminate political, social, financial considerations... But can you? You can overdo even Academic Prestige, Mr Palace. You can overdo it... For example, consider Dr Nicholas Murray Butler. That Carnegie Trust man. Most able. Splendid, if you could see the real man there! A great imagination. But – He's *encrusted* with the honours and decorations thrust upon him, all from the most respectable Founts, jewelled in *every* hole, so to speak, Mr Palace. No one could be so learned and wise and clever as Dr Nicholas Murray Butler is certified to be by practically all the universities in the world. It's too much. You can't see the saint for the halo. He ceases to be human, Mr Palace, he becomes a caddis worm of decorations. He's the Pearly King of the Academic World. And all the same – '

Mr Cloote paused to gather his instances.

'Does he rank with D H Lawrence – or Greta Garbo – or Einstein – or Colonel Lindbergh – in the world of Art and Thought and Achievement?'

Mr Palace had no estimate ready.

2

'But this folder,' said Mr Cloote, striking it very hard with his hand to enforce the significance of the word *this*. 'This folder is just one Folder. Let me try to make a conspectus of what I conceive to be your Predestined Career, Mr Palace. Let us try to envisage this business as a Whole.'

He threw the one folder down on the desk as if he had taken a dislike to it. 'Consider,' he said, and for a time left Mr Palace considering in the absolute.

Then with great intensity. 'First: *Personality!*'

'It was precisely about personality,' said Mr Palace, 'the establishment of a personality, that I was thinking, when I wrote my original advertisement. I did not mind being neglected but I realized I might be distorted and misinterpreted. That set me thinking. A personality has to be – conveyed.'

'We differ in our manners, we differ in our gifts,' said Mr Cloote, 'but we think alike. We are going to be a great combination.'

(It seemed horribly true.)

Mr Cloote's next move almost made Mr Palace jump. He took three wide dramatic strides across the room, half-circling Mr Palace, *passant guardant*, as the heralds say, and with the near hand making snaky gestures.

'Mr Palace,' he said, 'you have never been *really* photographed. Never. They just simply don't get you. What I've seen – what your publishers issue – is more like a passport photograph than a picture. What I call – statistics about a face. Recognition notes. Diagrams of You.'

He came towards Mr Palace, holding his head rather to one side. It was as if he himself was taking a photograph. He framed Mr Palace with his hand, retreated to a better standpoint. 'A mere head and shoulders of an author. Or a politician. Or any public character. For all practical purposes – it's just nothing at all. An author should always be shown in an atmosphere, in an entourage. He should be grouped. He should be doing something. The Public wants that. The author in his Native Habitat. Your photographs hitherto...'

He paused. He threw out a hand of critical disgust. 'A stuffed author. The Sportsman's Club dining-room. Head of an author shot by Mr Schroederer in 1930. A Trophy, not an Ad. Not in any sense of the word, an Ad. *His* Trophy. Rows of heads. Decapitated heads. Bloodless heads. Drained of all reality. What do they convey? Nothing!

'Now let me give you *my* idea,' Mr Cloote continued, though Mr Palace was doing nothing to prevent him.

'I see you' – Mr Cloote raised his eyes to heaven and for a time spoke after the manner of one who sees visions. 'I see you… May I use a word – a key word, Mr Palace. About you. A quality. The word – Debonair!…'

He calmed Mr Palace with an extended hand, deprecating any interruption while his vision continued. 'Let me make myself perfectly clear. Debonair. You could easily be *very* debonair, Mr Palace. I've always thought Il Re Galantuomo a most attractive title. Il Scrittore – No! – Lo Scrittore Galantuomo. A man, just a little aloof – aloof in his soul and yet not too aloof. Smiling but never mingling, friendly, assured, kindly. Capable of immense seriousness, but carrying it easily, lightly. Capable of – adventures. And naturally he had to be seen *unposed* – in transit – in action – caught unawares. A man rather heedless of his public. No standing at attention to be photographed. Good Lord! *No.* In an assembly among delightful people – good, well-known people or lovely-looking people. Smilingly making a repartee… But you get me, Mr Palace?'

'I think you have practically the whole philosophy of publicity there,' said Mr Palace.

'Perfect!' approved Mr Cloote. 'And then instead of saying, "What's this barber's block? Another escape from the waxworks!" they will say, "What's going on? Who's that? Of course, that's Mr Palace. What a lovely garden! Who's the lady? What can he be saying to her?" '

'That might be a little difficult to manage,' mused Mr Palace.

'Not so difficult as you suppose. I *am* a photographer. I have even been a Press photographer. I have even worked the railway termini and the boats. In times of adversity. Advise me of your friends. Advise me of some pleasant society grouping. I will appear – as from the Local Organ... The expenses and hire of the camera, a mere song... Simple...'

Mr Cloote smiled radiant reassurances.

Mr Palace walked to the window and looked out. How far could he confide his own secret spectacular ambitions to this alarmingly energetic, preposterous, but extraordinarily intelligent man? And yet he couldn't possibly get what he wanted unless he asked for it. A rather frequent, recurrent appearance with Lady Cytherea, for example...

There would be nothing in it yet everything would be implicitly there. Debonair wasn't at all a bad word.

Meanwhile Mr Cloote pursued the robust tenor of his way.

'I would like to put you in flannels, Mr Palace. I think you would look well in flannels. You play cricket? Well then, tennis. But why not cricket? A man's game. You must give me a list of your games, your sports. Climbing? An author of your build, Mr Palace, would look well on a rock, amongst snowy mountain scenery.'

3

They covered the ground pretty exhaustively before they had done. Some of the ground they returned to and covered again. There was a great air of thoroughness about it all. Some of the things Mr Cloote said seemed already vaguely familiar to Mr Palace. They were regurgitations from that intelligent letter of application which had secured Mr Cloote his appointment, or they were echoes and expansions of earlier contributions by Mr Palace to the discussion.

Occasionally Mr Cloote was seized with an incontinence of memoranda. He hailed the passing idea with a raised red hand as he might have hailed a taxi. 'I must put that down,' he said. 'I must put that down. I can't risk losing that,' and he would go to the desk and scribble, breathing hard, ejaculating fragmentary words, while Mr Palace went to the window and hummed and got new angles upon their projects.

And as they covered the ground and retraced their steps on it, they sowed the seeds of those various activities that ultimately were to expand Mr Palace from his status of a highbrow favourite percolating slowly into the general realm of intellectually snobbish bookbuyers to a writer of world-wide fame, influence, and distinction, a Great Writer. They were to send him on scores of railway and automobile journeys, make him step on to dozens of flower-adorned platforms, project him bowing and smiling from trains, stages and balconies, turn him about time after time, gaily waving a hand to ranks of cameramen.

That day they set in motion the forces that were presently to make Rowland Palace a suitable but not too frequent or regular contributor to the general thought and feeling of the country.

'Occasions for appearing,' Mr Cloote called them. 'As almost accidental as possible. But do them well. Do them memorably. A schoolmaster wants to advertise his school through you. An institution wants to get a press. Publicity swapping. As a rule you turn them down. Turn them down. But not always. Once in a while, as if out of sheer good-fellowship you yield. Some little picturesque country grammar school perhaps. And then you say something deep and moving to those boys which they will remember, which their mothers will remember, which people who write about schools will remember. A revelation of fine feeling.'

'Feeling? Not sentimentality, I hope. Not quite in my picture, is it? I don't want to wear my heart on my sleeve, you know.'

'You don't. And I don't want you to. But – Wear your heart *up* your sleeve. Give them a glimpse of it and then – Presto! It's gone, and you get that enigmatical Palace smile.'

Mr Palace looked sceptical and Mr Cloote hurried on. 'In all directions,' he said, 'there are occasions for appearing. What I should call your Natural Occasions. For example, Agricultural Meetings. Fire-brigade suppers. Poultry shows.'

'But what have I to do with poultry?'

'Exactly. Precisely. What *have* you to do with poultry? Arouses curiosity straight away. And you make good among the hens! See? And after that for weeks and weeks lots of people won't be able to look at a hen without thinking of those quaint, interesting, penetrating things you said. It's just the things you couldn't reasonably be expected to have anything to do with that broaden you out, widen your basis and (Mr Cloote rose to a deep full-bodied roar and made advancing threatening gestures with his hands) *get you there*.'

'But I don't want to appear a sort of know-everything, you know.'

'Nor I. Johnny Busybody-can't-keep-shut. No fear. It's just that once in a way you let yourself out. Inadvertently. And then you show that sure and certain Palace touch.'

'H'm,' said Mr Palace.

Mr Cloote swept on to a subject already dealt with in his opening letter; fan-mail, the great autograph question, the signed photograph. 'Why be boorish to these poor creatures?' he pleaded. 'Your compliance takes a moment and thereafter the happy recipient becomes, so to speak, your unpaid agent, he feels a sort of ownership, he follows your career in the papers – *he may even get your books!*'

Mr Palace made a sceptical grimace.

'It's happened,' Mr Cloote asserted stoutly. 'Some of them can read. I know it. And certainly those people who want your advice, who ask what you think of infant paralysis, or psycho-analysis, or crossing the Equator, or when to cut your hair, or books they ought to read... A little trouble for you, but then they quote you for years. And you know – I can do all that – just pass you a typewritten letter to approve. I can assure you... We must do it. We can't disdain these – these camp followers of literature. I can make it all perfectly easy for you. Sometime when you are at leisure you might jot down as few of what I might call "Mental Preferences and Characteristics". Then I needn't trouble you generally. Except to sign...'

'It's a bore,' said Mr Palace.

'It's Mulch,' pleaded Mr Cloote. 'Consider it as Mulch.'

4

They lunched together in that maelstrom of lunching business men, the Holborn Restaurant, and Mr Palace had an opportunity of studying the table manners of Mr Cloote. They were broad and inclusive manners, elbows well out. Mr Palace, in his insular English way, decided that they must have been acquired abroad where people feed so much better and eat so much worse. Mr Cloote never seemed to look at his plate, he just bent down and swept up the food into himself, catching it deftly with his mouth as it rose towards him. His amplitude of gesture was enlarged by knife and fork, and his discourse was sprayed with crumbs, but he kept on and kept on. Curiously enough this gave no offence to Mr Palace. He liked it. It opened a gulf between them; it mitigated that disagreeable sense of intimacy, of kindred, of something unpleasantly like being searchingly mirrored and told immodestly about oneself. A man who eats as one eats oneself is a friend and brother. But a man who scoops and engulfs food is an instrument. Cloote was much more endurable, Mr Palace was realizing, as an instrument.

The business men about them were preoccupied with their own affairs. Nobody seemed to be looking or listening, and that, Mr Palace felt, was just as well. For now Mr Cloote was dealing again with the broader aspects of a world reputation and returning to the subject, the very indelicate subject, of the Nobel Prize. He talked about that as though he were the trainer of a prospective World Champion. In imagination he set Mr Palace sprinting through the Continent. 'We must travel,' said Mr Cloote. 'You have to make yourself known in the Baltic countries and eastern Europe. You'd like Scandinavia.'

He reflected. He smiled at some memory. 'Can you stand a lot of drink?'

Mr Palace weighed himself. 'I have a certain resisting power. A normal resisting power.'

'Drink makes *me* – garrulous,' said Mr Cloote. 'I have to be careful.'

'I got drunk in Bergen once,' Mr Cloote reflected. 'It was Sunday. Ever been in Bergen on Sunday? Makes a Sabbath in Scotland seem giddy. It was raining. Ever seen it rain in Bergen? And there was a great temperance demonstration going on in the Square. Most uncalled-for. Wet banners. Wet umbrellas. Wet women in wet mackintoshes. The band sounded wet. There wasn't so much as a cinema open. I *had* to get drunk. It was troublesome to get but I got it.'

'And that broke down your usual – taciturnity?' smiled Mr Palace.

'I went out into that Square. I *tried* to tell them what I thought of them. In Norwegian. I was never very good at Norwegian. I broke their Norwegian badly. Inadvertent indecency. I was locked up... My salad days.'

Mr Cloote turned abruptly to other agencies of literary distinction and particularly to Academies.

'I doubt if we really want Academies,' said Mr Palace, 'at least in the English-speaking countries. A British Academy would be bound to exasperate feeling in American literary circles – none too good, anyhow.'

'Lots in that,' said Mr Cloote. 'They'd be sour. Certainly they'd be sour. An Academy would be worse than Olympic Games in really keeping the sores open. All the same, Mr Palace, you have to consider it. It may be undesirable, but it may come. It is comes, you want to be on the bus. It really isn't fame in itself. You can't expect the public to adore a mixed bus-load of forty literati. Sort of troupe. But all the same, they might notice it if you weren't there. Americans, for example. Think nothing of you if you had it, but think there was something damned wrong with you if you hadn't. They're used to branded articles. You can't ignore Academies, Mr Palace, for one simple reason: you can't afford they should ignore you. You've got to make your calling and election sure. The project of a real group of Imperial Academies isn't dead; it's sleeping. Some chap might think of reviving it presently – to build up the dignity of the Crown. Empire of the mind and all that. It's a wonder to me that Ramsay

Macdonald never had a shot at it. He'd love to be a great lord of literature and tell them all what. Booming away. Think of it. Think of the satisfaction it would give all round to heaps of people with a pull. Canadian Academy with a President. South African Academy with a President. Australian President. New Zealand president. Dublin Academy. And so on. A majestic one in London. You can't be *out* of that. You can't be late. You must be *there* – in position. And the whole question of literary circles, the swing of literary gossip, the fermentation of a reputation, the harvesting of criticism, I can assure you, it's a most fascinating department. Gossip particularly. Most fascinating.

'Gossip particularly,' said Mr Cloote, twiddling his fingers in front of his face in a strange hypnotic manner.

He looked through the mist of quivering fingers at metaphysical things. 'One of the greatest ideas of our time – Relativity!'

'We aren't going to Parnassus via the Fourth Dimension, are we?' exclaimed Mr Palace.

'We're going direct to Parnassus. But all the same – all the same there's Relativity!'

Mr Cloote leant over the table. 'There is no such thing, Mr Palace, as *absolute* greatness. Your advance is relative. You want an outstanding position. If you are surrounded by others, by clustering others, how can you outstand?'

'I don't quite get this,' said Mr Palace.

'Nature red in tooth and claw,' said Mr Cloote.

'You don't want me to *eat* other writers?'

'No.' Mr Cloote took counsel with himself for some time. 'This,' he said, 'is a service I do you and nothing I ask you to do. In fact the word for you here is – pardon me – "keep out". But we have to be chary of the growth of other reputations. A false reputation, shot up in the night, fungoid, that might take the wind out of our sails... We can't ignore it.'

'I am the least competitive, the least envious of men.'

'Exactly! Perfect! It is in your picture. Careless. Debonair. Yes. Nevertheless, when one sees other people, sinister figures, illegitimate competitors... This queer man from nowhere, for example, who had just loomed up, this boomster Bunter.'

'He appears to be a very harmless person.'

'I mention him only as a type – and because I happen to know a few things about him.'

'I want to know nothing about that man's private life – or any one's private life.'

'Precisely. Perfect. As I desired. That sort of thing... Invisible... Ignored by you.'

Mr Cloote became intensely confidential and breathed close to his employer: *But not ignored by me. No.*

Mr Palace waved the evil suggestion aside with a graceful impatient gesture and turned to the waiter for the bill.

'I love all this,' said Mr Cloote. 'I love it. I am a born Yes-Man. When other babies were saying "Pa-Pa", "Ma-Ma", I must have been saying "Ya-Ya". Loyalty is a secretion with me. It oppresses me. It has to be discharged.'

5

When Mr Palace returned home from Multiple Buildings, he had a bath. At times he liked to soak in a bath and think. He was thinking now.

133

He remained for quite a long time in his bath, thinking over the vulgarity, the verbal exuberance, the pretentiousness, the utter lack of scruple or delicacy, the probable dishonesty and the undeniable energy of Mr Cloote. And Mr Palace told himself he would not have things otherwise.

The man was an instrument, a tool. 'A mercenary. A bravo. My Minion,' said Mr Palace, feeling like a Florentine nobleman of the best period. 'My creature. My henchman. By the way – what is a hench? Hench? Hench? Some sort of a horse perhaps? In a panoply. Rowland Palace on the high hench with his trusted henchman beside him.'

Mr Palace applauded himself by swirling the water. Then he became still again.

Joking apart, Cloote was necessary. In this swift, crowded, violent new world in which we live such agents are necessary. You don't dine with your dustman, but you have to avail yourself of his services all the same.

It was a Florentine nobleman who towelled himself in Mr Palace's bathroom.

At dinner that night he was unusually debonair. Brynhild couldn't imagine what had got hold of him.

CHAPTER NINE

Mrs Palace Meditates on the Lot of Women

In the October of that year there came a run of golden days in which Brynhild found herself rather alone and much occupied with her own thoughts. Her husband had gone off to Scotland on one of those novel excursions that were becoming now recurrent variables upon the pattern of their existence. He was to give an address on *Strength and Delicacy* to the students' association of Dunbuttock University College. And then he was to stay a week with the Burnadips at Garvie Castle.

These new and lengthening departures puzzled her. They had a flavour of disentanglement. She felt, and she felt that he behaved as though he also felt, that an implicit treaty was being tacitly broken.

He was as little communicative as possible on each occasion about the places and objectives to which he went. But invariably for some days after each excursion a multiplication and distention of his bundles of press-cuttings occurred and from these she did what she could to understand the drift of his proceedings. With all the will in the world to find some coherent purpose in them she was drifting more and more towards the conclusion that for some reason for which perhaps she was partly but very obscurely to blame, a long suppressed exhibitionism had been released in her husband, and that he was now, as they used to say at school, 'showing off'. He went from her to have a good show off. But why?

Before this present journey to Scotland there had been four of these expeditions in which she had played no part and of two of them she had been quite unaware until the report of them had reached her. One she learnt about for the first time through his sudden appearance on the newsreel at the Curzon Cinema, as a brilliant batsman in the annual charity cricket match at Long Marringbury between Actors and Authors. She had never suspected him of cricket and she had attached no importance to his spending the August Bank Holiday weekend with a few other writers in Essex. She did not know he had been taking secret intensive lessons from a professional for a fortnight before the event. But then to her intense astonishment he appeared in bright new flannels, carrying his bat, chin up and debonair to an extreme degree, the best-looking author in the bunch. He stole the picture.

'The Author of *The Supple Willow Wand* shows he understands how to wield the willow,' said the picture.

'But the "Supple Willow Wand" in his book was a Chinese lady!' protested Brynhild to herself.

And then came the cuttings. Hitherto the Actors and Authors had had their happy little match in Wiltshire, usually in lucky weather, indulging in an amiable blend of real and fictitious puerility and really being boys-together with a very minimum of gentle genial publicity. But this year with Mr Rowland Palace as the new boy – nobody quite knew how it was he had been brought into the eleven – things were insidiously different. No direct responsibility could be traced to Mr Palace, but there was a new and formidable camera-hound on the scene, with abundant dark curly hair, a vertical squint, a voice of great range, clutching hands and urgent hypnotizing gestures, and his concentration on Mr Palace was undeniable. He took shots indeed of everybody, but few of these other shots survived. He was also, it became apparent, the representative of Topical Films. Very few of the players – not even among the Actors – realized that a movie take was afoot outside the marquee until it was all over. Then there was no opportunity to pose. There may have been a faint surmise about the state of affairs, but Palace under scrutiny remained as debonair as a flag in a good breeze. And most of them were too worried trying to remember how the movie camera might have caught them to think about him.

The cricket match spate had hardly died out of the English press-cutting and was just beginning in the American packages, when Mr Rowland Palace was discovered to have discovered Quilp Crake, the artistic strawberry-grower at Westerbridge.

Brynhild had never heard of this Quilp Crake. Rowly had never said a word about him to her. Then suddenly here was Rowland opening a local show of 'glowing roseate pictures' he called them and making it a national event. He had run down from London by road it seemed the other afternoon and with him was a Bloomsbury contingent hitherto unattained by him, and the Duchess of Shonts and Lady Cytherea Label and so on and so forth, with the usual competent photographer. There stood Rowland expatiating on the peculiar colour sense that had lifted Quilp Crake at one step from the status of a secret shamefaced amateur in a greenhouse, to that of a universally astounding artist. She stood at the breakfast table with the cutting in her hand as Rowland came down.

'I didn't know you cared for painting,' she remarked.

'Dear, dear!' said Rowland, featuring a vexation that would not have deceived a lap-dog. 'Have they got all that again?'

'You didn't tell me.'

'It happened impromptu – so far as I was concerned. I was carried away. Did they get my speech?'

'Verbatim I should think,' she said, handing him the cutting.

He read. 'Fairly good,' he said, sitting down to his breakfast.

'I would have liked to have seen those pictures,' she remarked after an interval.

He stopped with half a sausage on his fork and reflected gravely. 'If you had been there, my dear,' he said, 'I should have known those pictures for the daubs they are. And I didn't want to do that.'

'Why?'

'It is like that.'

'They were daubs?'

'With something else. I tried to say it...'

She regarded him sideways. What had he tried to say? 'Do you like these new sausages?' she asked quite needlessly.

'That man gets his effects like a sunset,' he explained. 'Not a shadow of any intention. But he gets his effects. I was asked to go down quite suddenly... And anyhow you wouldn't have liked it.'

The next surprise for Brynhild was the presence of her once so reluctant husband, very grave and thoughtful, at a Summer Peace Conference which had met to discourage warfare in an inoffensive way amidst pleasant surroundings just outside

Birmingham. Here the photographer got him rather close and large and seriously downcast. He rose from out amidst ferns, and his background was a bishop and a liberal peeress, both out of focus. The speech was on another page of the paper and it was given at some length. He would be the last, he said, 'to deny the noble tradition of the Warrior in the past. In his esteem the Knight in Armour stood beside the Saint. In those days the Weapon was the Sword. It chose. It looked to see whom it slew...' And so on.

Bryn read all that with an expression of meek edification. Then he 'ventured to make a suggestion or so, but with little expectation that what he had to say would be heeded'.

His proposal was a simple one, the total prohibition of air-warfare, of the use of gas, high explosives, and incendiary substances. Simple.

Never yet had Brynhild come so near to thinking her husband an ass. She was moved, as she was rarely moved, to express her criticism. 'But, darling,' she said, putting down the paper, '*who* will prohibit air-warfare, the use of gas, high explosives, and incendiary substances?'

He did not look at her. How rare it was becoming now for their eyes to meet!

He stood up. 'It's just that want of faith,' he said slowly, 'that makes this modern world the horror that it is.'

That was all.

He walked quietly out of the room. 'Either I am a leering sceptic,' thought Brynhild, 'or Rowly is a touchy child of eight.'

It was rapidly becoming clear to her that unless Rowly was a child of eight her married life was becoming unendurable. And even on that hypothesis it was anything but satisfactory. She pushed the newspaper aside and turned to her housekeeping.

The fourth expedition took Rowly to the popular seaside resort of Morganspool for an afternoon to open 'Ye Fleet of Odd Ships', and that again was done before Brynhild had news of it. The Fleet of Odd Ships was a collection of nefs, ships' models, silver ships and ivory ships, votive ships, ships in glass and china to hold flowers, ships made in prisons, and ships cunningly inserted by sailors and prisoners through the necks of bottles. The collection had been left by its creator to the borough of Morganspool and on the spur of the moment and at the invitation of the mayor, Lady Cytherea had motored Palace down from London to inaugurate the exhibition. Here again the thoughtful side of Rowly was uppermost. 'Man the eternal wanderer makes himself a home and then over his very hearth, he puts the model of a ship.'

But the latest departure of Rowland in this new moth-like career of his towards the blaze of fame, had put his wife out much more than any of the previous occasions. It went further in the direction of separation. Hitherto it had seemed to be tacitly agreed between them that socially they went together. For weekends and mixed dinners and so forth they had been a brace. She had to dress well, look beautiful, behave nicely and be a credit to him. And she had been. Up to quite recently he had shown an unquestionable pride in her. She had seemed an essential part of his ensemble.

She had found a cheerful pleasure in these visits. There was real amusement in a quizzical Who's Who? of the arrivals, in the conversations and the games, in the inspection of the village hall or the parish church or the ruined castle, and it was pleasant to come at last to her chintzy bedroom and an exchange of observations about the company. Generally he would wind up by telling her that never in all the world had he known so lovely a woman as she was and that the more he saw of other people the more he adored her. And so to kneeling beside her armchair and tender intimacies.

If that sort of things was to be cut out and Rowly was going to do weekends and even whole large portions of week unencumbered, then Mrs Rowland Palace was beginning to realize she would find herself with more time and energy on her hands than she knew how to use.

What was she going to do with herself?

It wasn't that she was an abandoned wife. It wasn't that Rowly had ceased to be in the common acceptance of the term her lover. He wasn't deserting her; he was just overflowing beyond her limitations. He was flooding the adjacent country. He was greedy. But he came prancing back from these new expedition an ardent and appreciative husband, rather greedy, very self-satisfying and quite oblivious to the possibility that he could ever be unwelcome to her.

Some streak of pride in her was provoking her to disillusion him.

She had locked her door at Valliant Chevrell but then he had never found out that she had locked her door. Supposed she locked her door now at home?

He would be the most astonished and hurt of men.

The provocation to do something of the sort, if only to hear him argue about it, was very considerable.

She smiled faintly and added it to an unwritten list of Agenda in her mind.

She reflected on the evanescence of her memories of love-making. Did all people forget those intense moments as she did? Are there no fast-colour phases of passion? Are they semi-realities, hybrids of time and dream? Once it seemed, unless her memories betrayed her, he had been a divinity and love had been wonderland; and then there had been a long phase of hearty mutual appreciation. At least that is how it seemed to be now in that peculiar region of her mind, that restless region where some recurrent stir is continuously dissolving away the edges and the details of events. But certainly making love had been lovely, and now it was no longer lovely. Now at any rate he was just a pampered thing that she embraced and tolerated out of habit.

2

And then suddenly it jumped into her mind that she was quite out of love with Rowly and that equally he was out of love with her. Nothing led up to this idea. It appeared suddenly in her mind as a self-evident fact that had been there, quite disregarded for a long time. Her thoughts were like some chemical mixture that quietly reaches the exploding point and then explodes.

Abruptly it was plain to her that she did not love him, that she did not admire him, that she had only the scantiest respect for him, that she knew him as exasperatingly vain and disingenuous. There was no process of gradual suspicion and discovery in this realization. It was like a shutter falling to expose a plate. It was like an electric light turned on unexpectedly in a darkened room.

'Of *course!*' she said.

For a while her mind stopped dead at that. By sheer inertia she went on with the seemly routine of her daily life. She attended two linen sales to repair the wear and tear of her household stock. She visited an infirm great-aunt, played bezique with her and discussed transferring her from her present boarding-house to a much more comfortable and hardly more expensive residential hotel. She went to a show of the Royal Horticultural Society. She attended, to vote rather than talk, a meeting of the committee of a Marylebone Housing Society which was slowly buying up slums and rebuilding them as tolerable but not too costly working-class dwellings. It was a meritorious common-sense enterprise in which she had invested three hundred pounds of her own money – in spite of a certain disapproval on the part of Rowly. He didn't think it wise to mix up monetary affairs with public service.

Then, while she was sitting at the table listening to the secretary's report, her mind began working again.

What does a modern married woman who finds she is not in love with her husband and that he is very plainly losing anything but a physical interest in her, do about it?

This new train of thought once it was started, started off so vigorously that the chairman of the meeting had to ask her twice whether she voted for the motion or against it, before she could be recalled to the business in hand.

3

Once this train of thought had come out of its incubatory tunnel and started openly upon its journey it bore her along relentlessly. She thought all day and for a considerable part of a very restless night. 'What am I going to do about it?' she asked. 'What sort of outlook have I before me?'

She tried hard to recall when it was she had stopped loving Rowly. The astounding thing was that now it seemed that right back, far back, even to those remote days among the lakes, she had known that she did not love him.

Had life played a trick upon her? Or had she through some fault of her own stumbled at the threshold of life? Perhaps she had sailed into life too confidently and too confidingly. Had she assumed too much about it? In those buoyant days between seventeen and twenty, her hope and expectation had been of a tremendous companionship which was to go on developing through the years. Rowland had seemed to be just the predestinate companion she needed. They had been immensely in love with each other, or at any rate she had been immensely in love with him. Surely. Surely! There was to have been work together, adventures together, travel together, success together, a continual rich mutual endorsement. That was the essence of the handsome offer life had seemed to be making her, the most popular girl in the school, the easy first in classics, Brynhild of the unruffled good manners and the pleasant voice. In the background of this picture, with a faint modern flavour of postponement about them, there had been children. More remotely the companionship attained maturity and dignity in the midst of a constellation of starry offspring.

And so she had gone off to the honeymoon and the Alps and then – nothing more. By imperceptible degrees indeed something less. Less and less co-operation, less and less mutual confidences, less and less frank talk, less and less assurance. Seven years of ebb.

For a time the Great Fair of Life which she had learnt about from literature and art, had seemed to be a going concern. If she, in her little corner of repetitive and decelerated love-making with Rowland, felt she was rather settling into an eddy, the natural expectancy of youth assured her that this was only a transitory recession. It hadn't at first struck her as significant that the chief entertainments in the Great Fair of Life seemed to be swooping to and fro in the swings and circulating faster and faster on the roundabouts and returning perpetually in each case to the point of departure. That wasn't evident to the spectator at first because sweeping up or down in a swing or holding tight to a roundabout horse gives the human countenance and bearing a purposive quality such as no sustained forward advance, with all its scaring novelty and uncertainly, could ever possibly produce.

But now the vain repetitions of life displayed themselves to her with an appalling clearness.

She was caught in that eddy. She was just spinning round in that eddy while the stream of life was flowing by. The eddy was flatter than it used to be but it held her just the same. And there was no prospect, no open door at least, of escape from this futile circling about Rowly. Was this the universal lot of women? And of men too? Did they just begin – and circle? All of them?

It was certainly a very common lot. 'Everything goes round, my dear, and comes back – a little different – a very little different – but it comes back.' It was her father's voice. She remembered a night with him and his old brass Georgian telescope, in the vicarage garden, and how he had made her conscious of the circling life of the sky. Even the stars in their orbits went about and returned, and if there was indeed a general drift in things they circled unconscious of it, perigee to apogee, perihelion to aphelion, hurrying exaltation and prolonged recess.

Was that all life was?

A brilliant evanescent promise as gay as the breeding plumage of a humming-bird and then this dullness, this pointless recurrence of small and diminishing excitements. A broken promise? She began casting about in her mind for instances of other people who might be escaping this fate. But they all seemed to be spinning. Hitherto she had always thought there was something distinguished and significant about herself. Now, belatedly perhaps, at six and twenty, it was dawning upon her that her life was probably going to be a quite ordinary life, just another among the ordinary lives that were eddying about her. And she found this an extraordinarily distasteful idea. She found a very strong urgency in her to break away.

But how can any one break away?

She was a satellite of Rowly and he was tracing some incomprehensible orbit of his own.

How was it possible to break away?

4

The recognized code of morality, the legal conception of social duty, forbade her to break away at all. This was the situation to which she had been called, this was the way of life she had chosen, and she had to endure it.

What would her father have said about it? Not exactly that. He would have said, 'My dear, it is for you to decide. I have done my best to put the established code of morality before you. As a churchman I was bound to do that, but as a Protestant and a pagan I am bound not to anticipate your decision.'

Who believed nowadays in the established code of morality? The romantic spirit which had always run counter to morality and seemed nowadays to be triumphantly in control of our conduct, was dead against any such submission. It was dead against complaisant wives. If Rowly and she were no longer in love, said the romantic spirit, that was the end of the affair. The next step was to fall in love afresh and begin all over again with another man. Or rather to let another man being all over again with her. Her marriage was to be treated as a point of departure and some remarkably different male, some entrancing Perseus, was to come fluttering down the sky to release her.

All fiction is full of these fluttering Persei, they are as common there as white butterflies on an early day in summer. They take the initiative. They overcome all your scruples. They do everything for you. It is very misleading to the young. Brynhild could not persuade herself that in real life she had ever so much as glimpsed a specimen. She had never felt that slightest disposition to fall in love with any one but this difficult and acutely disappointing Rowly of hers, and she had very grave doubts whether any one had ever been to any extent in love with her. And if now she was out of love with him, that did not mean she was in love with any one else. She had not the slightest desire in her for a Perseus.

Perseus seemed to offer no solution to her difficulty. Suppose there was a slightly super-Rowly hovering just beyond the limits of visibility, and supposing there presently arrived a triangular situation, confrontations, generosities, elopements, a tangle of embarrassing complications, a sort of torn, mangled, and spread-out second honeymoon; what would it bring her to? Could it end on anything better than other sexual roundabout, another cycle of board, bed, and *da capo;* another home which had to be housekept somewhere – with a studio perhaps or a factory or an

147

office, in place of a study to which after the roseate days, husband number two would increasingly withdraw. Could it be much better? She tried to imagine some sort of super-Rowly who would restore meaning to life for her. Not a shadow came. If the Creator had sat down beside the green park chair in which she was sitting and offered to dispense at once whatever prescription she chose to give him and put the new man before her, she could not have specified a single detail: appearance, profession, character. So that not only was there no sign of a super-Rowly in the world, but also no desire in her heart for one. Apparently whatever there was in her in that way had been taken by Rowly and used up and left spinning emptily.

'Emptily,' she said aloud as though she was definitely pinning down that part of her meditation before going on to cut out the next.

'So I'd better look for something else?' she mediated. 'It's up to me.'

Something had to be done, some way of mitigating this concentration of her life that had put her so entirely under the sway of Rowly's behaviour, so entirely dependent on his presence. And it had to be something that would not put her at the mercy of the behaviour of any one else.

'Independence,' she considered. 'A life of one's own.'

She sought through her married acquaintances for examples of women who had at some phase or other in their careers, got detached, as apparently she was going to be detached, from close and habitual association with their husbands. Mostly they were women older than herself. They got along – they got along from day to day – many of them with an appearance of great brightness and self-satisfaction. How deep in, did that self-satisfaction go?

Quiet Lovelies observe much, they are obliged to observe much, and she doubted profoundly the inner contentment of these smart, brisk, incessantly active matrons – childless or with one or two parked-out and negligible children – who fluttered from one thing to another, playing bridge, playing tennis, going out, seeing everything, putting in an appearance everywhere, gossiping, scandalizing, befriending, consuming cocktails, doing exercises, dieting, having treatments, developing personality in pets, furnishing and refurnishing, making gardens.

Some of them had followers of a sort – not so much lovers as hangers-on. So far as this class of women went the hangers-on didn't seem to be of any real importance. Mild exercises in competition and jealousy seemed to be all that happened. The husbands on their rare detached appearances did not seem to be uneasy.

In her private classification of human beings she called these ladies the bridge and club lot. Perhaps playing bridge and eating at clubs was not the profoundest quality they had in common, but it marked them all. There was Mrs McGree, for example, there was Rose Lavender who had been her senior at the High-farthing school, there was Lady Alice Armand, and they all kept up an appearance of being particularly competent bridge players. Mrs McGree, in addition, was interested in a furniture shop. And Lady Alice professed a highly developed interest in the turf and Monte Carlo. But that was rather off the beat of the Palaces. Lady Alice gave Brynhild to understand she had immense passions for loss and gain, that 'thrilling' crises occurred.

For the passion of loss and gain, Brynhild with her vicarage-classic origins, had a profound, an almost formless contempt. You simply did not either risk or grab money; it was an indecency. And as for the bridge. As a game it was interesting for a time and then fatiguing. You sat with your thirteen cards and guessed from rational indications the lie of the other thirty-nine. It wasn't so overwhelmingly difficult if every one played in simplicity and good faith. But it was overlaid by a complex of systematized signalling systems, this convention and that, which nothing could persuade Brynhild was not elaborate half cheating. About these systems Rose and Mrs McGree were swiftly technical and very touchy. Lady Alice had a mystical manner and a mysterious smile. In practice on such rare occasions as when Brynhild made a fourth with all or some of these friends, she found them without exception extraordinarily woolly about what was actually going on. A mixture of undigested conventions enhanced their natural inadvertency. Jacks, tens, nines went by them unobserved; they never seemed to be quite clear whether there were fifteen cards to the suit or only eleven. But the one convention they never broke was that at the bridge-table they were existing in a state of alert super-intelligence unknown to the uninitiated, a state of super-intelligence which never extended to any other aspect of their days.

Brynhild would play bridge with close attention for three or four hands and then give way to boredom, stop noting and remembering. Her partners never seemed to observe her early acuteness or her subsequent lapses. If her cards were good and her play fortunate she was treated with respect. If not, the oddest manifestation of irritation might appear. Somewhere in the back of it all there was a marvellous pretence of expertise. The game was not indeed a game of pure chance but it was preposterous, she thought, to pretend a game of impure chance could ever be made more 'scientific' than was involved in a wary evasion of risks and the prompt grabbing of occasional opportunities. 'Scientific Bridge' was just a way of glorifying one special sort of fiddling with one's mind. Backgammon was in another grade in the same class of futility. These were substitutes for any real use of the brain. But these other women became flushed, snappy, and exalted, questioned if their games was 'improving', excited themselves with the thought of a perpetual dribble of gain, became uneasy if the game was delayed or withheld.

Said Lady Alice Armand one day, 'If you went in for bridge, you know, you'd play it quite well in no time.'

Brynhild found that an illuminating phrase. 'If you went in for – '

Was that what she had to do now? Go in for – ?

They had 'gone in' for bridge. Other women she knew had 'gone in' for tennis, swimming, mountaineering. Just as they went in for cures or diets. And some 'went in' for literary appreciation, for Proust and modern poetry, and some furnished houses and arranged gardens for occupation rather than profit. They were all indefatigably busy. They did these things, she realized now, because something central had dropped out of their lives, because they were in headlong flight from the most terrible of monsters, a devouring disappointment, an enveloping vacuum, the relentless tentacles of nothingness. And that queer feverish unreality she detected in all of them – for their emotions, their judgments, their values were as much painted on them as their eyebrows and their complexions – was a warning beforehand of the futility of 'going in' for any of these opiates against the pursuing sense of frustration that overshadowed her.

She sat down in a green chair in the park in the afternoon to have it all out with herself. Slowly she ticked off the items on the menu that life, as she knew it, put before her. What lay ahead for her? Social occasions? Meetings with people all most desperately attempting to keep it up that they were doing something and that something was happening to them, when, as a matter of fact, they were doing nothing and nothing whatever was happening to them, except the inexorable passage of time. The shows of life, concerts, theatres, sport, and the general gadding about of social existence had no appeal for her. Books – some amateurish art? Painting? Sculpture? If one had companionship one might get 'fun' out of these things perhaps. But now she knew plainly and harshly that she had no companionship. Without an intimate to give it substance the succession of shows and social events was revealed in all its flat, unprofitable insignificance.

She couldn't do these things, she couldn't 'go in' for them. Whether her inability arose from a lack of will or whether her lack of will was due to her inability seemed an open question to her.

'It's queer,' she said. 'I'm not a fool. And yet I'm not a bit clever at any of these things. And I don't want to be.'

Games, gambling, little businesses, shows, plays, books, pictures, sculpture, charities and good works. She couldn't see herself filling the emptiness ahead with any of these.

5

'It isn't good enough,' she said.

'And who are *you*,' said an accusing voice within her, 'to refuse to live the sort of life that countless women live with a reasonable contentment? All life is compromise.'

'I've heard that before. I don't care a rap whether I am good enough for anything. What matters is that none of these things are good enough for me. I am so made that they are not good enough for me. They do not satisfy me. I may have to compromise in the end, but *may the Almighty damn and destroy me for ever, if I compromise a particle when I am thinking in my private thoughts.* (I got that from my father.)'

She had remembered for years her father's strange outbreak, and now it seemed that suddenly for the first time she understood it. It had happened when she was eighteen, a little before his sudden death. The old man had been sitting at dinner with her one Sunday night, brooding after his manner, and apparently as oblivious of her as he was of the glass and silver and flowers upon the table. Suddenly he had dumbfounded her with a question that made her doubt her ears.

'Brynhild, my dear,' he asked. 'What did you think of my sermon tonight?'

She was quite unprepared to say anything about it. It had perplexed and yet attracted her. But the old man took her inability to criticize as a matter of course. He did not bother her to defend herself. He went on talking in his slow, deep voice, without looking at her; his sombre eyes on the distant twilit downland, his closed fine hands resting on the table.

'Over your head it was,' he went on, 'and over all their heads. And yet I was trying to talk to some one. All through life one goes on thinking, trying to get it right. Never getting it exactly right. The one precious thing in life, my dear, is integrity – an inner integrity. The hard, clean, clear jewel, the essential soul. No matter where it takes you. I've never tried to give you much religious instruction. I've never tried to build up any blind Faith

153

in you. It's time I told you that. Creeds are incantations, my dear, and Faith is a stampede from Reality. High time I told you that. One has to make one's compromises, accept unopened packets at times – better eat canned food than starve. Yes. But remember always, it's canned food. Don't woosh and pretend that stuff is marvellous like these damned young fools from Oxford. Know what you are doing. I hold this living. I go through these services. You saw me tonight kneeling for a moment in silent prayer before that sermon which was too plain and clear for any one to understand.'

He paused, and father and daughter looked at one another with a mixture of wonder and intimacy.

'What I pray more and more frequently nowadays, Bryn, is this: May the Almighty damn and destroy me utterly and for ever, if I compromise in one particle when I am thinking in my own private thoughts. You think that over. You remember that. That's what I want to get over to you, my dear, somehow. And the creeds, all three of them, and the Old and New Testament and the Prayer Book and Hymns Ancient and Modern may get up and quit in a body if they don't like that little addendum.'

She learnt that by heart from him, she wrote it down that night in her bedroom and she repeated it to herself now.

It was as if he had just said it.

'And so,' she reflected, 'I can say it's not good enough. Even though it is equally true that I am no good at all. If I'm no good at all – and I tell you I don't believe it – then that is just as much *your* fault as the other thing.'

Noiselessly but obstinately she shaped the words.

'I tell you. It isn't good enough.'

6

But there were some things that did seem good enough to her. And yet she knew that they were things she could not do. She could not bring herself to do them. Other people made of like flesh and blood as herself did them and lived happily by them. She could even say that among these things worth doing some might be found that it would be reasonable to say she ought to do.

The Palaces knew Oscar Geck the biologist and at their house she had met and listened to men like Lee Fredericks the mathematician who had become an economist, and Doctor Brad-Haughton and Lord Cray. And she had once met a young man at a weekend party who had talked to her about Geck, under whom he had served for a time as student and assistant. It was his enthusiasm had lit up all the rest for her. These scientific workers seemed for the most part unusually simple, often with a sort of shallow and obvious worldliness that did not conceal the fact that they were essentially absent-minded. Essentially their minds were absent, transferred to regions in a world far nearer to reality than this everyday world where façades existed perilously and crumpled as they arose. She had read and listened and asked about the scientific worker and she had come to believe that, in his way of living at least, an austere, sustained satisfaction in an undying advance could be found. She had had opportunities of watching Geck, of weighing him against her own master of unreality. Geck too cared for reputation, success, prosperity – yes. But as secondary things. When he went into his laboratory and put on his white overalls he left such concerns with his hat and coat outside.

The foundations for this immense respect with which she regarded Science had been laid in her girlhood by her father. Yet he knew practically nothing of modern science and was disposed to regard it with suspicion. But he knew the reality of science under the name of Philosophy. He had wisdom there in a stouter, more primitive form. His classicism was the classicism of Plato, Aristotle, and Alexandria, he despised Homer (who, he agreed with Butler, might very well have been in part an enthusiastic old lady), and he thought the comparison of Ancient and Modern art and literature a paltry discussion. Savages can produce art and barbarians epics. Most children can draw better than most adults and cave men better than English gentlemen. Music substitutes rhythm for reason. Little birds sing sweetly, though usually too early in the morning and at other inopportune times, but the human voice uplifted in song is disturbing and detestable to all calm-minded men. All art and literary art is trivial and debatable. But Philosophy is a gentleman's game. So that Brynhild's ideas had needed only a certain modernization by experience, for her to accept the immense detachment of scientific work from current unreality as one of the most sustaining and dignifying things in the human spectacle.

Which was the entirely adequate reason why she could not dream of 'going in' for science merely as an escape from her present devastating aimlessness. For science more was needed than a gesture of self-devotion. Scientific workers must be born and most elaborately made. They must have the predestination of an aptitude and the habits of a training. If these other things she had rejected were not good enough, scientific work, on the other hand, real, vital scientific work, was altogether too good. She knew she couldn't do it, couldn't hold herself down to it.

But was this quite right?

She sat forward, rested her elbows on her crossed knees and gnawed her thumb in the intensity of her concentration. Had she got it quite right?

Why was she, so to speak, letting herself off science in this way?

Why wasn't she now finding out what sort of work she might be able to do, what sort of work within her compass needed doing. Was that true about her not having any special aptitude? Or was it the first excuse her subconscious opposition could produce against this line of conduct? Special aptitude might be necessary for eminent work, but the finding of some trustworthy director and the gradual assimilation of his points of view and his needs for help was well within the range of her capacity.

Brynhild's intense pose relaxed unconsciously. She had dismissed an insidious pretence and felt all the better for it. That plea of unworthiness was an excuse. The truth was that she realized clearly that science could not hold her attention. It wasn't a question of ability; it was a question of will. The will for science wasn't in her.

It wasn't in women!

Her mind went off at a tangent to this generalization and she felt herself making discoveries. Why was one able to count the first-rate men of science by the hundred for one outstanding woman (and she almost always daughter or wife of an equal scientific man)? Why? The idea of an all-round inferiority on the part of women had always seemed nonsense to Brynhild. The brain-stuff of a woman was just as good as a man's and allowing for inequalities in the requirements of bone and muscle there was just as much of it. But they had no will, normally they had no

157

will, for laboratory, museum, observatory. These places were not battlefields for them; they were at best retreats. Men went into science for conquests but not women. It wasn't what they were for.

7

The will of a woman is different from a man's. As wide as any other structural difference between them whatsoever. Brynhild considered that new idea. There was sex in wills? There were male and female wills?

It seemed now obvious and yet hitherto she had never seen it quite in that light. Any particular woman might be subtler, cleverer, stronger, heavier, braver than any particular man; that didn't matter. What did matter was this, that determination in her always took a distinctive shape, just as distinctive as the rounder, more fluent lines of her body. The male will was crested and spurred. It was definite and versatile. It leapt out of nothing and took and kept clear shapes. The female will was invincibly obstinate and yet shapeless. It would not do all sorts of things. When it acted and it could act violently, it did so in response to suggestion. Essentially it was responsive. Normally it lay in wait. It waited for a call. Even when it seemed to be aggressive it was no more than provocative, demanding counter-attack.

Brynhild's mind went off after the feminist women she knew to ask how far the things they said and did defined that feminine will.

She had grown up when that great tide of Feminine Emancipation which had given women the entry to various professions, the vote, the right to go alone in hansom cabs, ride bicycles, smoke cigarettes, drink cocktails, use trousers whenever they chose and indulge in unchallenged self-exposure, was already ebbing. The beach was littered with such new-won liberties. Liberties galore and no achievements at all. A number of women who had been young during the crowning phase of that insurrection, still lived on as leaders of a movement that had gained most of its declared objectives, seemed at a loss to map out fresh spheres of emancipation and was quite unable to conceive of any purpose in the world except emancipation.

Remarkably at a loss, Brynhild took stock of the feminist movement of the day as she knew it in the light of this new idea of hers, that there was an absolute lack of positive initiative in women. She considered dear Lady Roundabout with her bevy of women writers and adorers, her broad, complacent face and her uneasy eye. Dear Lady Roundabout ran a weekly paper, *Wear and Tear*, which revealed from week to week the burthen of women. It was a burthen of discontent void of all positive aims. This troupe of women seemed to find a certain satisfaction in being generally disagreeable to the world at large, but its only palpable objective was to seat dear Lady Roundabout in the House of Lords. Where she would just sit. It betrayed a quite Victorian belief that, after all, the rôle of women was never to propose but always to decide. She was still clinging to her right to say Yes and 'name the day'.

From protesting feminism Brynhild's survey passed on to such positive revolutionaries as she had met or heard of, women who belonged to the Communist party, who carried messages to dangerous places, who did strange, devoted things. She knew that familiar fluttering figure; the woman in the procession, the woman in the demonstration, the woman in the barricade, carrying a flag, herself a flag. No doubt of her courage. But always she was being carried along. These women revolutionaries directed no more than the ardent woman figureheads of ships. They directed nothing. They killed and were killed, vividly, and there they ended. A revolution ought not simply to destroy things; it ought to replace things; to have something ready, something better. These Red ladies of the petroleuse type seemed to be emptier than the emptiest Marxists, emptier even than Anarchist syndicalists, of any creative contents. And even in that emancipated Russia which our younger generation instead of taking thought was still trying so desperately to believe in, not a single woman had produced a new idea, turned a corner, invented a deviation of her own. They achieved devotion, cruelty, made gestures of desperate defiance and passed away.

'I suppose *I* should like a tremendous revolution in life,' thought Brynhild – 'in *my* life. I should like to escape from this awful emptiness ahead of me. But I'm like Susan Wiles the dressmaker. I can't do anything until I have a pattern. We feel a want, but we don't give it a shape. We *can't* give it a shape.'

We can't give it a shape!

Her mind ran over the vital issues of the day, and the ideological barrenness of women became amazing. There was this question of money. What was money? What was to be done about money? What was inflation – deflation – reflation? What were monetary standards? What was the price-level? Men toiled at such problems like ants. They invented dogmas and plans and systems. They fought passionately and absurdly for their doctrines. They were not in the least ashamed to be bores and they seemed to enjoy unpopularity. They would go blind and round-shouldered pursuing some intricacy of the system.

And clearly the business was a vital issue for mankind. It affected the household, it affected the children, it affected social status and everything of importance in the life of a woman. Yet women left all that to men. Even when they had nothing else to do but play bridge! The bright young women who came out of the Cambridge Tripos 'above the Senior Wrangler' were just as indifferent to this issue as the shop assistants and the cocottes. It mattered profoundly to every human being, but it wasn't a woman's affair.

And then interlacing with this money tangle were the riddles of manufacturing and selling, and behind these again a vast complexity of political difficulties. What did women care for this riddle of power that every man was discussing? The men thought, debated, intrigued, organized, conspired, terrorized, fought, assassinated, killed, died sometimes quite magnificently. For them these things were real. Their minds struggled perpetually with them. Their will to grapple with and overcome these difficulties revived and resumed after every defeat. The plot of history was this fantastic, inevitable struggle for power, for direction, for the recognition and the achievement of a common aim. The continuation of human life depended ultimately upon the outcome, and the women didn't care a damn.

Into all these immensely purposeful things woman's will did not seem to fit, played no more than an ancillary part. Even when one went to meetings where these monstrous perplexities were discussed and wives, sisters, mistresses, secretaries, daughters graced the assembly the women's faces were — fatuous. Like mothers at the prize day of some classical school, listening to the little dears doing a Greek play.

Of course, if one of the little dears got hurt – ! Or developed spots!

'What in Heaven is wrong with us?'

8

There is sex in wills. She had got that idea from Lucy Hambledon. She had got quite a new outfit of ideas from Lucy Hambledon. Lucy Hambledon had been a great discovery.

Lucy Hambledon had given a lecture some weeks before in Lady Ilmain's drawing-room on the population question. It had been discovered that the population of the world was threatened by a catastrophic shrinkage, and something had to be done about it. Brynhild had gone to this lecture with no belief that the population question was any affair of hers, but simply to work off some vague outstanding obligation to Lady Ilmain. But she had found Lucy Hambledon, with her combination of good looks, slender neck, high colour, and glasses, her clear, protesting voice and her general air of spinsterish disinclination for the occasionally quite improper things she was saying, unexpectedly interesting, and the lecture had sent her reading that lady's books upon sexual psychology and social custom with considerable curiosity.

She had found them very disturbing and illuminating indeed. Lucy had a way of saying whatever she had to say in the manner of a reluctant but convinced learner, which is far more impressive than any eagerness of assertion. One would like things otherwise, she implied, but that was how things were.

'What is a woman?' Lucy Hambledon had asked and had answered her own question in a quiet lady-like voice and with a faint sigh, 'Either a baby-bearing specialist or a pervert.'

'Occasionally,' said Lucy Hambledon, 'it is necessary to re-state the most obvious things as though they were new discoveries. Woman is woman, because she is the breeding continuing animal. She is substantially the important part of the species. The biological prosperity of a species,' said Lucy, quoting very rapidly from Kuczynski and Enid Charles, 'is determined by the proportion of reproductive females in the population. If they increase, the species is biologically in the ascendant. If they decrease, it is biologically declining. The male,' said Lucy, 'is essentially an escapade. Sexually he is a lightweight, he flits and returns.'

'*Does* he return?' considered Brynhild.

'He goes off and does the most astonishing things,' said Lucy. 'We can't vie with him. Those of us who happen to be in a position when one, so to speak, vies, know best how impossible it is. Perverts and abnormalities of course exist and there are natural nuns. But not being completely a woman does not make one a man and the distinction of the masculine and feminine wills holds good. We can learn, we can repeat, we make really good executives. But such exceptions merely confirm the rule of the fundamental, ineradicable difference of male and female. Eliminate what is generally understood by sex and the difference is still there. As far as we can follow the modern psycho-physiologist it is perhaps a matter more of blood chemistry than brain structure. Anatomists can tell already that a scrap of bone or a handful of hair is a woman's and not a man's and a time will come when they will know a single drop of blood for male or female.'

'But what about transfusion?' asked the trained sceptic in Brynhild. 'What about women Givers who transfer blood to men?'

She struggled with that objection for a time and when she came up to attention again Lucy Hambledon had got on to still more provocative matters.

She was saying, in her carefully chosen and neatly spoken words, that there were two sorts of adult women – the quick and the dead – the quickened and the unawakened. 'Adult, mind you,' said Lucy, 'for human adolescence nowadays is a prolonged, delayed, and complicated business.' But either an adult woman was having a child or reassembling her forces after having a child or preparing to have a child, or she was leading an unnatural life. She was an apparatus out of use; a house wrappered up. Her will was dispersed or stagnating until her blood was quickened. She could not will under 'physiological disuse'. Quickening was as necessary for her mental as her physical well-being.

9

Brynhild had a great fight with these ideas. They broke up her sleep.

Her father had trained her to a scrutinizing habit of mind and she did not succumb to Lucy Hambledon's prim and courageous charm without a struggle. She put Lucy Hambledon to the test of her own inclinations. You would think, she reasoned, if Nature really intended woman to be first and foremost a child-producing, child-protecting animal and only secondarily a human being at large, she would have put a dominating philo-progenitiveness into the creature. But had she?

'Do I want to be a mother?' she asked. 'Not much... Hardly at all... Certainly no stress of desire... You would have thought Nature, if she had really been so obsessed with this drive towards multiplication, would have been too clever to leave that out of my make-up. But she has.'

Brynhild tried to recall the phases of her sexual development. She had been sincerely in love with Palace but had she ever, at any phase, had any ambition to reproduce Mr Rowland Palace? If she had, it had left no trace in her memory. What she did recall was an immense craving for companionship. And now – did she want to launch new little Rowlys in the world?

There might be some satisfaction, of course, in slapping Rowly by proxy...

'I've had enough of Rowly,' said Mrs Rowland Palace.

10

'I want some one to talk to about this. I'm spinning round again, I'm spinning round and round these ideas she has dropped into me and I'm not getting on. I want quickening. Mentally anyhow, I want quickening.'

Quickening?

It was curious how infectious some of Lucy Hambledon's phrases were, even if you were quite indisposed to agree with her conclusion. They set one off along the strangest of paths. This suggestion that minds and bodies could be under-stimulated until they wilted and shrivelled, and that any quickening process must affect both body and mind, continued to ferment in Brynhild's brain, almost in spite of her.

Am I too aloof for life? she asked herself. Have I been shirking life? This exclusiveness of mine, this fastidiousness, this reserve, this dignity on which I have prided myself; is it, after all, anything to be proud of? Isn't it three parts timidity? If you do not go out to people how can people react on you?

Minds to quicken one's own? If it was true that women's minds were all critical, resistant, or responsive minds, then it was men's minds, talk with men, initiative from men, aggressive ideas, that a woman needed. Throughout her married life so far, Brynhild had avoided talk about men, disliked it and killed it when it came near her. Was all that a mistake? The difficulty was that it seemed so difficult not to talk to men or about men without the sexual issue putting in an appearance. It seemed impossible to indicate a preference for a man without archness creeping in.

Women were extraordinarily variable in these matters. Some like Brynhild herself were punctiliously reserved, with nothing to hide. Others talked continually about this main relationship of life. For many it seemed to be the only reality. Some talked insatiably about the adventures of other women, speculated with the utmost indecency about the relations of lover to lover or of husband to wife. Others, again, made boasting about their own achievements in excitement, their central theme. They excited, but did they yield? Quiet Lovelies sat in the background and heard much. Brynhild had been shocked and interested by the discourse of an aggressively loquacious Swedish lady at a woman's tea-party given by Lady Roundabout. This lady had experienced two *grand passions* and a vast number of minor *passades* and she supplied much interesting detail of her experiences. The term *passade* was new to Brynhild. She tried to imagine the technique of a *passade*. How did it begin? How did they set about it? Where did they go? And how did one feel after it? Rather, she imagined, like a hen in the dust.

No. This wasn't what she wanted – these scuffling indignities. The feminine sex talk was a mere talk about preliminaries. It was really a sort of prolongation of early adolescent curiosity and sensuality. Most of these women were just smutty little girls of thirty or forty. They were always talking of 'taking lovers' and never really getting at them. Some of their 'affairs' sounded like collecting autographs or stealing spoons for fun. They went from lover A to lover B like cards being shuffled. In vain the onlooker asked, 'Why A?' 'Why B?' They had reduced immorality to a sterile formula about as fruitful and satisfactory in the long run as an excess of cocktails. And yet wasn't there something more in it than that?

Why did these more or less promiscuous women play at this game at all? Something attracted them, surely, graver than a slightly insane desire to drink from the wrong bottle. What, apart from the sheer torment of vacuity, was the reality that drew them to these affairs? What was the underlying need?

It came into Brynhild's head that they were all curiously like children who are fascinated by an important-looking doorway and, greatly daring, creep up and knock – only to fly headlong at the remotest sign of the door opening. Suppose that 'taking a lover' was really something very grave and important in a woman's life, something as grave and important as marriage. Suppose one marched up to that forbidden portal, and knocked and faced up to it and, instead of bolting, marched in and through to whatever lay on the other side?

At this point Brynhild pulled herself up. She was slipping away into metaphors. 'Never think in metaphors,' her father had said. 'Never symbolize. Strip your facts.'

She was not thinking of portals and buildings. She was thinking of the possibility of being unfaithful to Rowly. She was thinking of having another man as a lover, and she was thinking this because she had been so infected by Lucy Hambledon's phrases as to develop this queer idea that the only way she could get on such terms with a man as to get her mind 'quickened' was by becoming his mistress.

'What are you thinking of, Brynhild?' cried some lurking governess within her. 'Stop these strange thoughts. These *improper* thoughts!'

'I'm going on thinking,' said Brynhild. 'It's my business. It's my primary business as a woman. Go away. I'm going to have this out with myself.'

The governess went away.

'Now suppose I take a lover,' thought Brynhild stoutly, 'and he turns out wrong and I don't get any mental quickening out of him. Yes – yes, I know the idea is disgusting, but I want to face it. Suppose this new elixir vitae turns out to be nothing better than the sort of nasty cocktail one swallows by mistake? Then – do I begin over again with number two?'

The protesting governess could be felt in the darkness stirring uneasily.

'Then the alternative,' said Brynhild, 'is just to spin with Rowly until death do us part.'

The governess receded into absolute silence.

Brynhild continued to scrutinize her own chastity. Was she excessively monogamous? Was her reserve about sex in particular, morbid? Was she – latterly the idea had been rather frequently in her mind – a Prig, and an immature, damped-off sort of Prig at that? Had she missed a natural phase in her development? Perhaps this inhibition of hers was something she ought to have got rid of long ago. Perhaps passing over from a first exclusive lover to lovers was a natural stage in the development of a modern woman. It was a border crossed. It was like cutting your teeth. It was passing into a new, more adult human phase. You've become something else and nothing can ever put you back again. And when that border is crossed, perhaps you may meet men face to face and be on equal terms with them.

She was being as liberal-minded as she knew how, but she found the taste unpleasant.

11

Sooner or later every woman must have thoughts like this, insisted Brynhild, keeping to the cold rational line. Ideas of this sort had come to her perhaps later than usual because she was a backward type. That was all. What she had taken for pride and chastity was really just backwardness. She wasn't so different from these other women really, it was only that they had thought quicker, acted sooner, and arrived at this phase earlier. And yet it was odd she should be thinking to and fro among these ideas even now, while any possible lover still remained intangible and formless. That 'quickening' man was an impalpable fantasy born of Lucy Hambledon's phrases. So soon as Brynhild turned to actuality she found her world a loverless desert.

She began a sort of parade of specimen men. The governess was faintly audible making some indistinct stipulation about costume and then retiring reproachfully into nothingness at the remark that she ought to be ashamed of herself. 'I am going to think about all this quite freely,' Brynhild insisted. 'Modesty is a matter of behaviour and how you deal with other people. I won't have any nonsense about modesty in my private thoughts.'

The parade of lovers was a poor display.

Men were nice enough until you began to think of them in this fashion and then they became fantastically difficult. The men she respected most changed into grotesques which became oppressive and terrifying just as people change in dreams. Mr Alfred Bunter appeared to be just as he had been in the Valliant Chevrell gardens, quite close to her with his soft, full voice, his rather troubled brown eyes and his ruddy complexion, and then he became quite shockingly impossible. 'Is there something askew with my imagination?' she asked herself. 'I begin to wonder how I ever came to marry Rowly.' It was too monstrous a price to pay for the chance of some stimulating conversation. She could not imagine any other man taking her and embracing her – as Rowly did.

'No, I couldn't do it,' said Brynhild.

'I'm fastidious. I'm a prig. The dignity of chastity is an overwhelming tradition so far as I'm concerned. I'm clean and decent and moral and futile, but, anyhow, I couldn't do it. It's foul. It's inconceivable except with Rowly. And even with him – it's a thing so *private*...'

So here she was where she had started and as usual she hadn't made up her mind about anything at all.

Chapter Ten

Mr Bunter Tells His Story

She looked up and discovered Mr Bunter approaching her. She did not embarrass him by seeming to watch him but she noted every detail of his movements. He stopped short when he saw her, uncertain whether to advance or swerve off across the grass behind her. Plainly he did not want to salute and pass her, and as plainly he was too inept socially to know how to stop and talk to her. His feet, which was all of him that she had in her field of vision, wavered. She decided it was time to look up and see him.

There was something ingratiatingly shy and clumsy about his proceedings. He pretended to recognize her with a start and then came towards her. 'You don't know quite how you are going to behave,' thought Brynhild. 'But as a matter of fact you are going to sit down in this chair beside me.'

She rested her hand on the back of the next chair so as to constitute it part of their grouping and awaited his approach with the shadow of a smile on her face.

He stood in front of her and his eyes were led to the chair.

'So pleasant to see you again,' he said. 'I wonder if I might sit down for a moment?'

'I'd be delighted.'

He sat down.

'If I might talk to you for a bit? I'd be so grateful. You see, I've quarrelled with myself today and I don't like the company I'm in. I came out for a walk to walk away from myself – and I find I can't. And, anyhow, I'd like to talk to you. In fact – I've been thinking of you. Mrs Palace, I want some one badly... You're in no hurry? You really can talk?'

'I too was just wanting some one to talk to. You couldn't have chosen any one better.'

'Glad... I've been thinking no end about you since we met at Valliant Chevrell. More than is reasonable. And hoping that presently we'd meet again... You don't mind my saying that?'

'No.'

'I liked talking to you down there. It was an extraordinary party. I like Valliant Chevrell. I doubted if I should.'

'He is a born mixer. If he wasn't a host and an hereditary legislator and a very rich man I suppose he would make sauces and pickles. Or blend tobacco or tea.'

'Well, it was nice of him to blend us. I've been grateful ever since. Because in spite of everything – ' He glanced at her: ' – we did get on together.'

'Yes,' she admitted and then reflected; 'we said very little to one another.'

'But all the time we had – *I* had and I know you had – an extraordinary feeling of friendliness. I have that at times, just as cats and dogs have it. But rarely. Very rarely. And less often than I used to do. I see some one – I knew instantly that you could not possibly jar with me – not really – that I was safe with you, however clumsy I was. And down there I felt all the time on the very edge of being unusually clumsy.'

'Anyhow you seemed to want to go on talking to me – right up to Monday morning.'

'Doesn't every one?'

'Mr Bunter, for some obscure reason – I am incapable of conversation and most people get that quite soon. That you shouldn't have found it out – Or betrayed that you had found it out – Naturally I liked you. All the time I could see you thought that at any time I might say something. And all the time' – she smiled – 'you seemed to be expecting me to understand something that you didn't actually say.'

'Saying things that matter is the last triumph of the human mind,' said Mr Bunter. 'I did want to say something. For various reasons… There are things I want to say.'

The silence of the next thirty seconds seemed rather to support Brynhild's account of her limitations.

'People ought not to force confidences on others – ' Mr Bunter began.

He did not like that beginning and he left it at that.

She was acutely aware of him beside her but she felt instinctively that she must not look at him directly just then. He became quite still. Something within her counted; one, two, three… Ten seconds. Then suddenly an entirely different and remote Mr Bunter took up the conversation.

'Speech was a great invention,' he philosophized. 'I am sure the wicked gods were afraid when men got hold of it. They thought human beings would get together and it would be all up with Olympus. Needlessly. What use do we make of speech? What use do we make of anything? Triviality or mischief. It's the same story today with flying and the cinema and the radio. And everything. Oh! everything. With you, directly I met you, I wanted to talk. I had an extraordinary urgency to talk. And all I could talk about – Do you remember how entangled we got swapping information about pond-life and water weeds?'

'And indeed,' thought Brynhild. 'What are we getting to now?'

It seemed probable that the two of them would spend the rest of their time together, circulating awkwardly round this theme of their mutual attraction and their common inability to express it. With parenthetic comments on the general inexpressiveness of life. And part at last with their amiability completely unexploited. Brynhild broke away. She realized it was her job to break away, but it was chance rather than intention which made the break for her. He could never, she realized, make her talk, nothing could ever do that, but there was talk in him, he wanted to talk – hadn't he just said so? – and somehow she had to help him get it out. Then he would talk for the two of them. He made her feel extraordinarily socially experienced and responsible. Considering how fiercely he thought and wrote, her sense of his plasticity with her was amazing.

2

The topic she hit upon to get them out of their personal spin was the weather. Not perhaps a very rare or original topic. But it was the only one she could think of. There seemed to be nothing else at all in that vast vacuum her mind had become, except him and herself and that universal interest. By sheer good luck it turned out well. From having nothing to say they fell into a widening sequence of exchanges. As we will tell. The first sentence was unpromising. 'Do you remember Henley's line,' she said, breaking a pause apropos of nothing; 'October mild and boon? Was there ever a day that fitted it better?'

'I was too cross to see before. But now – ' He diverted his attention from her for a moment. 'Yes, it's a glorious afternoon.'

'Like a crystal – only with warmth in it.' She felt that was like a quotation from a descriptive passage in a novel. There was nothing to do but stick to it. 'My father would have called it a Good in itself.'

That was the happy release.

'Your father? Now what was your father?'

'He was a Stoic – he was a classical scholar. And he held a living in the Church of England.'

'That's the sort of thing I find difficult to understand.'

'He said he swallowed the Thirty Nine Articles at a gulp and thought no more about them. If he had masticated them they might have got into his system and given him trouble. And he said it was good for the soul to have knowingly done one dishonourable thing.'

'What was his name?'

'Loader.'

'Dr Loader, the great scholar?'

'No, his cousin. You mustn't misunderstand my father. He was cynical on that point, but he tried to teach me what he called honourableness of mind. One can wear Anglicanism in comfort, he said, because it fits loose and easy. It needn't touch. It needn't constrict and hamper. It leaves your soul alone. But you mustn't profess things you more than half believe. That gets into the system and cankers the mind. Faith, he called an invalid's trick.'

'Not a bad idea,' Mr Bunter replied. 'I like that.'

'And my father said,' she went on, feeling that with a little more of this she would get Bunter started; 'that until we knew better – had something positive – Anglican practice was as good a social cement as any. But I think all the time he was dreaming of knowing something better… Mr Bunter – '

She paused. She had a faint impulse to laugh at the immense demand she was going to make.

He looked at her interrogatively.

'What do *you* believe? What do you *know?* What keeps *you* going?'

'I wish I could tell you. I wish I could tell myself. Today, just before I saw you I was saying to myself, I'm damned if I stand any more of it. Any more of any of this. Never mind exactly what. It's something I've been enduring alone. Not a soul to speak to about any of it. Life, Mrs Palace, can sometimes be intolerably exasperating. I was just howling inside when I saw you. About – all of this. I wanted some one to howl to… At least I thought I did. But I'm so used not to talk about – all this business. Down I plumped beside you – full of it. Gods! I said. I'll tell *her!* And have I told you a thing?'

(Have a care, Brynhild, or you'll be getting back to the old eddy!)

'I wasn't thinking very much of life today myself – except for the sunlight.'

'But *you've* got no quarrel with life. You – poised in your place, assured, serene!'

'Never mind about me, Mr Bunter. What makes you find life so exasperating just now? What is it all about? What is it?'

'Not just now – altogether.'

'Well – altogether. Tell me. Howl. I'd like to hear some one who has words, give this life a thorough good damning.'

'My case?'

'Your case. And then everybody's case.'

'Well,' Mr Bunter stopped and considered. '*My* case!'

He seemed to weigh a monstrous proposition. 'Suppose I tell you. Suppose I really tell you.'

'Why *not?*'

He sat round and scrutinized her. 'I believe I am really going to tell you.'

He turned his face away again. 'I've never told anybody for six years. I've been carrying the whole business...'

Pause. She considered it best to remain quietly expectant, watching him. She noted that his ruddy complexion was clear and good with very delicate golden hairs upon his cheeks and the modelling of his profile rather fine, particularly about the now rather drooping mouth. But there were queer lines about that mouth now which she hadn't noted at Valliant Chevrell.

When he emerged from the pause, he was back in his bookish style.

'Life,' he remarked abruptly, 'is tantalizing in the things it offers and monstrous in the things it gives. We find ourselves in the world – well and good. It's a spread-out of lovely – intimations. Almost every dawn – if you get up and see dawn, Mrs Palace – is like the prelude to something splendid. You know that sense of a curtain rising. Very well. We try to live. And we are tripped up.'

'Yes,' said Mrs Palace.

'We jump out of bed and right away we tumble over our stale selves of the day before.'

He remained for a second or so as if he was digesting this disagreeable reality. Then suddenly he looked up at her with that faint disengaging smile of his. 'Which is only another way of saying, Mrs Palace, that I've got my life into a pretty considerable mess.'

But was this getting on?

'Tell me about it,' said Brynhild patiently.

'Oh, it's a frightful mess. I don't see how I *can* tell you. You of all people. Yet somehow I want you to know. Some of it at least I want you to know. It's just you of all people I want to know... You see... Yes, I'll you something I've never told any one yet. I'll give myself away to you. Within reason. I was born just over six years ago.'

He stared at her to see how she took it.

'Well-grown child,' said Brynhild, waiting for more.

'We'll put it like that anyhow. Alfred Bunter, Mrs Palace, was born with a manuscript under his arm. He was, you see, precocious from the first. He walked into a publisher's office and sold his story on his zero birthday. He seemed to me elated and a little scared. And at the same time a discontented young man with quite another name, a pharmaceutical chemist, let us say, whose affairs were in a tangle, disappeared from, so to speak, the city of Birmingham. He was "caught up," as the Second Adventists say, and vanished. Like that. He had resigned from a life he found altogether too much for him, and he left no address. Queer, isn't it? Subsequently some human remains were found in a deserted – no, in a canal – that might or might not have been him. It wasn't quite like that but never mind. That is near enough. That, Mrs Palace, is why among other things, you never see any portrait published of that industrious novelist Alfred

Bunter. He's afraid some one round about – well, Birmingham –
might see and recognize him.'

'Why did he call himself – Bunter?'

Mr Bunter met her eye cheerfully. 'It doesn't strike you as –
an attractive name?'

'No.'

'Alfred Bunter – Alf for short. "Elf" in London English.
Anything but an attractive name. It was not the sort of name you
could imagine any one taking of his own accord. No one has ever
suspected it was assumed. I think that was rather bright of me.'

'Yes,' said Brynhild, and then with an air of extreme *savoir
faire*. 'And those human remains? You said something about
some human remains?'

'They,' said Mr Bunter reflectively, 'were a coincidence.'

'They happened to be there – in the canal.'

'They happened to be there.'

'And you just took advantage?'

'I just took advantage.'

Brynhild reflected. Mr Bunter was behaving rather like an
oyster which feels it has been indiscreet. His face had assumed a
closed expression and he was looking away across the lake. She
realized that the next move was with her. 'And you really got
away from being that pharmaceutical chemist in Birmingham –
for some reason you didn't like his life – and you really did begin
again in London and pulled it off?'

'I did.'

'I couldn't have imagined that anything of the sort could be
possible!'

'Practically it wasn't. That's why I'm bothered. It never has
been *quite* possible. It's been touch and go ever since. You see –

he – the pharmaceutical chemist who vanished just when I materialized out of nothingness in Paternoster Row, had lived twenty-seven years and some months. And he had had an extraordinary knack of producing consequences. Quantities of consequences. Voluminous, unfolding and unfolding... Perhaps everybody has... But I don't know why I'm telling you this. I've kept it bottled up for six years. It's become too much for me. I've bluffed everybody so far but for some reason I can't bluff you. I've got to tell you.'

'It's that *friendliness*, I suppose,' said Brynhild. 'And anyhow, are you telling me very much?'

'I'm trying not to tell you too much. I'm so drawn to you – let me be frank – that I feel compelled to tell you things that – it's absurd, isn't it – are almost certain to estrange us... I want to tell you everything about myself and at the same time I want to stand well in your eyes. But I've been so lonely. I've been so damnably lonely.'

'I'm more broad-minded than I seem. And friendlier. You tell me.'

His next words seemed at first absolutely irrelevant.

'Mrs Palace, what do you think about my books?'

But – stay a moment. Was that irrelevant? She suddenly felt subtle.

'They, too,' she said, 'are like somebody trying to say something that is difficult to say.'

'Noisy books they are. And they pretend to be saying a lot and getting down to the real red core in things – and they don't. I'm trying and I don't succeed. It's just like my trying to tell you now – and not telling you. I write those books in the intervals of dodging my past and preserving my incognito. Every book, every *real* book, maybe, is a confession of solitude. It's an appeal. And I tell you in spite of the bawling confusion of these books I write, which keep on saying and then not saying, I am most desperately and honestly trying to get something said plainly about life, that hasn't been said and *has* to be said... And say it to some one...'

'I know. I read you. Since we met I've read most of you.'

'Since I came out of – we'll call it Birmingham – my books have been my life. Inadequate though they are. At times I've had a tremendous sense that I was getting something said, putting a shape upon the muddle of existence, finding something out, as I wrote. I've felt I was cutting down into things, getting below superficial and hasty assumptions. Secretly, I've been full of my own importance. I felt as I suppose the early anatomists or the early microscope and telescope men felt. Laying bare things long hidden. And then – '

He turned to her interrogatively. 'Does Palace get into states of mind about reviews?'

She found she didn't want to talk about Palace to Mr Bunter. She didn't want them both in the same picture. 'Every author,' she said, 'gets into states of mind about reviews. But the ones who suppress their states suffer most.'

And anyhow, what had reviews to do with the story of the vanished Birmingham chemist? What was he saying now?

'I *feel* reviews. Since I don't go about very much, it's the only way I have of judging whether this stuff I write gets over to any one – seems in any way to signify. Of course lots of reviews are negligible, obviously written by trite hacks who have never discovered that real books are alive. They review like – like tired ushers marking exercise books while they think of something else. And others are just inexperienced people who don't realize

181

that judgment is a duty. The stuff they do is bad but not wicked; trite stupidity yes, but not dishonesty or hate. They fall to prestige, gossip, and current catchwords and they follow the fashions. Not much to object to in all that. No. Never mind them. Once in a while you get understanding. A living mind detects you in your book – responds. Generally speaking. Generally speaking that is how things are. All that I can allow for. All that is natural. But not this time. *This* time the stupidity has an air of being concerted. *This* time the misunderstandings are not careless and casual. *This* time the reviews of my book are like a line of obdurate faces, a drilled line. They are all harping on the same idea, that I am a man of extremely limited social experience. They are all asking for my origins and credentials. You see? Review after review. They turn my book down, practically unread, and then attack me. It is as if some one had been going round spreading hostility against me. Nothing pleases them. My style is "raucous". The word turns up in half a dozen notices... Do you think I am imagining things? Do you think I'm giving way to suspicion mania? Because I've been bottled up, so long? I don't think I am. But it isn't that things are moving against me. It isn't coincidence. Things are being moved against me...

'And, you see, it's practically all I live for now – this bookish ambition of mine – this desire to get something disentangled and said, to get something over to people, in books. If suddenly they won't read them – If suddenly they stop listening to what I say and become excited about what I am or what I've done...

'Even if that was all...

'I don't think that that trouble alone would have got me so flamingly raw as I felt before I saw you. But you see, Cardiff and its consequences have been also blowing up like a bank of clouds before a southwester – filling the sky. In the most extraordinary way. There too, there is the same effect of a deliberate hostility. I'm – in a way – I'm afraid.'

(Let him talk now, Brynhild. It's Cardiff now – not Birmingham. He's going to tell you everything before he's done. Because he's beginning to talk to himself.)

'It was queer – that hejira from Cardiff.'

'Cardiff – not Birmingham?'

'Yes, it was Cardiff.'

'You began again?'

'Yes – let me tell you about it... I had a little money with me – but practically it was beginning again. For a time, it was exciting. And for a while it went better than I deserved. "I've got away from all *that*," I said. Queer how quickly the new circle came into existence. For a week or so I knew no one in the world except the publisher who had accepted my book and then I went out to lunch in Soho with him and a reader of his and Lesser, the critic. I confessed I was a newcomer to London and Lesser put me up for the Parnassus Club. Then I dropped in to one of Bedlow's Book Teas and made a little speech and found myself having tea with two rather intelligent women. One thing led to another. I overcame my first impulse to hide away completely. I shaved off my moustache and altered my shirts and collars. I had reason for that. In a little while I had a social circle of bookish and journalistic and artistic people. I went to meetings, cocktail and night parties – joined two more clubs – shifted to socially possible lodgings. People in the literary world ask amazingly few questions. Even the clever women who are' – he looked rigidly in front of him – 'kind to one – don't seem to care who you are really. And I liked the escape to a desk and a quire of clean paper and a room in which nothing could possibly happen unless I let it happen. Now, I said, I will really stop living in a series of responses and take up life in my own fashion.'

'That's in one of your books.'

'Yes, I've written it – somewhere.'

Mr Bunter became philosophical.

'I suppose greediness for life, or anyhow the frank release of greediness, is something new. Modern. Perhaps I don't really mean a greediness for life at all. Perhaps I mean a greediness for reality. Which is something quite different. Yet, come to think, there has always been something of the sort going on. Dissatisfaction. Men used to renounce the world, become hermits, go into monasteries. Do stranger things than that. It made me plan this flight – though not as I actually made it. At first it was only a flight to a writing-desk. It was a dream long before it materialized. To get right away and somehow – *penetrate*. When I came to London I already had a book written and practically accepted. And another planned. The story is more complicated than that. You see –

'If I had had no idea whatever of writing books and getting down to reality I should still have come away from Cardiff. I *had* to come away.'

Now for a bit he will just philosophize and quote himself, thought Brynhild. But we shall get back to Cardiff.

Mr Bunter resumed after something very like a consultation of his mental notes. 'What is modern, I suppose, is the relative absence of restraint. There never was a time when "Why not?" was asked so impatiently and universally. But as a child even I was outrageous. I think I was exceptionally uncontrollable. I wouldn't take No for an answer. I had extravagant expectations.

I resented punishment. All punishment I felt was injustice. I can remember a violent weeping fit – oh! inconsolable sorrow it was – at the end of an afternoon's play because suddenly I discovered it hadn't been good enough.'

'A lot of things aren't good enough,' said Brynhild.

'But *you* surely never had storms of that sort?'

'All the same, a lot of things aren't good enough. Go on. Tell me.'

'I had a feverish imagination. It was full of – I think psychologists call them, escapes. I couldn't believe that life was just the slow procession of dusty greyish events it seemed to be. Dusty greyish events with a lot of rather forced laughter and streaks of downright painful and disagreeable experiences. Uncalled-for inflictions. And a perpetual menace. I couldn't believe it. For some years, round about eleven to thirteen, I think it was, I was persuaded in my private mind that the whole of the life about me was an elaborate deception being practised on me.'

'I have thought that.'

'It didn't seem reasonable that one was permitted to live and then *persecuted*. Unsatisfied cravings. Greeds so that you made yourself sick. Aches. Teeth. Growing pains.'

'It isn't reasonable,' said Brynhild. 'But it seems highly probable that things are so. Seeing that they are so.'

'Presently somebody or something, I imagined, was going to draw back the curtain. "Prince, your time has come." '

'I believe every one has had something of that.'

'It grows stronger with adolescence. My brothers and my sister were older than I; my mother was an overworked, tired woman, my father a dull routineer – he was a solicitor. Adolescence came to me haphazard, a stir within, glimpses, evasive suggestions without. Something intense, thrilling, beautiful – and forbidden. That sense of menace growing stronger. Sex, I should think, comes dismayingly enough to a girl; to a boy it comes tauntingly, provocatively, shamefully, and pesteringly. Sometimes you say, "I shall get something splendid out of this." Sometimes you scream, "My God, I will get *something* out of this." Sometimes you are just bothered by something with a close face and hot breath tugging at your sleeve – something you can't shake off. First, I was shy and secret and then I was desperate.'

She understood as she looked at his profile his aptitude for either rôle.

'My two elder brothers joined up at the beginning of the war with pride and enthusiasm. I was only fifteen then. The world was already considerably disillusioned about the war before the searching hand, that blind implacable imperative to join up, found me and gripped me and put me in khaki. "Give me one taste of life before I go," I said.'

He sat up back in his chair and looked her in the face.

'These crucial years. It's about seven years, I suppose, for most of us. Eighteen to twenty-five. War or no war, it's much the same. My generation blames too much upon the war. Inexperience, a wild impatience, storm of desire. So it has always been. So for a long time still it will be. Six or seven years. And then we have made our lives.'

He sat and lifted his open hands. He repeated with intensity. 'We have made our lives...'

Brynhild had nothing to say.

'Well, I said, I would be damned if I stood it. That's all.'

186

'And the life you left behind in Cardiff?' said Brynhild, judicial and intelligent. 'That life you put behind you and escaped from. Sister, brothers – other entanglements? It all goes on?'

'Exactly. It all goes on. Yes.'

Mr Bunter was at a loss again.

It was not the first time that Brynhild had observed an author in difficulties about the opening of a new chapter. But she meant to have that chapter if she sat in Regent's Park until sunset and the evening dew. And he meant to give it her.

3

'I knew I could write,' he said.

'But for a time I was distracted by these other things that had got hold of me. I was just living. That is to say, life was playing football with me. Then battered and dirty I was kicked into that place in life into which it had pleased God to call me. And I found I still wanted to write.

'A lot of us wanted to write about the war. I didn't. Never. The war never really impressed me. It was monstrous and horrible, but it didn't seem to be anything fresh or new. It wasn't even outside you – spectacular, I mean – like an earthquake or a tornado. It was like paying a bill, that had been run up for you by some one else. Finding you're the last heir of a line of idiot spend-thrifts. And finding after all that your cheque wasn't acceptable because some one has mortgaged your balance. I didn't want to write about the war. In itself it was the most God-awful bore conceivable. It wasn't any the less secondary and second-rate because it was so bloody. The generals, the officers, the kings and politicians knew it was a bore, knew they were bores and that history would damn them to hell for it. Chaps like Winston Churchill and Duff Cooper try to get a kind of tootle out of it – but what a tootle it is! Haig! And all the memoirs. It wasn't my business to write that sort of thing. I wanted to get through that and write about the queer twists and treacheries in nature and us, that make disasters like the war possible...'

'In a way you *are* doing that.'

'You really think – ?'

'Tell me about Cardiff.'

'Suppose, presently,' said Mr Bunter, almost as if he was sheering off from Cardiff deliberately, 'we get a whole world that begins to say what I am trying to say. Suppose every one asks *Why?* and insists upon some answer, though it kills them to do so? Supposing what was your father's secret philosophy spreads and spreads. Suppose the two thousand million people on this planet all start saying: "We refuse all plausible interpretations. We shut our eyes to nothing. We refuse to put a brave face on it. No more tootle. It isn't good enough." '

Brynhild thought. 'Perhaps quite a lot of them *do* now.'

'But look at the newspapers.'

'Anything of that sort would take a long time to get into the papers.'

'We should blow the planet to fragments – or make it such a glorious storm of living...'

He was at a loss for words. Perhaps, too, he was at a loss for substantial ideas about that glorious storm. Most of us are.

'You were going to tell me about Cardiff,' said Brynhild.

4

She knew now perfectly well that he was not going to tell her all about Cardiff. Quite probably he had never told himself all about Cardiff. Probably he had told himself a score of different stories about it – whatever it was. If today he began to tell her about Cardiff, he would probably go away and begin to realize all sorts of things that were now untellable.

'It isn't a nice story. I want you to know. And at the same time I want to look well in your eyes.'

'Plaster image?'

'Not quite that.'

'Painted in the natural colours. You're better alive.'

'I have to tell you. To begin with there was a war baby.'

Brynhild betrayed no signs of shock. 'Is it a nice child?'

'I didn't stick to it. I mean I never saw it. There was another marriage. I mean I married some one else.'

Brynhild remained attentive, not helping him.

'You see, I got rather crazy about women in those early twenties. A sort of fever of the imagination. A desire for insatiability. Aldous Huxley gives you all that. Not bodily lust it was so much as lust of the imagination. I had affairs, adventures, and this particular woman I'm speaking of became my mistress and then we married. I didn't want to. I had strong reasons for not doing so. But a situation was created... She said *she* was going to have a child... She didn't.'

'But you married her?'

'Yes.'

'And you weren't happy?'

Mr Bunter shrugged his shoulders. 'This sort of thing is so difficult to tell. Telling things about a woman you have lived with. And then haven't lived with for six years. I never meant to live with her at all. I wasn't even reasonably fond of her. But there she was, excitable and exciting. I'd have been ashamed not to have been her lover. Another score in the rake's progress. God knows why such events are regarded as scores! They are. The trouble one takes to make a new one! She seduced me, she hardly made a pretence of being seduced. She meant to have me. She knew my family, she was related to business connections of mine. She was all over me socially. She threw herself at me and then threatened to make a fuss. At that time I had no idea of leaving Cardiff. I had hardly begun to write and I had all the unworldly ex-officer's dread of leaving the only business I had learnt. All that seems very feeble, doesn't it? I thought I could marry her and get on with her. I knew her only as a bright-coloured, bright-eyed eager thing. I had only been with her for an hour or so and a few half-hours and so on before we were married. She had cheated me into marriage but it wasn't her fault that she had cheated me. She wanted a child. Honestly. She wanted anything and everything that would fix me hers. But she couldn't have a child. She was the most possessive and jealous of human beings, and I was a provincial Don Juan. She didn't love me. She thought she did. Her egotism demanded that she should be a Great Lover. But she didn't love a thing in me. She hated almost everything I was and everything about me. She hated my family and estranged them. And particularly she seemed to hate anything I took a pride in. But she had fixed upon me, she had grabbed me. Love me, she said, listen to me, attend to me, owe everything to me...'

'How old were you then?'

'Nineteen twenty-two. I was twenty-three.'

'When a boy looks like a man.'

'When a boy makes the fetters for the man he is going to be.'

'And she was?'

'Twenty-six.'

'Go on telling me about her.'

'She talked incessantly. As I sit here now I seem to hear the onward looping rhythm of her voice. Low and hurried and then rising to a harsh shrill edge. About herself and about me in relation to herself. And how wonderful her love was and how little I deserved it. She vocalized life. She reversed St John's gospel. In the end was the Word and the Word was the end. She could not think that anything was or that anything had happened, unless she had said it. An audience had to be told; an audience had to be impressed. She loved to brag and outbrag. The actual facts of her life were just the point of departure for a torrent of fanciful misstatement, dressed-up claims, picturesque assertions, fantastic showing-off to herself and everybody. She made an odd screaming household for me in which the one servant was driven by sheer word-power until she rebelled and gave notice, and was thrown out in a storm of recrimination. And then *da capo*.

'And about me Freda wove a sort of legend to which I had to listen, as it developed, about my remarkable abilities, about my excessive virility, about the profound and perplexing kinks in my character. I had been dreadfully misunderstood by my family. She had saved me from that. Rescued me from the inferiority complex they had given me. We were to have a tremendous career. I was to become a Force in Welsh politics. I was the leader the world was waiting for. We were to stand for The New Wales and then we were to descend whooping and jabbering upon London and the empire. A queer, vague, pretentious couple we made. Freda had a good deal of social push, and, wherever we pushed, this legendary me was exposed and laid bare and flourished about. People knew I was just the junior partner in a firm of house agents and grinned. The future leader of The New Wales couldn't get a word in edgeways to disavow the impression.'

He paused. 'And yet you know I find I owe a great deal to her.'

Brynhild appreciated the change of tone and noted without comment that the pharmaceutical chemist was now a house agent.

'This torrent of talk without intermission stirred my mind, my reluctantly listening mind. Her headlong greed to be all sorts of things, her pretences and fantasies, made one ask oneself what sort of thing one was. And what one might be. I was forced to bottle-up my denials and criticisms of her talk because, as I said, I could hardly get a word in edgeways, and if I did get in a word it was usually a fatal word, and if it could in any way be constructed as a criticism of her, all the vain-glorious proclamations ceased, she would resort forthwith to shrewish insults and *tu quoques*. So, as I say, I was bottled up.'

Mr Bunter turned a wan smile on Brynhild. 'Funny, isn't it? A young man returns a few ardent kisses in the dark, and so forth, whispers a little mutual flattery, brings the encounter to a climax and thinks himself a dog of a fellow. And then things happen very rapidly, there are a few forced decisions, and he finds himself fixed as the permanent baffled centre of an incessant whirlwind. For life. For all the life he's ever going to have. Life, you know, is just one series of traps. We're all in traps. From the king captive in his duty to the people to the kid crippled for life in the accident ward. All of us.'

'But you broke through.'

'*Did* I break through? Have I broken through? I began this writing in secret I have told you of, and it dawned upon me I could write. I began to like the steady deliberation of setting things down, correcting them, choosing a better phrase and a better word, more and more. After one has heard words coming in a whirling rush like a spout of muddy water bursting a dam, it was marvellous to find they could also be still things, shining in their depths like crystals in a setting. Often I would go to the office, push letters and engagements aside and sit, letting my mind get clear, letting the sediment subside. Things would get so much clearer that at last it seemed possible to see down through the appearances...'

'Where was that office? What were you doing?'

'House and estate agent. I was a partner. I could pretend to have "books" to "do" in the evening.'

'You never were a pharmaceutical chemist?'

'No. I meant that by way of illustration. Before I decided to give you the facts.'

'Go on, Mr Bunter.'

'Don't be hard on me, Mrs Palace. I'm doing my best. I've been practising concealment for six whole years.'

'You went off. You took part of your life away from her. And then more of it. Hid it in an office. Hid it in a book. Hid it in your thoughts. And at last went off to London with it. Yes, I can understand something of that. Was she – provided for?'

'It didn't happen quite so simply as that.'

193

Mr Bunter was obviously now in trouble with another considerable mass of undigested particulars.

'There was that brother of hers. You see, she had a brother. My wife, I discovered after I married her, had this brother, an elder brother. He was in America at the time. He had travelled in the East. He was, I know now, a cocaine addict. He came back to England and drifted down to us, deep voiced when she was high pitched, but as garrulous as she was. He hung about us, living in a dingy lodging. He borrowed money from me and all her family. He came and went. He was extraordinarily cunning in getting money from us without any of us knowing what the others were doing. He would tell us things to set us against one another and so prevent us from acting together about him. He had a malicious ingenuity. He professed to take my part against his sister. He tried to touch one of my brothers. Then he began to blackmail me.'

'But what could he blackmail you about?'

'Somehow he had got wind of or guessed about that child in Scotland. I told you... *Yes*, I told you that... He was never clear about it, but his hints were broad and close. It would have been intolerable if Freda had known. Always he was trying to get money from me or else creating a scandal about his destitution. Like that. He combined his exactions with the most fantastic boasting. I can see him now, heavy, lumbering, portentous, fishy-eyed, with his lower lip drooping, coming into our little dining-room round about a meal time, but refusing to eat, too ill, sulking and menacing and then, after a little drink, beginning to talk. Of how he would write plays if he had an opening. Of how he would make a fortune if he had a little capital. Of the countries he had seen and the women he had had. He was the only one who could silence his sister even for a little while, and then her pent-up feelings would explode. She would scream and scold at him and he would become grossly pathetic. Why did he not work? Why did he not succeed? Why didn't he succeed or get rid of himself?

'But if I said a word about him, she took it as a reflection on her family and her breeding and turned the storm on me. She would insult my brothers and my sister. Any chance admission I had ever made about them would reappear distorted. "You yourself admit." Her hostility to my sister was insane.

'Cocaine was never mentioned in these rows. I don't think we knew certainly about his drugs, any of us. None of us knew much about that sort of thing. But we knew that he would come and sit in on us and devasate us until we gave him some money. Then off he would go to get it – whatever it was. He seemed to find no difficulty in getting the stuff in Cardiff. Then he would disappear for a day or a week or more. The bigger the sum we gave him the longer he would stay away... You *do* realize I was living a pretty intolerable life?'

'It wasn't what one calls a successful marriage.'

'No. It was intolerable. Something had to be done. I would sit with Freda above my head scolding and gesticulating with her long hands – how I got to hate those hands! – and Gregory rumbling and booming at ground-level. Something, you see, *had* to happen. It wasn't very wonderful running away from that.'

'But you did it.'

'Not at once. I developed that idea of getting out, first as a consolation fantasy. I think I got it first from a tale of old

195

Tolstoy's, *The Living Corpse*. Then I thought *why not?* Why not really do it? Then when I had *Blind Alley* – '

'That was your first?'

'Yes. It's the shortest too. I thought: why not get this published under another name? And slip away to that name? I certainly *had* got a sort of alibi already prepared in my imagination. I was beginning to realize the thing was possible. I had got a postal address in London – as Bunter. I really don't know now how far I had it cut and dried at that time. But the point is that there was a crisis.'

'You flung out of the house?'

'No. It wasn't like that. Let me tell you. As exactly as possible. My wife had gone to Cornwall to a married sister who had appendicitis. My brother-in-law hadn't shown up for weeks and weeks. I was temporarily in heaven. I was writing and writing well in my own home. And then Gregory turned up. Heaven knows where he had been and what he had been doing. He was in filthy clothes, black with coal-dust; he had no shirt. His black hair was unkempt. I was shocked and angry at his appearance and then I decided to treat him kindly and get rid of him as soon as possible. I gave him a hot bath. I gave him a good supper and plenty of whisky. I rigged him out in old clothes of my own from top to toe and I gave him a couple of pounds. This heartened him enormously. To begin with he had been the wettest dog that ever cringed, but before we were through with supper, he was boasting like a visitant from heaven. He would never forget my goodness and in a little while (trust him) he would make my fortune. And then – I don't think he meant to reflect upon me – he began to extol the life of wandering and adventure. He'd just had an affair with a woman who had been left alone in a farm in

Cardigan. Prime she was. Always he was having such adventures. He'd been out upon the hills and sleeping in the open. Nobody knew what sunrise was who hadn't slept in the open. This life people led in towns wasn't life. These clerks and people who sat in little offices and had their little villas and went to bed before eleven – "I'm not meaning you, old chap," he said. "You've got your political career and all that. You play the long game."

'But I knew he meant me. I knew that it was necessary for his self-respect that he should get over these taunts at me. And at last, drunk and glorious, he went out of the house – with his old clothes done up in a bundle...'

Mr Bunter hesitated. 'This is a queer story I am telling you. I've never given a hint of it to any one, but I've turned it round in my mind a thousand times. The man, you know, was drunk and crazy...

'Behind our house was a patch of open country and then some disused workings. There was a fence of barbed wire round them, but one could scramble through that, and across it was a short cut to our suburban station. The light was uncertain, ragged, black clouds across a low half-moon, but I knew the track by habit, I used it two or three times a week. I led the way, but halfway across he began to shout that I was going astray. "You stay-at-home fool," he said, "you don't even know your way about your own back garden." And then he went off to the right at a run, singing "Men of Harlech". I went after him expostulating. It was rough going. He stumbled once or twice, he fell and got up again and then, in an instant, the earth had swallowed him up. I crept forward to the hole and listened. There was a sort of scraping sound, a muffled shout and a splash. There I stood...

'I suppose I stood there for a considerable time...'

197

'You went for help?'

'No.'

'But why *didn't* you?'

'Because I felt I might have pushed him in.'

'But you didn't push him in?'

'I was a good ten yards behind him. I was certainly ten yards behind him. But all the same I felt that I might have pushed him in. Freda knew I detested him. She knew I was capable of violence…'

Mr Bunter made a clean breast of it. 'You see – once I hit her.'

'What did she do?'

'Boasted about it all over Cardiff and tried to make me hit her again. She liked people to think we lived a life of violent passions.'

'Why did you hit her?'

'She said something disgusting about my sister. The elder sister who brought me up. Never mind that. There I was in that ugly night in that grey-black squalor of dumps and dismal weeds, squatting beside the hole which had swallowed up this – blackmailer. I didn't call any help. I could hear nothing down below there. Perhaps if a rope had been lowered… I doubt if he was alive by the time he hit the water. I wasn't resourceful, anyhow. My minds seemed a mixture of liquid mud and drifting grey moonlight. A sluggish muddle. I had had some whisky myself. And also I had been struck by a fantastic idea. One thing was working with another in my mind… So I didn't think of calling help. I went back slowly and furtively to the house. The cloud shadows moved along with me like bad advisers.

'It's difficult now to recall how it looked to me. Still more difficult to make you see… Nobody, so far as I knew, had seen us together going across that waste land and I doubt if any one on earth knew he had been with me that night except our servant, and she had gone home after serving up our supper. She had, I knew, a sort of fear of Gregory. Maybe he had bothered her. A man like that...

'Anyhow – there he was, done for, at the bottom of the shaft and tomorrow Freda would be coming back from Cornwall. The prospect of the morning was overwhelming. I saw an immense vista of questions, explanations, accusations opening out before me. And maybe there were people who knew he had a hold on me. It was more than probable that he had boasted in public-houses and dope-dens of his hold upon me. He might have given endless hints. How far might I not be accused?'

'Mr Bunter, what was the hold he had upon you? Just having a war baby – '

'I've got to tell you all. When I was a soldier, in the war, mostly in training for the war, for I had only eleven weeks at the front, I told you I had this war baby. But I didn't explain that properly. I lived with a Scotch girl for some weeks at Aberlowson, outside the camp, and called her my wife. We went through a sort of declaration and I gave her a signed paper. I believed she was legally my wife. I am not sure whether that is so now, but I was sure then. Somehow he had got hold of that. I never knew how. That's what he held over me.

'I thought it over as I crept home. It's easy to be lucid now but it wasn't at the time. He's vanished, I thought. But that may not become important for weeks or months. Unless I say something about it. Nobody is going to miss him and look for him for a long time and his body may not be found for years. He was the sort of man who could vanish without any sort of disturbance. "Think it out," I said to myself. "Think it out." And then I had what seemed to be a bright thought at the time, though really it was a profoundly silly thought. He was wearing my clothes, with the tailor's mark in the pocket and my name on the shirt and socks. When they find him, I thought, if ever they do, he will be unrecognizable, rotten, macerated in the water. I forgot that his hair was straight and black and what is odder I forgot that the servant had got supper for us. I overlooked the fact that if the body was supposed to be mine, people would want to know what he had done to me. Where had he gone? If it was me down the shaft, what would they think of him? About him I was entirely unfeeling. Then and afterwards. I hadn't the slightest twinge of pity, regret, or compunction about him and I haven't now. Nothing so destroys human kindliness as insulting self-assertion. But I thought thick-headedly that night. I was in a muddle. There, I thought, is a body – and some day that body might well be taken to be mine. Good.

'I went back to my house. The shadows and the moonlight drifted about me and changed the face of the world continually. The long-elaborated scheme of a flight from this life I was leading became dominant. I went back into the lit and littered dining-room with its broken food, its dirty plates and the empty whisky bottle. I thought of all the crowding troubles that were gathering against tomorrow. Already I had behaved queerly in giving no alarm. Ought I to ring up the police now or pretend I had seen the last of him at the door? I should have to spin a yarn to Freda. I should have to tell her of her brother's visit and describe his departure. And away up the hill was that crumpled body waiting to be found. It would always be there waiting to be found. If ultimately that body was to become mine I must vanish now. I looked round the dining-room. "This is my time," I said. "Not a day more of it."

'I slipped out with a valise and my manuscript just before dawn. I tramped across country to another station. I rested on some felled timber in a wood until about ten o'clock so as not to be noticeable at the station in the early morning, and I took an ordinary train in an ordinary way. That night I was in London. I had burnt my boats.'

'And things worked out as you had expected?'

'Nothing worked out as I had expected. As soon as Freda realized in a day or so that I had gone she raised a frantic hue and cry. At first the search wasn't very thorough, but she was infuriated by my departure. Subconsciously she had been apprehending my intention to get away for some time. She pestered the Press; she pestered the police. She got herself interviewed, she got articles going on the David Lewis Mystery. It became a journalistic stunt. All South Wales was combed for me and within a month they found Gregory down his shaft, broken up, decayed, but pretty manifestly, I should think, not me. And after that you realize the relations of Mr David Lewis to Cardiff became – difficult.'

'But all this was years ago?'

'Nineteen twenty-eight.'

'That is some time – six years ago.'

'Six years.'

'Hasn't it blown over?'

'There was a tremendous fuss down there. A fuss that went on. I think the sheer impudence of my beginning again so close to it in London was a help for me. My wife behaved fantastically. First, she identified the body as her brother. There was his black hair, there were his large, coarse hands. Then she changed over suddenly, disavowed her evidence and said it was me. She had jumped to the conclusion that if she said it was her brother she might hang me. She would as soon have hanged herself. She said it was me and she proclaimed her dread that her brother might have done me a mischief. With equal emphasis she proclaimed that she did not care what happened to her brother where my life was concerned. From the indignant Deserted Wife her pose changed in a night into that of the Desperate Woman protecting her Lover. Nobody believed her new attitude. I doubt if she wanted them to. There was nothing to be done for her. She elaborated her rôle. In the background of the audience she must have imagined I was looking on. Somewhere, she hoped, I knew of all this. For the most part people believed her first story and not her second. That they appreciated. I guess they watched her pretty closely for some indication of collusion between us.

'At the inquest my brothers and sisters were ambiguous. They too had caught the idea that I was in danger. They irritated the coroner by their reserve. They knew very little of Gregory, they said. They swore to my clothes.

'When presently Freda claimed my insurance money there was a revival of public interest. I think she was forced into doing that by neighbourly comments. I doubt if she would have done it without that compulsion. The insurance company refused to accept the evidence of my death. Having got a considerable publicity in the matter, they made a grand gesture of it and paid up. Most embarrassingly for me. Under protest, they said. As an advertisement. Five hundred pounds. Then slowly the affair sank down again out of public attention.

'For three or four years I did not find out precisely what had happened, and then I took a risk and dug it all out in the newspaper-room of the British Museum. I said I was in search of dates and local colour, and I began with a study of some Yorkshire papers. Then I had out the files of various Irish Free State dailies together with two Cardiff papers. It was as if they were of minor importance to the matter under consideration. You perceive my elaborate cunning. But so I got all I wanted.'

'What has become of your wife?'

'That is one of my bothers. It was not so much a question of money. Her people were not badly off and she had our little house, some hundred pounds or so of mine and that insurance money. For a year or so she must have lived imaginatively upon my disappearance, made it her social distinction, talked it out from five hundred different angles, said she was sure I was dead, said that she was sure that I was alive. You know, it's an odd thing to say, but though I detest her I have nevertheless a tenderness for that woman. I understand the tortures an unstanchable insatiable vanity may give itself. In a sense she is mine. That she made life impossible for me, cannot alter that. I think I understand why she talks and talks. It is something she cannot help. She is driven. It is like skating on thin ice. You must go on and go on. Pause and you fall in. Below the thin surface of Freda's noise and violence was a horror of the cold and uneventful commonplace. Self-discovery. She boasted to keep herself warm in the eternal night. There is something of that in all of us, but with her it was quintessential. Lest the vociferous nonentity should be laid bare. And, after all, we'd been husband and wife. I couldn't bear – and I can't bear – to think of her silenced and going under. I'd feel better if I knew she was fixed up somewhere so that she could tell herself and every one just how glorious she was. But what can I do? How can I help her? How can I find out about her? I daren't ask about Cardiff. I daren't go near Cardiff. To this day I'm not safe. I know I'm not safe. The story isn't forgotten. It hasn't blown over. It's dangerous still. At the least hint of the real state of affairs she would revive it. The David Lewis drama would be billed for a new run.

'Always,' said Mr Bunter, 'that side of my life has been like a leaking patch in the side of a ship... Sometimes one lapses into a sort of security. Sometimes something trivial but alarming occurs. You find some one up from Cardiff looking at you from the top of an omnibus. Some one you knew slightly. Was he really looking at you – *as* you? Or you say something that might give you away. And now – recently – I've had a sort of feeling – like hearing a rat gnawing in the night – that some one is at work upon the problem of Mr Bunter, where he was born, where he went to school, what he did before he became a writer of books. I have a certain feeling that I am looked at, that people come to look at me. It may be a touch of persecution mania. But the other day in the tube a man stood holding a strap and looking down on me. I had an impression he had followed me along the platform and into the car and that saved me.

' "If that isn't David Lewis!" he said aloud.

'I went on reading my paper unconcernedly. A year or so ago I should have looked up at once and given myself away. You do not realize, until you think it over, the number of people in the world who know things about you, who have watched you go past in the morning or noted something characteristic in your voice or speech, schoolmasters, room-mates, men in your platoon, men who have done business with you. They don't forget. If they were young at the time they never forget. And after a newspaper mystery they are all alert. If they desist for a time a trifle will bring them back to it. "Oh, yes!" they cry, "*I* knew David Lewis." Then if some one, some one hostile, begins to look for gaps and pick up loose threads…'

'But it was six years ago.'

'All the same – No. It isn't over. I know it isn't over.'

For a minute perhaps Mr Bunter lapsed into silence.

'Suppose they bring Freda to London,' he said. 'Suppose some one had the idea of bringing her to London to identify me!'

'*Who* would bring her to London?' asked Mrs Palace.

6

The chiming clock of the newly erected Abbey Road Building proclaimed in a decorative manner the end of an hour and then slowly and regretfully struck seven.

'Well, Mrs Palace, we can't say now that we don't talk together. I've been talking to you here for more than an hour. There's my whole life story. Practically. At last I've told some one. I've got it off my chest. Thank you for listening.'

'Thank you for telling me. Mr Bunter, I find it a queer story with something in it… It's absurd, I know, to make such a comparison, but it reminds me – Have you ever seen a chick struggling out of an egg?'

'I knew you'd understand. That, Mrs Palace, is exactly what we are. No! – not "exactly". How easily these unqualifying words slip in! But that is what we are. Struggling out of a shell. All of us. The criminals and defaulters just as much as the leaders and philosophers. This human world isn't half-hatched. Struggling out of an egg. It's a beautiful image... "Let me out," we say. "Let me out." And then, "Don't pursue me!" And in the end – like a Monte Carlo pigeon – one may be brought down in the full delight of escape.

'This is the first time I've ever told this to any one,' said Mr Bunter. 'Perhaps I haven't done it very well. I've been getting in my own light, I expect. I wish I could begin it all over again... There are such a lot of ways of telling the same thing. But now perhaps you understand the quality of my particular exasperation. To some extent anyhow... Does it horrify you at all?'

'No.'

'Disgust you?'

'No.'

'Not about Freda?'

'I think I can understand that. You *had* to do something. And after all there was the other wife. Mr Bunter, I can't judge. How can I judge of things like that?'

'This talk isn't to be our only talk then? If you're not horrified; if you're not disgusted, why shouldn't we talk some more? I want to go on talking to you. I want you to know me. I can't tell you what breaking down this loneliness I have been living in, means to me. And never have I wanted to be known by any one as I want to be known by you. I open new gulfs between us, I know, with everything fresh I tell you, but then there always were gulfs... You have an effect on my imagination. If I can get you to know me I feel I shall begin perhaps to know something about myself. And I want you to tell me something about yourself.'

206

'I can never talk about myself – or anything.'

'But I can learn. Some of your silences are – expressive. It's just because you don't put up any screen of statement. *And you understand!* You seem to *take* everything... I must go on with this talking. If you'll let me talk. You can't imagine the blessedness of getting out of solitude and silence at last! To some one who gives you a fair hearing. Mrs Palace, would you care to lunch with me some day next week?'

She assented gravely.

'There is a Basque Restaurant in Dover Street or Albemarle Street,' he said, 'a most confidential place, where there is no band and no crowd and no fuss and admirable cooking... And we can talk in undertones...'

CHAPTER ELEVEN

Mr Alfred Bunter Goes to Pieces

Brynhild's mind was so filled with the remarkable story of Mr Alfred Bunter that practically she thought of nothing else for the rest of that day and most of the next, and she even woke up and thought about him in the night. She was immensely impressed by the natural and convincing way in which he had given himself away to her. His unqualified assumption that in a peculiar sense he belonged to her and that it would be impossible for her to betray or abuse his confidence, went unquestioned. So it was. She had to believe him, she had to help him as much as she could.

She was thinking about him and hardly at all about herself. She wasn't indeed keeping any sort of watch upon herself. It did not occur to her for a moment to think she was in love with him. She did not desire him, she did not look up to him, but she wanted enormously to know a lot more about him. He had quickened her mind tremendously. No doubt of the quickening. He was intensely interesting, from that elusive streak of gold in his complexion and the mixture of sensitive weakness and great obstinacy in his face, to the manifest hesitations in his account of himself and his passionate effort, nevertheless, to be sincere. It was that passionate effort appealed to her most; it was as though something in him was wanting to get born through her. In her, he had intimated, for the first time he had found a chance of self-knowledge. It made her feel incubatory. Nobody had ever asked her for help or indeed for anything, since the connubial demands of Mr Rowland Place established a sort of monopoly over her. She could give help to Bunter, she perceived, and she alone could give it. She could not imagine herself not giving it. She could alleviate his loneliness, be his fellow-conspirator, probably do things – she didn't know quite what things – to help his concealments and releases.

Here was just the mental occupation she had needed.

It would be friendship, a great and relieving friendship for them both. Later on, when she had found out how to put them, she might even tell him things about herself. She saw no reason why she should not develop a reciprocating friendship with him. He was the only man she had encountered since marriage with Palace had enveloped her, who had talked to her gravely, sincerely, and intimately for more than an hour without a single lapse into commonplace gallantry. He was at last what she had come to consider that impossible thing, a man friend. So often had she found a grave and respectful opening the mere smoke-screen for some stupid little amorous advance. Such an Eros, that furtive Eros of the genteel! A foolish-faced, indelicate, rather middle-aged faun, as tiresome as an intrusive, insufficiently clad beggar, invaded the serious conversation. But this man, it seemed, had need of her without any of that.

She realized that he wasn't a very wise man, that he needed protection from himself. She wasn't by any means sure that he was perfectly truthful. Not that he lied, but he was weak about the truth. Maybe all novelists get that way. She wasn't by any means sure that there were not one or two rather significant things about his story still to be told. But she felt she had power over him, so that he would be strongly disposed to do anything that she seemed to think fine and wise.

She tried to work out some aspects of his problem. She was all for his making good his escape. She was all for Alfred Bunter and against the obliterated Lewis. She felt singularly little compunction about the two abandoned wives. She had that very common disposition in women to consider that a woman who cannot keep a man deserves no pity. Her concern was for him. She surveyed his proceedings in an almost maternal advisory spirit. Had he really set about his business in the right way? For example, was he wise to go on living in England now that he was becoming a conspicuous figure in the literary world? He could reduce any risk of recognition by old acquaintances to a tenth if only he went to live in Paris. David Lewis didn't speak French perhaps, but why shouldn't Bunter learn? She did not realize as Mr Cloote did that the more subtly one learns to use one's own language the more difficult it is to use any other. And certainly – and soon – he must put his relations with the two abandoned wives – and the insurance company – on a less vulnerable footing.

Brynhild had an innocent belief in the honourable inhumanity of solicitors. She thought they were profoundly wise, resource-ful, loyal, illegal if necessary and absolutely silent – and that they did it for six and eight-pence a time. She did not see why Bunter should not settle all the practical side of his problems through a solicitor. And his father had been a solicitor. He must know solicitors down there that he could trust. He would find a solicitor. This solicitor would go to this incessant dangerous wife and say to her very firmly that if she became quite silent about David Lewis and particularly if she asked no more questions about him she should be paid a regular annuity...

At this point Brynhild pulled up in her scheming. She had a vague feeling of something unsubstantial in this planning. Perhaps she was overrating the effective firmness of solicitors. Perhaps she was underrating the power of that Cardiff wife to do novel and formidable things. She tried to recall everything Bunter had said about her and to evolve some sort of picture of her. She had to be reckoned with. She was keen, he had said – a formidable word – and bright-coloured and bright-eyed, incessantly voluble, so vain as to be unaware of the protests and resistances she evoked. Brynhild had met talkative people but she had never been the objective of a really voluble, inconsistent, and uncontrollable person in her life. She tried to imagine it. It must be very difficult to hold one's own. It must be like walking through a blizzard. A *hot* blizzard – a sandstorm. It might not be so easy, even for a family solicitor, to tell such a woman not to do things.

And then her mind came round to the question of that extinguished brother Gregory. He seemed to be a terrific person. Quite calmly she arraigned Bunter for murder, justifiable murder or manslaughter. What had he really done? Had he told the truth about that? Did he himself know the truth? Did he know exactly what had happened for a moment or so that night? Murder had never struck her as an unnatural thing to do – difficult it might be perhaps and reprehensible but not unnatural. If it was unnatural why should it be forbidden in the Ten Commandments which after all are meant for normal men? The Ten Commandments do not go out of their way to forbid unnatural

212

things. It seemed to her quite natural for him to have given this exasperating, shouting drunkard a push, a sudden, impulsive push. It didn't strike her as at all a dreadful thing for him to have done that. She could think that a possibility and still think none the worse of him.

But anyhow he said he hadn't. There was nobody in the world to contradict him. All the same there might be grave trouble. What could they do to him on that score? That incalculable, exhibitionist wife might turn against him again.

Was it really possible that some one would bring her to London? Who could do such a thing? Could there be plots and conspiracies against Bunter? Had he enemies? Had he made people dislike him? What could they find to dislike in him? He wasn't the sort of man any one dislikes. Rowly didn't seem to like him, but that was just Rowly's sensitiveness to competition, even to inadvertent competition.

'He must go abroad,' she said that night, and she stopped brushing her hair to tick the points off on her fingers. He must go abroad. He must keep abroad for a time and move about. He must get a solicitor. A Good Solicitor. He must pay that money to the insurance company under a strict pledge of secrecy. He must arrange those annuities somehow. It was a pity she did not know quite the solicitor needed but that was a detail. Then he could settle down over there, go on writing those really very fine and subtle books of his, and all would be well. And he would be very grateful to her. It would really be a tremendous thing in friendships.

In bed she recapitulated these really very sound suggestions so that she should have them at her finger-ends for their lunch. They seemed to be getting simpler and sounder as she went to

213

sleep. But that lunch with its further elucidations and its wise counsels, was never to happen.

᛭· She was rung up the morning after their talk and she found Bunter on the telephone. 'Mrs Palace?' His voice sounded near and yet very small. 'Mrs Palace, I can't keep my appointment with you. I'm sorry. I have been... I have got to leave London almost at once.'

A pause. What should she say?

'I suppose – I couldn't see you, could I?' he asked.

'But why not? Where?'

'I've left my place. I think it's being watched. I'm in a little flat belonging to one of my brother's clients. He's abroad and my brother had the key.'

'But I thought your brothers didn't know – '

'I'll explain all that when I see you. Everything has collapsed. I *must* see you again. I can't endure it if I don't see you.'

'Tell me the address.'

2

She found him in a queer, squalid little flat in a building between Portland Street and Tottenham Court Road. She went up an uncarpeted stone staircase to the door. On every landing were two doors at an acute angle and he was four flights up. He let her in himself. He led the way into a minute sitting-room furnished with the meanest-looking furniture she had ever seen. There was a cast-iron fireplace with a gas fire, a fairly commodious sofa and an armchair covered in dingy tapestry cloth, a square table, and a built-up arrangement of glazed book-shelves with books. 'Sit down,' said Bunter. 'Shall I get you some tea? I'll have to get it – if there *is* tea.'

'I didn't come for tea,' said Brynhild. 'We won't have tea. Tell me.'

She was beginning already to know his face rather well and she saw that he was changed. He looked uneasy – rattled. Hitherto he had moved and spoken in a consciously self-controlled way that she had found rather likeable. Now his nerves were at the surface. She had, she realized, over-estimated his firmness. He had the manner of some one who had rehearsed a speech several times and now finds he has to say things quite differently.

'I wanted to talk to you – just once more… Mrs Palace, it's all up with me, I'm afraid. For a long time, anyhow. I'm in a net.'

(His mouth was wincing. He wasn't an infinite distance from tears. Amazing!)

'What has happened?'

'My silly secret is practically out.'

'Yes?'

'The whole thing's gone phut. *I've* gone phut!'

'Tell me.'

'My eldest brother walked into my flat suddenly this morning at half-past seven. I was up at work already – in my dressing-gown. I often do that. When he sent in his name I hesitated and then decided to see him. He cam in, rather stouter, rather more like my father, rather more the perfect solicitor, but the same old Evan. After six years. He scrutinized me for one brief moment. "It's young Dave right enough," he said – in front of the servant.

' "Why have you come like this, without notice?" I asked, as soon as the servant was out of the room.

' "I only got word of it last night," he said, sitting down. "I came right up at once. Dave, you've got to clear out."

' "Why?"

' "I didn't realize what I was doing. I'm afraid I've given you away… This is a brave place you've got. You must be doing well. But you'll have to get out from it."

'He went on in a slow, deliberate, precise way that always used to irritate me. But what he told me was grave enough. I can't tell you all the particulars of the story we pieced together. I remembered a foolish thing I had done. It's great fun running a deception while you're getting away with it. But when you slip – Then you see what an ass you are! Such a silly thing! A year or so ago. At one of those Bedlow Book-Teas. Some one had quoted a Welsh proverb in Welsh. I capped it with another. You see? Alfred Bunter, supposed to be from the Midlands, talked Welsh! Somebody journalistic had remembered that and thought it over and remarked upon it and begun to look for evidence of the past of Mr Alfred Bunter, in the Welsh Press. Why should any one do that? I don't know. Somebody did. Then yesterday, yesterday morning, a man turned up in my brother's office wanting particulars about the missing David Lewis. Rather clever questions. Wasn't he rather a genius? Hadn't he written some poetry? Something like Chatterton? It was an urgent, dark man, my brother said, with a face as broad as it was long, and a squint. He said he proposed to write a book on the Tragedies of Welsh geniuses. One in particular he wanted to know about – David Lewis. Keen on David Lewis particularly. Would my brother be surprised to learn that David Lewis was probably flourishing in London under the name of Alfred Bunter? It was becoming an open secret, he said. Clever to say that. He produced two rather oblique photographs, one of a public dinner and one of a public lunch party, and several snapshots, and before my brother knew where he was he had accepted the identification. With surprise. He came to his senses in the afternoon and took the night train to warn me.

'My servant interrupted us with my overdue breakfast and my brother joined me at that. Neither of us ate much. We wanted the servant and the breakfast things out of the way, and then we sat down to talk it all out.

'We went into all the aspects of the case. What would happen next? Nothing was quite clear to us. It was just a tangle of disagreeable possibilities. The most probable thing was that this man with the effusive manner and the squint would take his discovery to the local Press. They might accept it forthwith, but they might wait and check up for verification with my other brother and my sister. But Evan had put both of them wise. They were going to admit a slight resemblance, they agreed, and then hesitate. No – no, come to look at it again, it wasn't me. Evan was going to keep out of the way. That would hold things up for a bit. But only for a bit. The story was too good not to come out, even if it came out with notes of interrogation all over it. It was bound to come to London. Then the insurance company would wake up, and then would come the question of how Gregory had come by his death. My brother could not recall the terms of the coroner's verdict. He thought it was death by misadventure. "But let's face up to it," said my brother. "I'm for you heart and soul, Dave, as you know, but there's going to be an imputation of murder. And, I must tell you, your sister and I know now of a possible motive. I'll be plain with you, Dave. We know of Mrs Dave Lewis away there in Aberlowson and her boy. Working in a factory. Why didn't you tell us, Dave? A Scotch marriage. Bigamy. That, again, may come out. How far the powers that be, will go into that murder inquiry, I can't tell. And now, what's to be done?"

'We spent two hours beating about that question and getting no further.'

Bunter stopped short.

He gave vent to a noise of extreme exasperation. 'Aaah!' – a quite remarkable noise. 'I just can't think about it! I can't think about it! I have no patience with it. I think up to a certain point and then I give way. I give way to the exasperation of a caught animal. I want to rush about the room. I want to break things and bang the walls. Let me see. What happened next? Yes. About half-past ten we got a ring from the gossip correspondent of the *Hourglass* to ask if he could speak to me. It may have been only a coincidence. My brother said I had just gone out. "Something may have appeared in the Welsh papers already," he said. "How can one tell? This is no place for you just now. They'll besiege you when the mystery thickens. You may get them outside. Freda is bound to rush up headlong directly she gets wind of the story. Safety first. Come right away to a little flat I know of." (This flat.) "It's a queer little hole, but no one will dream of looking for you in it. I'll scout around for a bit. I've got some business of my own to do in Brighton. And you'll have time to think and turn round."

'Good advice. I packed a bag and came. I remembered our luncheon engagement for next Tuesday as soon as I got here and rang you up at once. Here we are. My silly little card castle has collapsed. I'm done. I had to tell you. You're the only soul in the world to whom I can say a word. And anyhow, you had to know.'

He looked at her almost as if he expected her to invent some solution to his trouble there and then.

The confident, brown man she had met at Valliant Chevrell had changed into a distressed and appealing boy. Never yet had Brynhild come so near to feeling like a mother.

3

'It's the stupidest thing in the world to ask,' said Bryhild, 'but what *are* you going to do?'

'That's exactly what I wanted you to ask me. I *have* thought of something... And if I can watch your face as I tell you of it...'

'You tell me,' said Brynhild.

'It's this...'

'One thing, please. What has happened to your wife – your Cardiff wife?'

'My brother tells me she's gone to Ilfracombe, where she runs a sort of boarding-house. Unless somebody traces her there, she may not get into the drama for days – or even weeks. She doesn't read newspapers very attentively...'

'Go on.'

'Mrs Palace, the one person I care for in all this pother is Alfred Bunter – and his work. And you, of course. You, somehow, are in it too. But the others they're pauses in a game. You like – you have liked – I know you have – Alfred Bunter. For me he is reality. For you, too. That's the man you know. I dislike, I despise, young David Lewis beyond measure. I am quite prepared to kill him. I consider him a pitiful failure in life. He's over and done with. Or at any rate he ought to be. I would, if it wasn't for the feelings of his relations, kill him now. But Alfred

Bunter I mean to save if I can. *This* life. This life – which so far has been – only the promise of a beginning. I want to save it. What I can of it. And so far as I can see, the one person who can deny that Bunter is David Lewis and outface the man with the squint and all the rest of it – is David Lewis himself. Yes. Me! Really, I know exactly what I have to do. Up to the present time, you see, Bunter has been careful not to document himself too deeply. Consider the material unreality of Bunter. No photographs except a few bad snapshots and these public banquet pictures. I think I told you that. Rather aslant and a little out of focus. He can go abroad to France, Switzerland, Italy, Morocco – anywhere. He can even get photographs of somebody rather like him and obviously not like David Lewis, to send to the papers. It's not difficult to get Bunter off the scene. Not at all difficult. All that can be done. Mr David Lewis can resume his trimmed army moustache and reappear in Cardiff, penitent, explanatory, with money in his pocket, endorsed by his brothers and sister, ready to settle matters with the insurance company, ready to tell the story of the accident at the pit-shaft and his foolish panic. And ready to swear he has never heard of Bunter. They can't do *much* to him. And afterwards he can go back to America – where presumably he has been all the time – and we shall never hear of him again.'

He stopped and questioned her mutely.

'And the wife in all this plan?' she remarked mildly. And still more mildly – almost apologetically: 'The wives?'

'That *is* the real trouble.'

'That tenacious, loquacious wife in particular?'

'Yes – tenacious and loquacious. Good words for her. I agree. I shall have to tell Freda I love some one else. I *can* tell her that.'

'In America? Some one in America?'

'In America. Yes – in America.'

'And she'll accept that?'

'I don't know.'

'Nor I. She's a strong character.'

'No. She's a forcible character. Not a strong one.'

'But you admitted – "tenacious". I want to get all this right, Mr Bunter, or else how can I advise you? Suppose David Lewis *can't* get away again? Suppose his Freda lays hands on him – those long hands you said you got to hate – and won't leave go?'

'Murder, then.'

Brynhild considered him gravely. Was it in him? Not that sort of murder.

'If David Lewis can't get away, then Mr Bunter abroad in Europe, will fade and fade until he fades out altogether.'

'It won't be like that. No. In some way I must do a deal with Freda and get my liberty. I don't know how. There must be some way...'

Brynhild meditated for a time. 'The extraordinary thing is that by all accepted standards you are a very immoral man, Mr Bunter. And I don't feel the slightest disapproval of you. Except... In all this – There is something... You seem to disregard the other wife in Scotland.'

'She doesn't appear – I believe we may be able to keep her out of the Cardiff drama altogether.'

'But have you forgotten her?'

Mr Bunter searched his mind. 'No.'

'Doesn't *she* matter? How did your brother get to know of her? You *loved* her. You *did* love her.'

'She saw my name in the paper at the time of the mystery and wrote to him – a wise, discreet, little letter. She wanted to know if I was in trouble – that was how she put it. Could she perhaps help, she said.'

For some seconds Mr Bunter looked profoundly ashamed of himself, regarded the frayed carpet, and said nothing.

'Well?' said Brynhild. 'Tell me some more about the wife you loved.'

'It was a long time ago.'

'Your brothers contribute to her support?'

'She will be taken care of – and the boy... I know it sounds callous, Mrs Palace, but if I saw her now, if we met, I doubt if we should know each other.'

Brynhild said nothing, thinking darkly. Reality went into these unromantic patterns. The 'boy' must be seventeen. The boy he had never seen... Far away in time in another world, those two youngsters had loved. She perhaps was fresh and pretty then, and he must have made a glowing ardent boy lover. He must have been a delightful lover. Before he had got himself muddled up. The Scotch girl had had that anyhow.

And now all that was forgotten!

'Perhaps when you came home and got married in Cardiff you were still thinking of that Scotch girl?'

'I couldn't go back to her now,' said Mr Bunter. 'It's inconceivable. I will do all I can for her – if I get out of this tangle. I'll see the boy and help him. I've always meant to do that...'

He stood staring at Brynhild.

4

Then he spoke with a sudden access of force. 'You mustn't blame me for all that. You mustn't blame me now for that. You must not. I was a different being. I cannot recall how I thought or how I felt. Blame me then. But I'm paying for it now. It's the *me*, here and now, you have to think of. It's not the inexperienced man who ought to count now. It's the experienced one. Shall I do as I am planning? Shall I go through all this now with David Lewis and *end* him, end him as completely as possible, and then take Bunter out of cold storage again and go on with *him* and get the work I want him to do done? That's my idea – my fantastic but just possible idea. Bunter is worth something. He is indeed worth something. His work at any rate is worth something. You *know* he's worth something. Or why are you here? Lewis was worth nothing at all. Hadn't I the right to be born again and escape from this eternal game of consequences? Is human life to be a scheme of infant damnation for evermore?'

Brynhild sat on the one mean little armchair, elbow on knee and chin in hand, trying to seem and be absolutely clear and intelligent and feeling all the time the most irrational stir within. She took refuge in argument.

'*When*, Mr Bunter, do you think we ought to become really responsible for ourselves? No one expects it of infants. No one expects it of children. Now *you* are going to escape – if you can – from six-and-twenty, seven-and-twenty years of your life. That, we agree, was just the husk, that was just the egg-shell. When do we really *begin for good?*'

'Even the law doesn't let us incur debts until we are twenty-one,' said Mr Bunter. 'And, after all, I'm proposing to clean up my obligations first. Not so easy. I'll have no life now for endless months, anyhow; nothing real, nothing I can control, nothing but a rigmarole...'

223

He remained silent for a space. His face was getting red. Abruptly he exploded.

'*Damn!*' he said. 'I can't do it. I can't *do* it...

'I've got you here to tell you I was going to do it, because then I thought I could do it if I told you. I thought somehow – *if you knew*... And now it seems a more monstrous bore and toil than ever. And as hopeless. Utter separation. I thought I had got away and I haven't got away. And that breaks me. That's the essence of the situation. For weeks, months, years perhaps now I shall have to be lying and scheming and doing hardly anything else. For all that time I shall do no thinking, no writing worth speaking of. I shall be just trying to clean up David Lewis. In the vital years of life. The situation is like a monstrous octopus. You cut one tentacle and find there's another round your waist. What will Freda do? She may do any fantastic thing. She may disbelieve me, see through me, and take up this chase for Alfred Bunter again directly I get away from her. I can get away from her, but can I get clear of her? And while I am denying Alfred Bunter, there will be these people, this journalist, this man with a squint, whoever he is, who will be feeling about, feeling about for some thread that will hold and drag Alfred Bunter back...'

He made an ineffective gesture with his hands.

'It bristles with trouble. It crowds upon me and crushes me. Take one little thing. I suppose somehow I've got to invent something about that time David Lewis spent in America. That, you know, is going to be extremely difficult. If I'm too reserved about what I did in America that will look suspicious. Every one, you know, who goes to America comes back full of American slang and a sort of varnish of the accent. Intonation rather than accent. It happens to every one. There's something so vital about that American slang. It hits them, I think, at the first impact, and impresses them and they get it. But how can I manage that? Perhaps after all it had better not be America. No. It's too near and too well known. Why not Australia? Or the Cape? I shall have to think all that out. That's only one of a hundred little snags. Always on my guard. And I want to get on with my work, Mrs Palace. I wanted to get on with my work. I was getting in my swing. Meeting you somehow – I don't know, but it made me want to do something bigger and finer. I don't want to spend months, years perhaps, of pretending and play-acting. All this is more than a calamity; it's devastation. At this time. Just in my best years, just in the full swing of my thoughts.'

'You go back to reality,' reflected Brynhild. 'And you go back to falsehood. As if falsehood *was* reality. You will have to be thinking all the time of things that don't matter, things that are forced upon you. Plainly.'

'Life is a flight, Mrs Palace. The past hunts us. And by God! Now the hounds are hard upon my trail... And all the same I *mean* something. It isn't a delusion. I have something. I have an idea...'

But what good was that now?

5

She kept her pose of calm wisdom but she was more profoundly stirred than she knew. She was indeed as bitterly distressed as he, at this sudden collapse of a great expectation. For she had been elaborating, expanding, decorating, and dreaming about this fantasy of an intimate friendship and a great secret and a sort of collaboration, since the moment of their parting in Regent's Park.

And manifestly he also had been making some sort of similar if different elaboration. Disappointment acute and tragic hid behind their poses. But still they had to pose with one another.

'I know what to *say* about this,' he said. 'While I have been waiting here I have been saying it. Saying it over. Making imaginary speeches to you. About this tremendous struggle I was in for, about this tremendous lesson I had to learn. And how splendid we have to be. And it's true – and it's rubbish... I shall fight it out. Really I shall fight it out. I shall do exactly as I say I will do. But somehow – '

He stood in front of the sordid little fireplace and he stared at the built-up bookcase before him over her head.

'What right have I to grumble?' he said. '*My* case is only the common case, one variation of an everlasting tune. What *is* human life? What is any life? Fear – incessant fear. Hesitation. Baulking at everything out of fear. Precautions. A mind perpetually thinking of mistakes and dangers. Never living – *outwardly*. Forced to be wary – continually. Attention incessantly diverted – to perplexities, entanglements, threats. The war maybe wounded me more than I knew at the time, yet after all, did it do more than open my eyes to the truth about life? The war was nothing but ordinary life, hurried up, intensified, underlined, made plain by exaggeration. Life raw. Always on the look-out, we were. Always on the defensive. I was never seasoned. I never got used to it. The mine beneath your feet, the sniper in the thicket, the pitfall in the captured trench, the whiff of evil in the air, the queer taste in the food you found. Always on the alert, always on the defensive. Always distracted from calm and sane and lovely things.

'It's as if my eyes were opened then. All life is like that...

'It goes on. It goes on and men stand it. Because I suppose we don't really know how to set about rebelling. It's rebellion somehow I want to say. That is my great idea. Stop to think, life hustles you. Flowers and sunsets, art and music just mock us, as we get pushed and beaten past them. Every sort of loveliness mocks us – and gets snatched away. Love?... We're hustled. Mind your head! Mind your step. Get on with you. Consequences! Take the consequences. We were born conditioned. The past sold us.

'We won't stand it,' he cried. 'All that I'm saying, what I am trying to say in my muddy, noisy books... That's *me* – the essential *me*. Somehow, some day we will get the better of this predestinate world. Somehow we will turn round and get hold of the weapons. Find the magic word. Against all this hunting by the past... I'll get to it somehow. I'll go through.'

He stared at her with miserable eyes. He had an air of saying a premeditated piece, while beneath that surface quite other things refused to be shaped into words. 'It's not ranting, this. It sounds like ranting. But I'm trying to tell you – though I know I sound like ranting to you. God knows when we shall meet again. So I'm trying to tell you now. You asked me in the Park – what I believed, what held me together. *This*. Really I believe *this*. Man – all the sanity in man – has been struggling to escape from the past – continually. Always. Forgive us our debts! What does that mean? Through the ages men have been wiping off debts, as one wipes off dirt and filth. Haven't we tried a hundred ways of repudiating – years of jubilee, statues of limitations, statutes of mortmain? Amnesties. Forgive. Stop. Liquidate. Begin again. Let the dead past bury its dead. It's even in Christianity, you see, even in Bible teaching – mixed up with other things. That's the one saving idea for us. Being born again. I believe that. I hang on to that... Wherever you are in life, whatever you are in life, you are only starting. Against nature, you say? This whole world of nature may be a scheme of fate and damnation. Then we have to fight the whole scheme of nature.'

He stopped again and stared down at her.

'Why I should spend our last moments talking this rubbish,' he said, and left his sentence incomplete.

'It's not rubbish,' said Brynhild. 'Everything that is worth saying seems almost impossible to say.'

Mr Bunter ceased to look or speak like an over-straining prophet making the best of it. His manner, his voice, changed. 'Heroics,' he said. 'I've done my best to say it over. In a sort of way you asked for it. But today, it's hard to keep it up. I may think myself as something creative – rebel child of nature and all that, but today I feel shot through. I feel shot to pieces... Of course, this is an end.'

She looked up sharply at the catch in his voice.

'This is our end,' he said in a voice of calm misery. 'Manifestly.'

6

But she did not see it like that...

An overwhelming pity and tenderness for this distressful man had taken possession of her. She wanted extravagantly to comfort him. And perhaps she wanted to comfort herself. It was impossible to leave him in this state to end things like this. She would as soon have abandoned a nestling that had fallen out of a nest, or a lost, blind kitten. For some years her rôle had been that of a comforter. Wherever else Rowland had failed to bring out in her, his phases of petulance, disappointment, and distress had always turned him towards her as a consoler. From him she had learnt that there is only one conclusive way of consoling a nerve-torn man, and instinctively she resorted to it.

She stood up and drew Bunter's face down to her own. She held his face between her hands.

'Don't mind about it like this,' she murmured to his lips. 'Nothing is worth minding like this. My dear!'

There was nothing more to be said and nothing more was said.

She was seized upon hungrily and she yielded herself responsively.

7

The little clock upon the mantelshelf marked the passing of an hour...

A remarkable calm had come upon them. It was like the passing of a thunderstorm. To her in particular the world had taken on a complete matter-of-fact quality. It was a world now without emotion, without a shadow of desperation, in which nothing is surprising any more.

Certain things had to be done and they were going to be done.

'*Now* I don't mind going back to Cardiff,' said Mr Bunter, breaking a silence. 'I don't mind anything.'

'How shall I know what happens to you?' asked Brynhild.

'I can't write?'

'No. You can't write.'

'But perhaps – if you wanted to say something – if it was only "Stick it" to Mr Alfred Bunter, he will be away somewhere, but his agent – Mr Blatch – A letter, I mean, would be forwarded to him.'

'I won't forget that.'

'It mustn't be a rash letter. It might go astray.'

'Do you think I write rash letters...?'

'Something will appear in the newspapers. Something will certainly appear in the South Wales papers. If an unmarked newspaper came to you from Cardiff?'

'Once.'

'No more?'

'If an autograph hunter with the Christian name of Brynhild and perhaps my surname, writes to Mr Bunter care of his publishers, she will give him an address where he can write his news freely and fully...'

'Maybe it won't be so long. Maybe it won't be so bad. Maybe I'll liquidate David Lewis for good and all. And there'll be no hitch. Maybe Mr Alfred Bunter will be assembling himself again somewhere over there – some place like Nice or Ragusa – in quite a little while. And be coming back.'

Brynhild curiously enough had nothing to say about that.

'When we meet again,' he began, and stopped short.

She said not a word.

'If we meet again,' he said, 'we shall find we have a lot to tell each other.'

He glanced at her brooding face.

He laid his hand timidly on her bare shoulder and spoke in an undertone. 'Anyhow, thank you for this.'

He clenched his two hands together between his knees. 'Whatever happens I shall adore you. Love calls once. Or never. I loved you from the first moment I set eyes upon you.'

8

At seven o'clock Mrs Palace found herself in her own room surveying herself in her dressing-table mirror. She saw a lady surprised perhaps but not dismayed, and looking unusually animated and well. She was feeling rather indolent but by no means exhausted. And tragedy had evaporated from life.

She looked down at her hand mirror which was prone on the table as though hiding its reflections from her. Then by an effort she raised her eyes and met the grave but by no means despondent face in the glass. Brynhild scrutinized Brynhild.

'Yes,' said Brynhild aloud, and did not trouble to say more because the other Brynhild understood it all without her saying it.

'We have always been simple because we have never done anything out of our pattern. And we didn't think anything *could* surprise us. We didn't think we could surprise ourselves. But now we begin to realize...how life can be complicated...

'Now we shall understand other people better.'

She ran her fingers round the ivory back of her hand mirror slowly, thinking out a practical problem.

She came to a definite conclusion about something hitherto unsettled in her mind.

'It just didn't happen,' she said.

But presently she began to doubt whether accomplished events can always be dismissed so easily. Even memories are not easy things to hide.

CHAPTER TWELVE

Mr Rowland Palace Goes Upward and On

When at last after two days' delay Mr Rowland Palace returned home and could be heard downstairs in the hall, his wife had a moment of panic. She felt that unless she went down at once and looked him in the face, she might have a difficulty in looking him in the face. Yet why should she wince? But she need have had no such apprehension, because for some reason that did not at once become apparent, he displayed an unmistakable disinclination to turn his countenance to her. He backed up to the foot of the staircase, kissed her *over* her, so to speak, on the forehead, and immediately went upstairs without once looking back.

At tea she had her first inkling of his reason for this unwonted aversion. Something had happened to his left cheekbone and brow; his normally flexible skin had been replaced by a harder shining pink expanse, that sent lighter extensions on to his eyelid where they mingled with powder.

'Has anything happened to your eye, Rowly?' she asked.

'I thought you would see it,' he said bitterly.

'It shows against the window,' she said, to mitigate her remark. 'The slanting light just catches it.'

'It is a – contusion. In fact – it is a black eye painted over. A black eye. There was an accident at Dumbuttock. Those young men had what they called a Rag.'

'I saw something in one of the papers.'

'It ought not to have been in the papers.'

'It was in a letter in some local paper. Somebody protested against – stupid exuberance – was it? I couldn't understand.'

'Stupid exuberance describes it. Those young barbarians staged a Student Rag for me… These rags are not natural things at all. I never realized that so fully before. They are self-conscious exaggerations of a silly custom. One university or medical-school apes another and tries to do something sillier. I was met at the station and taken in a sort of procession of rather extravagant costumes to the hall where I was to give my address, and the joke – if you can call it a joke – was a raid to capture the Mascot.'

'The Mascot?'

'Me. It's all too silly. And they threw what they called bombs and hand grenades with flour and so forth. A pelting, in fact. And one lout hurled this turnip… After that they expected my address to be a success… This Ragging doesn't give you a chance with them. It's derisive. Essentially.'

Evidently he wanted to talk no more about it. She suppressed her imagination in the act of presenting Rowland dishevelled and with a black eye – still being debonair – still doing his best to dominate the undergraduate mind. And she had a transitory vision of the bright young things in the galleries applauding their damaged plaything, and listening very little, not quite sure whether they had indeed gone quite far enough with him.

'It was a good address,' she said, 'and the *Daily Telegraph* gave it the best part of a column. It read very well. And then you went on to Garvie Castle. Did you have a good time there?'

'Except for this eye.'

'And the motor trip to John o' Groats – and the yacht?'

'Some of the scenery was quite unexpected,' he said, with a sort of defensive aloofness.

So that too had not been a perfect success.

'Betty has made some of those soda-buns you like,' she said.

He took a soda-bun with an air of not caring a rap whether he took a soda-bun or not.

2

Mr Palace had called in at the office in the Multiple Building on his way home, and had a rather disturbing interview with Cloote. He thought that the entire Dumbuttock affair had been mismanaged; that Cloote had exposed him to indignities and deserted him and he wanted to say so clearly and forcibly. Cloote should have been on the spot to intercept that turnip. Mr Palace had arrived unannounced about twelve in the day, and the state of the office had greatly increased his discontent with Cloote.

It looked frowsty and deserted. It had not been cleaned out for days. There were signs of a hasty departure. A Bradshaw lay in the armchair open and face downward. The desk, the floor, was littered with burnt matches, cigarette ends, scraps of paper. There were three empty beer bottles on the sofa, and an empty glass with a fly drowned in a heel-tap of beer. There were a number of unopened letters and bales of press-cuttings scattered over the floor under the letter slit. Mr Cloote had apparently been called away, urgently called away, while struggling with a game of Patience. The little cards remained spread in lines and packets as he had left them.

'Phew!' said Mr Palace, and opened a window. One of the patience cards shifted slightly and thought better of it.

There was nothing to indicate when Cloote might return and Mr Palace thought it might be worth while to take this opportunity of examining the folders in which the projects for their various campaigns gathered form. The first he took up dealt with Continental Prestige. It seemed to consist mainly of manuscript notes and he discovered for the first time the extraordinary quality of Cloote's handwriting. It was a large unformed schoolboy script with long slanting loops and occasional convulsions and it was written in long ascending curves across the page. And it diminished in size downward and to the right. Mr Palace had seen straight manuscript and slanting manuscript before but never this parabolic inclination. It was fragmentary stuff, evidently intended only for the writer's eye and it was interposed with what appeared to be sketches or hieroglyphics.

One group of these Mr Palace found particularly intriguing. They gave him the impression of being attempts made with a bad pen and a bad eye and a very unsteady hand, to draw his own profile. Certain characteristics were seized, a certain proud carriage of the head, for example, and a graceful movement of the hand. Others were as certainly missed or disregarded.

It is often difficult to determine when bad drawing ends and caricature begins, and Mr Palace was still pondering the subtle boundary line when Cloote returned. He became audible on the stairs without. He seemed to be having difficulties with the stairs at the bend. The first impulse of Mr Palace was to replace the folder hastily. Then he decided rather to be discovered holding it reproachfully in his hand. His general intention was reproach. This untidy office, Cloote's absence, the pervading evidence of negligence – and in particular Dumbuttock – merited a wigging. A warning.

But when after a tussle with the latchkey the door opened, it was immediately plain that Cloote was in no condition to receive either a wigging or a warning. He was manifestly very drunk.

He appeared in the doorway trying to hold on to the door and make a triumphant gesture with the same hand. He seemed obscurely puzzled to find that his right hand was not ambidextrous. He manifested no surprised at the presence of Mr Palace. He seemed to take him for granted.

'Where have you been?' said Mr Palace sharply, without any preliminary greeting.

'Cardiff... Fascinating. Simply fascinating. I say – what's the matter with your eye?'

'Cardiff? Why Cardiff?'

'Why Cardiff? Why *not* Cardiff?'

Mr Cloote advanced into the room leaving the door to close itself behind him on its own initiative, which it did with a petulant slam. He focused his attention on his employer, so far, that is, as his attention could be focused – having regard to his temporary and permanent disabilities. His large red hands framed Mr Palace unsteadily. 'Let's look at you! *You* been in the wars? What you done to yourself?'

'Tell me why you have been to Cardiff,' said Mr Palace stiffly.

'You don't need to know. S'not your business. No. Deb'nair
gents don't do this sort of thing. Still, if you must know, *Bunter
is dished!*'

He seated himself on the sofa and for a moment his attention
was distracted by those empty beer bottles. He took up one and
examined it closely. He dismissed them as irrelevant and
returned to the main topic in his mind.

'Bunter is down and out,' he said. 'The job's done.'

'It's no job of mine,' said Palace. 'What do you mean, "Bunter
is down and out"?'

' 'Zactly what I say.'

'You don't mean you've been doing anything against Bunter?
Doing anything about his private life?'

'Doing *everything* about his private life.' He swept his arm
about to convey extreme amplitude.

'I wash my hands of this,' said Mr Palace. 'I won't stand for
it.'

Cloote regarded his employer as if he looked at him through a
mist. He tried to brush the mist away and then desisted.

'Lousy Ungrateful Swine,' he said very deliberately.

'*What!*' cried Mr Palace, stiffening.

'Lousy Ungrateful Swine,' Cloote repeated. 'No! hold up for
a minute. Hear me out. The context justifies the means.' His
large flat hand went up as if to arrest any precipitate action on the
part of Mr Palace. 'Have I ever shown you the least want of
respect? Never! Never once! Have I ever allowed you to doubt
that I regarded you as the greatest, noblest, grandest writer alive?
I have not. So it has been, so it is, so it always will be. *Saecula
Saeculorum.* I have loved you this shide – this side of idolatry. I
do. Your career has been and is and will be more precious to me

than rubies. That's in the contract and no man on earth can ever say I broke a contract. No. I'm your Yes-Man. Your obedient servant. And all the same – All the same I tell you you're a Lousy Ungrateful Swine.'

Mr Palace took a pace towards the window, swung round and demanded of his disordered henchman. 'What does this mean? What are you driving at?'

''Zactly what I say. Here was this Bunter – '

'I don't want to hear about Bunter.'

'Here was this Bunter, the most dangerous man in your way to a wide publicity. Why, they were asking him to lecture in Warsaw and Oslo next spring! Yes – sir. Oslo. And now, they won't. He won't. Nobody won't. He's out of the way. He's off the map. And the road is clear for you.'

'What have you done?'

'Nothing. Just asked a question here and there. Flut – fluttered the dove-cotes. It wasn't certain but it was a damned good guess. Even now, I don't know anything plositive. Absolutely proved, I mean. We needn't. But Mr Bunter has always been very shy of a camera and just now he's shyer than ever. Nobody knows where he's gone these last few days. And all this idea of lecturing about the capitals of Europe and all that, he's thrown it up. He threw it up yesterday. Said he wanted to go abroad and concentrate on his work. That's all.'

He had an air of closing the discussion. 'I wish there was a nip of gin and some Worcester Sauce or red pepper in this office,' he said. '*Badly* furnished. Never mind.'

'I suppose now I know so much I might just as well know all,' said Mr Palace after an interval.

239

', 'I expected that,' said Cloote, and for a time he brooded sadly on the want of trustfulness in his hero. Then with an affection of great weariness he told what he knew of the probable identity of Mr Bunter with the missing David Lewis. He was not very complete in his knowledge. His ideas centred on the possibility of an impulsive murder. 'There's a wife somewhere but I couldn't find where. But it would be easy to find her... There it is, like a mine with a train laid ready.'

He told his story quite unaware that at that particular moment Mr David Lewis, back from an imaginary exile in Belfast, was sitting at a table in his brother's office in Cardiff, explaining the particulars of his flight from home to a doctor, to the news editor of the second Cardiff paper and to two responsible police officials, and so beginning the long and intricate task of detaching Alfred Bunter from his past. It never entered the head of Cloote that Bunter might take his dilemma by the horns in this fashion.

'We've got him taped,' said Cloote. 'And that's all about it.'

'All this I wash my hands of,' said Mr Palace.

'It's never been *on* your hands,' said Cloote. 'And so why should we talk any more about it?'

His manner suddenly became very grave.

'Mr Palace,' he said, 'I think you ought to realize that I am, in a stale and incomplete sort of way, drunk. I have to be worse before I am better. You may have noticed a certain defliciency, deficiency (Hell!), deficiencies, in my manner. I came up from Cardiff by the night train. I have eaten nothing on an empty stomach. Tomorrow I shall suffer terribly from my liver. Spots on everything.' He seemed desirous of indicating spots of everything by an appropriate gesture and to find the effort

beyond him. 'Active spots. Wandering spots. A Dalmatian world.
I believe I have gallstones. I think if you will leave me here
now and let me struggle with my – well, with my fizzy – my
physiological entanglements – all twisted they are – in my own
fashion for a day or so, I shall be able to get on more efficiently.
With my mission. My self-appointed mission. Self-chosen. This
has been a curious time in Cardiff. An exciting time. I've had to
stand an extraordinary number of drinks altogether, and I'm
overwrought. Maybe I stood too many drinks. It was confusing.
There were times when I seemed to be standing drinks all to
myself. Standing drinks in the absolute.'

3

Three days later Mr Palace found the office swept and garnished
and Cloote restored to his usual state of animated sobriety. He
seemed to have forgotten the obliterated Mr Bunter.

'The time is ripe, Mr Palace, for you to make the grand tour,'
he said, pacing up and down the room and making passes with
his hands. 'The time is ripe for *us* to make the grand tour. For
this is my business quite as much as yours. The expenses need
not be excessive. Though of course we must do ourselves well. I
have a flair in these matters, an instinct. There is a Dunne region
in my brain. A Dunne ganglion. Intimations. Foresight. The
time is ripe. The moment comes. I can hear the whirr of the
clockwork before the striking of the hour.

'And besides,' he added, with a burst of frankness, 'if I stick
much longer in this damned office my liver will overpower me...
It needs stimulation and it demands stimulants... There are
times when I feel a craving... Drink. My spirit revolts against

241

that. Passive stimulation. No, sir. Let me *do*. Let it be movement! Let it be action!'

Mr Palace was perched upon the writing-desk in an easy, graceful attitude. 'But I thought,' he said, 'that all that was to come much later on. When my position here and in America was established on a broader basis.'

Mr Cloote drooped and cut the air before him into a number of thin slices with his hand. 'The time,' he snarled, 'is NOW.'

He paused impressively. 'Mr Palace, there is at present a Conspicuous Dearth of Great Men.'

Mr Palace featured a modest sense of irrelevance.

'There is a universal Dearth. A shortage. New Great Artists. None. New Great Lit'ry Figures. None. It is becoming a matter of world-wide comment. This distracted world has ceased to produce them. The World Output of Great Men, in Art, in Literature, in Thought, is dying away. The End of an Age. It is like the alarming fall in the birth rate – or – Anyhow, it is very similar. Conditions have changed. Publicity has become disordered. It is no more possible for poets and novelists to grow steadily and surely into a hard, infrangible greatness, than it is for crystals to form in a whirlpool. Nothing forms. We look round. The Nobel Committee are looking round. Governments are looking round. Particularly some of the new governments. Nazi Germany – urgently. They want men to honour, to glorify, to reflect credit back upon them. As Longfellow, Tennyson, Dickens, Thackeray, Tolstoi, Goethe were honoured and glorified and reflected credit on their particular cultures. One or two great figures still remain. Vestigial figures, rather lonely in their greatness, noble monuments to themselves, great men in their sixties and seventies. Autobiographical. But when we look for new Successes what do we find? They come, they go. Today they are best-sellers. Tomorrow they are cast into the oven. A struggling, tropical forest. "Too many of us" as the small boy put it in *Tess*. Where there is everybody there is nobody. An indeterminate crowd. A universal indecision. Criticism undecided. Loud praises today. Running away tomorrow. The public undecided, governments afraid of making mistakes, of making themselves ridiculous. It is a period of suspense, profound suspense.'

All this Cloote recited very rapidly. Then he changed his note to one more wary and confidential.

'*Schroederer*,' he said, '*is no fool.*'

Mr Palace became more attentive.

'I happen to know that he had an option on no less than the next three – *three!* – books of Alfred Bunter. And so the mystery of Mr Alfred Bunter being invited to lecture at the Sorbonne, in Oslo, in Warsaw and here and there, stands explained. A searchlight fact! Schroederer discovered – naked. Nose and all. Well, well, never mind about Bunter. He's all over. I mention him only for purposes of illustration. For once Schroederer has backed the wrong horse. His celebrated flair has been double-crossed. The pea was under the other thimble. The twigged the moment and mistook his man. At present there is only one figure fitted, entitled, called upon to come out into that vacant limelight, that *aching* unsatisfied limelight of the Nobel literary situation. That limelight, Mr Palace, is yours, legitimately yours. It is up to you to emerge now. It is imperative upon you to emerge now. An author who is treated with respect owes something to his supporters if only in the way of dignity. *Noblesse oblige.* There are times when modesty becomes a crime.'

'There are times,' said Mr Palace with a humorous smile, 'when I might suspect you of flattery.'

'There is such a thing as the flattering truth,' said Cloote. 'But a truce to that. Now I have been making inquiries, I have been pulling strings. Mr Palace (never mind how) that Sorbonne date is yours. You must go to Paris. I am in touch with a small but efficient publicity agency in Paris. And after that Gargalia.'

'Gargalia?'

'All that large region of Europe which gargles when it speaks – guttural Europe. The shores of the North and Baltic Seas! Scotland to Finland, the lands of prohibition and earnest private drinking. There we still find the legend of the literary personality surviving. We have to seize upon it and revive it before it is too late. We have to strike up by Holland to Denmark and go through Norway, Sweden, Finland, lecturing, being received, making friends, bowing right and left, blond, Nordic, debonair. Your personality has immense Scandinavian possibilities, Mr Palace – immense... In these folders my scheme grows. But there is one point – '

Cloote featured tact and embarrassment.

'I have never had the honour of meeting Mrs Palace.'

'No,' Mr Palace agreed.

'In presenting you to the attention and curiosity of the various Continental publics, it is unavoidable – Your wife, Mr Palace, is part of your ensemble. I have heard that she is a very quiet, charming, and dignified lady.'

'You could not describe her better.'

'I am thinking of Paris, Mr Palace. No foreigners really understand the intense regard of the French public for respectability. Whatever they were in the past the French are now a people of what I might call an intense rational sobriety. Sexual methodists. Morally *neat*. Nothing is so calculated to gratify their national craving for regularity, logic, and stability as the presence of a wife, a wife who is also, in every sense of the term, a lady. Presentable. Presentable. Frenchmen have wives, many of them have mistresses also, but in both cases the relationship is formal and regular. Every Thursday afternoon, for example. Nothing shocks a Frenchman so much as to hear a man is unfaithful to his mistress – or his wife – when there is no mistress. Many external observers fail to understand this extreme orderliness. The French, if I might say so, can practise adultery without depravity. Bohemia has been defined and regulated, codified, and put in its place. The large, careless promiscuity of the Anglo-Saxon peoples is absolutely alien to the modern French mind. It disgusts it. And the ordinary Frenchman's observations of the foreign visitor, leering about him, greedy for strange excitements, spoiling the vice just as he has already spoilt the cookery, *asking* for dirt in his dalliance, so to speak, makes an unaccompanied Anglo-Saxon in Paris suspect, antipathetic to every good Frenchman. You see my point?'

'H'm. I think it would be possible for Mrs Palace to come to Paris.'

'Perfect! And if you could stay at a good hotel and visit, say, one or two well-known dressmakers and a hat shop, in the rôle of the attentive husband...'

'I thought that nowadays all the Paris houses had London branches.'

'*No*,' said Mr Cloote. 'Not for the purposes of our picture. The spectacle of the debonair husband still delightfully in love with his wife! Don't you get it?'

245

'My wife has a certain dislike – almost a prejudice against publicity.'

'She need never know the camera was more than accidental... You see my point? You *do* see my point? Exactly! Perfect! And so we arrange for Paris.'

'Mrs Palace – Yes, I think she will come.'

'As far as Paris. So far as Paris is concerned. But after Paris, the case is different.'

Mr Palace with an attentive expression lit a cigarette, while Cloote executed a few magic passes to convey how different the case could be. Finally he came to a stop with his index finger pointing arrestingly to Mr Palace.

'In Gargalia it is not like that. No. In the Gargalian countries the man of genius is still supposed to be rather a wild and passionate creature. He is not supposed to travel *en famille*, to carry a *ménage* about with him. The unexpected is expected of him. He must yield to impulses. Outside Latinized Europe lies the picturesque. The more one goes eastward and northward the less weight domesticity carries. It's not that I suggest – Not at all... The point, Mr Palace, is that Mrs Palace might be bored. She might find herself talking Ollendorf with rather dull domesticated women. She would have a feeling of being left in the cloakroom. You would have to be the life and soul of men's parties. Essentially men's parties. And a certain gallantry – '

Mr Cloote hesitated.

'I have an east European side,' he said darkly. 'I could show you about. Joseph was never an Eastern hero. Something will be expected of us... Man is many-sided, Mr Palace, and romance rises in the east and sets in the west.'

4

It required some days of thought before Mr Palace could contrive that Mr Cloote should meet Mrs Palace and at the same time have only the slightest opportunity of breaking out into uncontrolled talk to her. He arranged that Cloote should call about a quarter to five while tea was being served and that he should bring a portfolio for some alleged urgent autographs. He could meet and observe Mrs Palace in the drawing-room. He would be given a cup of tea which would hamper his gestures and be fed bread and butter and cakes which would break up his discourse. Then he could be carried off to Mr Palace's study for the signatures and so got rid of.

It worked very well. Brynhild was aloof, surprised, and coldly polite.

As soon as the door of the study closed Cloote burst into panegyric. 'But she is *lovely!* Marvellous. Perfect. There is a grave dignity about her. A Junoesque Venus, if I may say so – with a touch of Diana. Paris, yes. Certainly Paris. A profound impression. But for Gargalia. Gargalia? Apart from all I have said already. There is something about her. She would never relax. She might chill the convivial warmth. Chill it very considerably...'

Brynhild failed to reciprocate Mr Cloote's admiration. It was rare that she took instantaneous dislikes but this time her reactions were hostile from the first.

She was unusually outspoken about him. After his departure Rowland rejoined her in the precious little patch of London garden they possessed. He admired her asters, and she spoke in answer to the interrogative silence that ensued. 'I don't like that amanuensis, secretary, valet of yours. No. No exact reason. But

247

his manners – are horrible. Waving his arms about like – like a hot polyp. As though he wanted to take hold of you and didn't dare. And he squints.'

A queer, a fantastic thought crossed her mind. 'I don't like men who squint,' she said.

'He can't help that. His energy is wonderful. He's a most indefatigable, useful man. And he's devoted. He sees my interests with a single eye. You can't think what he will do for me.'

That fantastic thought grimaced at her again. She stood side by side with Rowly and stared away from him at this monstrous idea in her head. No! The idea was impossible, quite impossible. Rowland was a complex character but she had never doubted he was a gentleman. And now more than ever she did not wish to doubt that. All the same she never wanted to see Cloote again.

'Mr Cloote makes me feel sick,' she said. 'I never met a more emetic man. But perhaps somehow I have a prejudice against squinting men.'

She turned to go indoors. Some neglected statistical-minded corner of her brain was asking just what proportion of the adult male population of Britain squinted today. What were the chances?...

But her conscience was protesting that there were things it was not fair play even to think about Rowly. Especially as things were turning out at the present time. She was all for fair play for Rowly as far as it could be managed.

5

Rowland had something to break to Brynhild and Brynhild had something to break to Rowland, and yet, for three weeks and more, neither got to the point of revelation.

Mr Palace wanted to make it clear, first, that Brynhild must go with him to Paris for the Sorbonne show – brushing up her very nice French accent and her very scanty French vocabulary beforehand – and then that she must not expect to be taken on to that personality display in Gargalia. Because quite apart from the fact that it was manifest she would find the indispensable Cloote an unendurable travelling companion, there was the more permanent trouble of her cramping effect upon Rowland's style. He would have to be florid; he would have to be *scrittore galantuomo* to his utmost. And so forth. It was absurd to go except in that spirit.

It seemed to him that the best line of attack would be to stress the exclusive masculinity of literary banquets in these lands, and to use Cloote's phrases about her being bored and left in the cloakroom. Still that diffidence which Brynhild always inspired in him, kept him tongue-tied day after day. When at last he did achieve an *éclaircissement* he found a novelty in the situation that eliminated the need for most of his carefully polished discouragements.

Brynhild listened with more than her usual quiet to his opening explanations. Then she spoke. 'I couldn't come on that expedition, anyhow,' she said. 'I couldn't take the risks of hotels and bad food just now. I have to take care of myself. I doubt if I can even come with you and Mr Cloote to Paris. You see – I ought perhaps to have told you before – you are going to be – a family man in – it may be a little more than seven months.'

'*What?*'

Nothing but blank annoyance was manifest in his first reaction.

'It will be expensive,' he said.

'But, darling, that isn't at all the tone – '

He didn't heed that.

'But I thought you always – ' he began.

'Well, I didn't,' she answered with deliberation, meeting his eyes.

And then with even more deliberation. 'You see, I'm going to have – *children*, Rowly... It's what I'm for. I've messed about with sex too long.'

For a moment it was almost as if they were two quite unexpected people who had come starkly face to face, and then this new personality he had been building up for himself resumed possession of the scene.

'It's rather wonderful,' he tried doubtfully.

'It happens,' she said.

'I should be glad to be a father.'

'I suppose I ought to have consulted you. But – I thought your attentions to me were getting just a trifle trivial. Maybe I was selfish. I wanted something of my own – really my own. I wanted a rôle of my own.'

And then, her natural truthfulness insisting, she said: 'It has happened. Anyhow. And I'm glad it's happened.'

'I shall be glad to be a father,' he repeated, with more assurance. 'Yes.'

He took a step or so away from her and turned. He was warming to the situation.

He allowed himself to brighten manifestly. 'Of course,' he said. 'A father!... Queer that I should be surprised... Bryn! I'm *glad* you've done it. I'm glad you thought of it. It was lovely and wise of you. And to do it so – silently. It – it completes us.'

'It *is* definitive, isn't it?'

'It will be a son.'

'Yes. I hope it will be a son. To begin with.'

'It means a new phase for me – for both of us. You've taken splendid care of me for seven years, my dear. Splendid care. I've had you all to myself... Now for a bit I'll have to take care of *you*.'

And as he spoke he began to see how he could be made to look as a father, a splendid father, the protective, expectant husband of this quiet, lovely, submissive wife, responsible though still debonair. She should go to Paris all the same, arousing respectful envy. To arouse envy is probably among the purest of human satisfactions. He knew Bunter had admired Brynhild, he had seen it in his eyes. The man had coveted Brynhild. Not for him and his like was a woman of her sort. The contrast of his own controlled and orderly mastery of the world with that man's impulsive and ramshackle life, rose splendidly before Rowland.

'I shall take *great* care of you,' he said. 'I may even be a little overbearing with you – for your sake – for *our* sake. For the sake of all three of us.'

Whatever other fluctuations there had been in her feelings towards him, she had never really faltered in her belief that he was the most amusing being in the world. The quality of her amusement had altered, perhaps, but the quantity had never abated. Never had she realized so completely that his most amusing phases were the unconscious ones.

'Darling,' she said, 'I know you'll take wonderful care of me.'

By way of earnest he advanced in an enveloping manner and took her in his arms. '*There!*' he said, as full of consolation as she was full of escape. He held her to him, he patted her shoulder. So for moment they grouped themselves, putting a brave face upon it.

What else, she asked herself, was to be done?

Silly old Rowly, she thought, gulling and gullible Rowly, and yet in a way tolerable and likeable Rowly. Substantial. Materially substantial. Smelling slightly of soap and tobacco. Married – extraordinarily married to her, about whom he would never know anything at all, about whom he didn't want to know anything at all. Married. And at the same time she was escaping – going away from all that had held her paralysed for seven years – to something profoundly her own, profoundly secret in its essence and profoundly real.

She had become real. Her priggishness had been reft from her. She was a cheat now – like everybody. She was a humbug – like everybody. She was a secret behind a façade. And altogether human. She had grown up at last...

Her thoughts flicked off at a tangent. The child? The child, though, was going to be different. Her child would never cheat like this, never humbug any one. Her child was going to be something better than had ever been before. In some way... This sort of thing wouldn't do for her child. That was what she had to see to...

'No,' she said, and drew herself away from him and stood alone. She seemed to be looking at something that had appeared suddenly a thousand miles away.

'*No?* I wonder what you are thinking about,' said Mr Rowland Palace. He reflected upon the limitations of even a penetrating and ironical novelist...

'*Often*, Bryn, I don't in the least know what you are thinking about...'

6

A rather ruffled young woman sat in an easy chair in her own room after this touching scene. 'That's that,' she said...

She repeated his words softly to herself. 'Often, Bryn,' she said, '*I* don't know in the least what you are thinking about. So how should he?'

And just now in particular her thoughts seemed less clear than they had ever been before, they flowed through her mind no longer like a ripple of clear water but in smooth milky patches.

'I *did* think I was in control of my own life...

'*Life has raped me...*

'Suppose after all there is a God?'

She found she was no longer an acute theologian. She had dismissed Omniscience years ago as an infinite, entirely inanimate encyclopaedia, she had lost her faith in a God of love who had nevertheless left the matches about for the children of the Great War to play with, and the landscape gardener of Wordsworth had been banished from her scheme of things by reflexion upon the hyena and the less attractive aspects of physiology and pathology. She had been a quiet Atheist who never said anything about it. Like so many people. But now she found herself wondering in a curiously excited state whether perhaps some Great God Pan, shaggy, redolent among other things of humour, and with little horns and pointed ears and a cloven hoof, might after all not be nearer to the fundamental realities of life.

She had recently become firmer, she felt, in her mental substance. Her discursive, indecisive will had been pulled together to a serene assurance. She felt, as she had never felt before, that she knew her own mind. And that instead of being the most aimless thing in the world, she now conceived her essential business plain before her.

'Not one child but *children*, and the best I can get...

253

'What I was made for...

'Jolly children and get on with it... Those men know even less about life than we do...

'A stormy little rebel to begin with who will batter at the façades. With trouble and stubbornness in those brown eyes of his...

'Somebody will have to pay. I can't see to everything. If Rowly cares more than anything else for his Nobel prize, and I find I care for a brawl of children, aren't we each entitled to get what we want? And the best of it? In whatever way we can?

'When all that is fairly under way, then surely at last I shall take an intelligent interest in – say – education. And politics. So that they don't kill or waste or starve my children or leave them alive with nothing sensible to do...

'If there *is* any sense in things at all.'

She turned sideways to the mirror on her dressing-table and surveyed herself. She had always cared immensely for her own long slender lines. It was her love for that gracious, slender body of hers that had helped her to consent not to use it. But now it did not seem to matter to her at all if that grace departed from her. Perhaps, said the Great God Pan in her, behind every lovely thing is the possibility of something lovelier. If things hadn't happened as they had happened, she would have kept that beautiful figure and it would have grown stale and fruitless upon her. From being a fresh young body it would have become a preserved body.

She bent down towards the mirror and studied her changed throat and bosom.

'Little blue veins,' she whispered.

She looked at her grave face in the glass.

Façade she had to be. Every self-conscious behaving thing must be a façade, must turn a face to the world and be aware of itself... All the same these juices in her blood that had taken possession of her, and filled her with this deep irrational satisfaction, had a very imperious suggestion about them of being real.

If indeed there was in human experience as yet any such thing as reality.

CHAPTER THIRTEEN

The Envoy

Sufficient unto the novel is the story thereof. And this is the story of how Brynhild Palace grew up and became a normal adult, façade and all complete. Of how Mr Palace and Mr Cloote fared in the literary capitals of Europe, of the ripening charm and dignity of Mr Palace, who grew more triumphantly debonair every day, of the temperamental aberrations of Mr Cloote, and the curious, intricate, subromantic adventures of these two gentlemen in Sofia, Stockholm, Tallinn, Oslo, Warsaw, and Prague, there is nothing to be told here, nor of the difficult and tortuous experiences of Mr David Lewis in Cardiff. Having cleared his character from the imputations of murder and bigamy, and made various minor restitutions, he faded quietly out of local attention – and vanished. Only in one abandoned home was his memory kept green. What Mrs David Lewis said about it all would alone fill a volume. That lady has never been anything so far here, but noises heard off. So for the present she shall remain. We have done her no sort of justice.

Nor will we go further with Mrs Brynhild Palace's new half mystical self-devotion to the physical rebirth of our world, or with the steadfast and ultimately successful attempts of Mr

Alfred Bunter to re-materialize himself as almost the only bearded British author. He lived behind a large brown beard, and more and more at Dubrovnic. A pipe was his natural complement. For some years he kept silence, and his later work, though profound, inspiring, and well spoken of, hardly redeemed the promise of his earlier books. He never became a serious rival to Mr Rowland Palace for the Nobel Prize. He shunned personal exposure. He kept away from Gargalia; he did not wish to compete.

Maternity Brynhild found a very interesting and satisfying rôle. 'The juices' played up loyally. She developed an increasing social confidence and dignity, and brought a bright and various family of three sons and two daughters into the world. Two at least of these offspring were quite debonair.

In New Zealand, as Mrs Ettie Hornibrook showed so ably and interestingly in her *Maori Symbolism*, the decorations on a beam or a pillar may be expended by an understanding imagination into the most complete and interesting of patterns, and so it is with this book. It is a novel in the Maori style, a presentation of imaginative indications.

Did Brynhild and Bunter ever meet again? Not for many years. And then with an entirely unromantic friendliness – and no revelations. The beard had made a great difference in him. Her eldest boy was a charming boy with a sort of natural sunburn, and as every one agreed, the very image of his mother.

H G WELLS

THE HISTORY OF MR POLLY

Mr Polly is one of literature's most enduring and universal creations. An ordinary man, trapped in an ordinary life, Mr Polly makes a series of ill-advised choices that bring him to the very brink of financial ruin. Determined not to become the latest victim of the economic retrenchment of the Edwardian age, he rebels in magnificent style and takes control of his life once and for all.

ISBN 0-7551-0404-8

H G WELLS

IN THE DAYS OF THE COMET

Revenge was all Leadford could think of as he set out to find the unfaithful Nettie and her adulterous lover. But this was all to change when a new comet entered the earth's orbit and totally reversed the natural order of things. The Great Change had occurred and any previous emotions, thoughts, ambitions, hopes and fears had all been removed. Free love, pacifism and equality were now the name of the game. But how would Leadford fare in this most utopian of societies?

ISBN 0-7551-0406-4

H G Wells

The Invisible Man

On a cold wintry day in the depths of February a stranger appeared in The Coach and Horses requesting a room. So strange was this man's appearance, dressed from head to foot with layer upon layer of clothing, bandages and the most enormous glasses, that the owner, Mrs Hall, quite wondered what accident could have befallen him. She didn't know then that he was invisible – but the rumours soon began to spread...

H G Wells' masterpiece *The Invisible Man* is a classic science-fiction thriller showing the perils of scientific advancement.

ISBN 0-7551-0407-2

H G WELLS

THE ISLAND OF DR MOREAU

A shipwreck in the South Seas brings a doctor to an island paradise. Far from seeing this as the end of his life, Dr Moreau seizes the opportunity to play God and infiltrate a reign of terror in this new kingdom. Endless cruel and perverse experiments ensue and see a series of new creations – the 'Beast People' – all of which must bow before the deified doctor.

Originally a Swiftian satire on the dangers of authority and submission, Wells' *The Island of Dr Moreau* can now just as well be read as a prophetic tale of genetic modification and mutability.

ISBN 0-7551-0408-0

H G WELLS

MEN LIKE GODS

Mr Barnstaple was ever such a careful driver, careful to indicate before every manoeuvre and very much in favour of slowing down at the slightest hint of difficulty. So however could he have got the car into a skid on a bend on the Maidenhead road?

When he recovered himself he was more than a little relieved to see the two cars that he had been following still merrily motoring along in front of him. It seemed that all was well – except that the scenery had changed, rather a lot. It was then that the awful truth dawned: Mr Barnstaple had been hurled into another world altogether.

How would he ever survive in this supposed Utopia, and more importantly, how would he ever get back?

ISBN 0-7551-0413-7

H G Wells

The War of the Worlds

'No one would have believed in the last years of the nineteenth century that this world was being watched keenly and closely by intelligences greater than man's...'

A series of strange atmospheric disturbances on the planet Mars may raise concern on Earth but it does little to prepare the inhabitants for imminent invasion. At first the odd-looking Martians seem to pose no threat for the intellectual powers of Victorian London, but it seems man's superior confidence is disastrously misplaced. For the Martians are heading towards victory with terrifying velocity.

The War of the Worlds is an expertly crafted invasion story that can be read as a frenzied satire on the dangers of imperialism and occupation.

ISBN 0-7551-0426-9

OTHER TITLES BY H G WELLS AVAILABLE DIRECT
FROM HOUSE OF STRATUS

Quantity	£	$(US)	$(CAN)	€
FICTION				
ANN VERONICA	9.99	14.95	22.95	16.50
APROPOS OF DOLORES	9.99	14.95	22.95	16.50
THE AUTOCRACY OF MR PARHAM	9.99	14.95	22.95	16.50
BABES IN THE DARKLING WOOD	9.99	14.95	22.95	16.50
BEALBY	9.99	14.95	22.95	16.50
THE BROTHERS AND				
THE CROQUET PLAYER	7.99	12.95	19.95	14.50
THE BULPINGTON OF BLUP	9.99	14.95	22.95	16.50
THE DREAM	9.99	14.95	22.95	16.50
THE FIRST MEN IN THE MOON	9.99	14.95	22.95	16.50
THE FOOD OF THE GODS	9.99	14.95	22.95	16.50
THE HISTORY OF MR POLLY	9.99	14.95	22.95	16.50
THE HOLY TERROR	9.99	14.95	22.95	16.50
IN THE DAYS OF THE COMET	9.99	14.95	22.95	16.50
THE INVISIBLE MAN	7.99	12.95	19.95	14.50
THE ISLAND OF DR MOREAU	7.99	12.95	19.95	14.50
KIPPS: THE STORY OF A SIMPLE SOUL	9.99	14.95	22.95	16.50
LOVE AND MR LEWISHAM	9.99	14.95	22.95	16.50
MARRIAGE	9.99	14.95	22.95	16.50
MEANWHILE	9.99	14.95	22.95	16.50
MEN LIKE GODS	9.99	14.95	22.95	16.50
A MODERN UTOPIA	9.99	14.95	22.95	16.50
MR BRITLING SEES IT THROUGH	9.99	14.95	22.95	16.50

ALL HOUSE OF STRATUS BOOKS ARE AVAILABLE FROM GOOD BOOKSHOPS
OR DIRECT FROM THE PUBLISHER:

Internet: www.houseofstratus.com including synopses and features.

Email: sales@houseofstratus.com
info@houseofstratus.com
(please quote author, title and credit card details.)

OTHER TITLES BY H G WELLS AVAILABLE DIRECT
FROM HOUSE OF STRATUS

Quantity	£	$(US)	$(CAN)	€
FICTION				
THE NEW MACHIAVELLI	9.99	14.95	22.95	16.50
THE PASSIONATE FRIENDS	9.99	14.95	22.95	16.50
THE SEA LADY	7.99	12.95	19.95	14.50
THE SHAPE OF THINGS TO COME	9.99	14.95	22.95	16.50
THE TIME MACHINE	7.99	12.95	19.95	14.50
TONO-BUNGAY	9.99	14.95	22.95	16.50
THE UNDYING FIRE	7.99	12.95	19.95	14.50
THE WAR IN THE AIR	9.99	14.95	22.95	16.50
THE WAR OF THE WORLDS	7.99	12.95	19.95	14.50
THE WHEELS OF CHANCE	7.99	12.95	19.95	14.50
WHEN THE SLEEPER WAKES	9.99	14.95	22.95	16.50
THE WIFE OF SIR ISAAC HARMAN	9.99	14.95	22.95	16.50
THE WONDERFUL VISIT	7.99	12.95	19.95	14.50
THE WORLD OF WILLIAM CLISSOLD VOLUMES 1,2,3	12.99	19.95	29.95	22.00
NON-FICTION				
THE CONQUEST OF TIME AND THE HAPPY TURNING	7.99	12.95	19.95	14.50
EXPERIMENT IN AUTOBIOGRAPHY VOLUMES 1,2	12.99	19.95	29.95	22.00
H G WELLS IN LOVE	9.99	14.95	22.95	16.50
THE OPEN CONSPIRACY AND OTHER WRITINGS	9.99	14.95	22.95	16.50

Tel:	Order Line 0800 169 1780 (UK) 800 724 1100 (USA)	**International** +44 (0) 1845 527700 (UK) +01 845 463 1100 (USA)
Fax:	+44 (0) 1845 527711 (UK) +01 845 463 0018 (USA) (please quote author, title and credit card details.)	
Send to:	**House of Stratus Sales Department** **Thirsk Industrial Park** **York Road, Thirsk** **North Yorkshire, YO7 3BX** **UK**	**House of Stratus Inc.** **2 Neptune Road** **Poughkeepsie** **NY 12601** **USA**

PAYMENT (Please tick currency you wish to use):

☐ £ (Sterling)　　☐ $ (US)　　☐ $ (CAN)　　☐ € (Euros)

Allow for shipping costs charged per order plus an amount per book as set out in the tables below:

CURRENCY/DESTINATION

	£(Sterling)	$(US)	$(CAN)	€(Euros)
Cost per order				
UK	1.50	2.25	3.50	2.50
Europe	3.00	4.50	6.75	5.00
North America	3.00	3.50	5.25	5.00
Rest of World	3.00	4.50	6.75	5.00
Additional cost per book				
UK	0.50	0.75	1.15	0.85
Europe	1.00	1.50	2.25	1.70
North America	1.00	1.00	1.50	1.70
Rest of World	1.50	2.25	3.50	3.00

PLEASE SEND CHEQUE OR INTERNATIONAL MONEY ORDER
payable to: HOUSE OF STRATUS LTD or HOUSE OF STRATUS INC. or card payment as indicated

STERLING EXAMPLE

Cost of book(s):......................Example: 3 x books at £6.99 each: £20.97
Cost of order: ....Example: £1.50 (Delivery to UK address)
Additional cost per book:..............Example: 3 x £0.50: £1.50
Order total including shipping:...........Example: £23.97

VISA, MASTERCARD, SWITCH, AMEX:

☐☐☐☐☐☐☐☐☐☐☐☐☐☐☐☐☐☐☐☐

Issue number
(Switch only):　　　　**Start Date:**　　　　**Expiry Date:**

☐☐☐　　　　☐☐/☐☐　　　　☐☐/☐☐

Signature: _____

NAME: _____

ADDRESS: _____

COUNTRY: _____

ZIP/POSTCODE: _____

Please allow 28 days for delivery. Despatch normally within 48 hours.
Prices subject to change without notice.
Please tick box if you do not wish to receive any additional information. ☐

House of Stratus publishes many other titles in this genre; please check our
website (**www.houseofstratus.com**) for more details.